Virginia Blackburn was brought up in the United States, Germany and Britain and read English Literature and Law at Newnham College, Cambridge. She then turned her hand to a variety of careers, including the law, banking and public relations before discovering her true calling as a tabloid journalist. She now lives in west London.

BLONDE WITH ATTITUDE

Virginia Blackburn

CORGI BOOKS

BLONDE WITH ATTITUDE
A CORGI BOOK : 0 552 14514 9

First publication in Great Britain

PRINTING HISTORY
Corgi edition published 1997

Set in 10½pt Linotron Bembo by
Deltatype Ltd, Birkenhead, Merseyside

Corgi Books are published by Transworld Publishers Ltd,
61–63 Uxbridge Road, London W5 5SA,
in Australia by Transworld Publishers (Australia) Pty Ltd,
15–25 Helles Avenue, Moorebank, NSW 2170
and in New Zealand by Transworld Publishers (NZ) Ltd,
3 William Pickering Drive, Albany, Auckland.

Reproduced, printed and bound in Great Britain by
Cox & Wyman Ltd, Reading, Berks.

To Caroline

1

I was crawling through the desert. My mouth was parched and my throat was raw. I was hardly able to see or move because of the rivers, no, torrents of sweat pouring down my face and body. They were dribbling into my eyes and mouth, gushing underneath my arms and between my breasts, and I was struggling to get just a couple of yards further . . . when suddenly a hand grenade exploded by my head.

I sat bolt upright in bed. The alarm stopped ringing. It was pitch-black, my head was pounding and my throat was sore. I reached across for the glass of water I always kept beside my bed. It was not there. Come to think of it, neither was the table I kept the water on. And the bed did not feel quite as usual. Oh no, I thought, not again. The dark shapes hovering around me did not look at all familiar – and what the hell was that? A primeval creature seemed to be in repose beside me: he grunted and snorted and then heaved himself into a sitting position beside me. 'Who are you?' he asked.

An hour later, still only 8.00 on a freezing cold and rainy November morning, I attempted to insert my key into the front door of the house in which I lived, failed and withdrew the key in despair. A second later I nearly fell into the hall as the door was yanked open from the inside by Nigel, my next-door neighbour, fetchingly dressed in a ghastly maroon tracksuit and repulsive running shoes. He had just started a jogging regime, in order, I assumed, to develop a bit of muscle in his decidedly unmanly figure. His hair, as usual, was unwashed and he had not yet had time to shave. 'You look a bit rough!' he cried, beginning to bounce up and down on the spot, prior to taking on the rigours of Holland Park. 'Heavy night?'

With a revolting leer, he set off up Napier Road. I dragged myself upstairs to my flat, fuming with rage, and shoved my key into the lock. Bugger, I thought, stomping into my tiny little hall, he has caught me *again*. It was only last week that he had seen me sneaking in wearing a little black dress, stilettos in one hand and hangover in the other, at 7.30 on Saturday morning. I threw my coat and handbag into the bedroom and kicked my shoes in after them. One of the heels flew off en route. And not too long before that he had come across me bidding an affectionate farewell to some swain, the name of whom I had embarrassingly forgotten as Nigel demanded an introduction on the doorstep.

Oh well, at least this time I was in work clothes so he might have thought I had been out to get the papers, I thought, going into the bathroom and turning on the taps. Unfortunately, I had been carrying nothing but a handbag: last night's excesses were a result of what was supposed to have been a quick drink with a few of my colleagues, before we had run into a few friends of friends and the whole evening degenerated from there.

Not that I could remember too much about the night before. I caught a glimpse of myself in the mirror and winced. My unnaturally blond hair was getting far too dark at the roots, and instead of rolling in gentle curls over my shoulders, as it was supposed to do, was standing up in a wild and frizzy mess. My eyes, which were normally puddle grey, were looking distinctly bloodshot. At least my complexion, which was quite pale, was holding up under the strain – odd really, as I never took off my make-up before passing out of an evening.

I gulped a few Nurofen and gingerly lowered myself into the bath, trying not to sway too much because I was paranoid about slipping and knocking myself out. Then I would be found days or even weeks later, drowned, decomposing and with smudged make-up by Nigel, to whom I had once foolishly given a spare set of keys and now felt too embarrassed to ask for them back – although I was constantly worried that he might barge in one night in a drunken stupor and attempt to have his wicked way with me, as he had been known to do with other women. Lying back, I tried to piece together the events of the night before, working back from this morning.

The monolith and I had exchanged names – Gary, I ask you – and even phone numbers (office only as I did not know him that well) and I had made my way back from some obscure road in Chalk Farm. But how the hell had we ended up in Chalk Farm? We had been drinking in Vic Naylor's, which was miles away in Smithfield. I had been paying for everything by cheque, because I was overdrawn as usual and it was nowhere near the end of the month. So if we went back by taxi, he must have paid for it, unless, of course, the taxi took cheques. I must remember to examine my cheque book, I thought; that was frequently the way I managed to trace my movements of the night before – except when my handwriting was too shaky to decipher.

Anyway, there we had been at Vic Naylor's, grouped at a couple of tables in front of the fire. At first there were only three of us, me and a couple of colleagues from work, George and Ian. Then I had seen first Natasha and then Jack, two very close friends of mine and, I seemed very blearily to remember, as if it had happened in another lifetime or another age, being introduced to the person who must have been Gary, who knew Jack very slightly because he had been doing some systems work at Smedley Nelsons, Jack's bank.

Systems work? I sat bolt upright, regretted it and settled back into the water. God Almighty, that must mean he was a computer programmer. I knew I had had a few drinks, but I did not realize it had been that many. I gazed stonily out of the bath. The bath water had sloshed over the side onto *Private Eye*, the *Spectator* and a few old newspapers, essentials that I always kept on the bathroom floor, turning them cold and grey and soggy. The hum of the ventilator fan (my flat was so tiny that the bathroom had been crammed into what must once have been a broom cupboard and had no windows) was making my headache worse.

Anyway, that would explain the name, although not Chalk Farm – what was a computer programmer doing living in Chalk Farm? That was one to think about later, though. There was something from the evening I could not quite remember, something important, something Natasha had told me. What was

10

it? Try as I might to concentrate, though, it would not come – oh well, if it was important, I would probably remember it later.

I heaved myself out of the bath, stepped over the sodden magazines and wiped a facecloth over my drawn, grey features. I was still shaking slightly, shivering and, despite the bath water, knew I was covered in cold sweat. At least my eyes were returning to their normal colour, but I could not face work just yet. Anyway, I was already late: in the public relations firm in which I was employed we were supposed to start at 8.30 and it was already fifteen minutes after that. I staggered into the sitting-room, stepped over various piles of clothes and papers, found the phone buried under a heap of unpaid credit card bills on my desk and called my secretary.

'Is that Camilla?' I asked.

'Yah.'

'Look Camilla, it's Emily. I'm going to be a bit late.'

'Yah?'

I fumbled desperately for an excuse I had not used too recently. 'Yes, the radiator in my hall's leaking, and I don't want to leave until the plumber gets here. Could you tell everyone I'll try to be in by ten?'

'Yah, will do,' replied Camilla. 'Hope it doesn't make too much of a mess, Emily. By the way, I hear you had a pretty heavy evening last night?'

Seething with rage, I put the phone down. Sanctimonious bitch. Just because she never had a couple of drinks too many, or if she did, certainly never ended up in bed with people called Gary. On top of that, unlike me she owned her own flat and even though she was my secretary, she was considerably better off than I was. Her father, a Major Dressingham-Whitstable, made up for what he reputedly lacked in brains in the bank account department, and had already passed a fair amount of it on to Camilla, his adored only daughter.

She had three elder brothers, I had heard, who all adored her as well, and who had spoilt her rotten. Her father now lived in retired semi-dotage in Gloucestershire, while her mother, as far as I could tell from eavesdropping on her phone calls, paid a trip to London at least once a week to build up Camilla's already extensive wardrobe. The brothers all lived in far-off parts, which gave Camilla the opportunity to take exotic holidays and drop them casually into the conversation, while I was striving to save for a week in Spain.

And her hair was straight and auburn and perfect, unlike mine, which always looked as if I had got up an hour or two too late and had not had time to comb it for a week or so. And I strongly suspected her jewellery was real. And although I would not exactly have claimed to have had an illustrious career in PR, ever since she had become my secretary four months ago – very much against her will – my standing at the firm seemed to have plummeted. The old cow.

I began to feel better. Anger and hostility were getting the juices flowing again – any minute now I would feel like putting some make-up on. I marched into my bedroom, found some clothes that did not look as if they had been worn too recently and started to get dressed.

About an hour later, I levered myself grimly down to my desk, dealt with a few tender enquiries from colleagues about the state of my plumbing – I said the plumber had only managed to do a temporary repair job, and would have to come back, in order to give myself an excuse for next week, should I happen to find myself in the same lamentable position, and turned towards the phone. It rang instantly. 'Emily, it's Nat,' came the abrupt tones of my friend. 'You remember what I told you last night?'

'Well,' I started, but she ploughed on, 'Look, I've got to see you right away. Can you get away for lunch yet? I'll meet you in the Fifth Floor Café in Harvey Nicks in half an hour.'

'But it's only ten o'clock,' I protested – too late, however, as she had already hung up.

I was not that annoyed. Natasha had been like this ever since we had met at university nine years ago and I felt too ill to do any work anyway, and so I pulled myself together and stalked to Camilla's office. She was wearing a new yellow jacket, which I was certain I had seen in the window of Paddy Campbell last week, and which set off her gleaming auburn hair. She was lying back on her chair with her phone against her pearl-clad ear. She had a certain poise which, combined with an icy coolness, always intimidated the hell out of me. 'Alex says Gerry's a good man. But Mummy always said Gerry would come to no good. Ever since he was caught in the lockers at school that day . . . Yah?' she enquired as I approached.

'Oh, don't let me interrupt,' I said, fascinated by what Gerry had been up to in the lockers.

'No probs, Emily, what can I do for you?' Her tone was that of the busy schoolmistress, interrupted by one of her more obstreperous charges. I was fazed by it as usual, but attempted to assert my authority. 'I'm just off for a meeting with Interbank, and then I'm meeting someone for lunch, so I won't be back until this afternoon.'

13

'A meeting with Interbank? That's not in your diary,' said Camilla, fixing me with the full force of her calm and dimpled features. Her dark brown eyes glistened suspiciously.

'Yes, well they've just called and said they want to see me about something urgently,' I lied, hoping Camilla had not been on the switchboard and thus monitoring incoming calls that morning, 'so I thought I'd better go right away. Bye.'

'Bye, have fun,' dimpled Camilla as I backed away from her desk, dropped my handbag and tripped over the rubbish bin on the way to the door.

'Anyway,' she continued, returning to the receiver, 'Mummy said that Gerry . . .'

My attempt to eavesdrop was ruined by a rather large sneeze which I suddenly emitted just outside Camilla's door, and which sent me scurrying off towards the lifts before she realized I was still there. What a life.

Natasha was not there when I arrived. I stomped through the doors of Harvey Nichols, made my way up to the fifth floor of the establishment and perched at one of the trendy modern tables in the café, glaring at all the beautiful, exquisitely dressed women with soft powdery faces and exotic and expensive smells, to whom the waiters paid far more attention than they did me. Gentle yappings about the fab new clothes in Moschino were set against a glittering steel and chrome background, while beyond the eating area, the Harvey Nichols Food Hall weighed up in all its modern and expensive splendour. I bet all these women know what to do with lemon grass, I thought sulkily, to say nothing of stocking their kitchens with at least ten types of extra virgin olive oil.

At least I have a career, I thought, and was instantly plunged in gloom as I cast my mind over briefings and debriefings, touching base and ballpark figures, client relationships and contacts in the press – all the paraphernalia that goes along with PR. But what do we actually *do*, I moaned to myself while licking the top off my second cappuccino. Really we are just parasites living off real industries. If real industries which actually make real things did not exist, there would be no need for us at all. And working for something like Interbank, really we are just parasites of parasites because they don't do anything of real value either. Even Natasha, who worked in an interior designers – well, it was actually an upmarket shop which sold very expensive sofas, and had an office in the back, but she liked to glorify her trade – at least did something a little bit creative.

My life was never meant to turn out like this, I thought dejectedly. Back at university, where I had read English Literature, I had planned to go on and do research that would change the world – well, change the minds of a few bored students, anyway – or travel the seven seas or be a vet like my brother Jamie, even though I could not stand the sight of blood and I did not have the right degree, or write a great novel or do something worthwhile. I had done a little travelling after I left Bristol, to say nothing of an abortive attempt at further research which is why, overdrawn and lacking in imagination, I had ended up in PR.

At least if I worked in a factory making sprockets or frocketts I would be doing something useful and would not have to go out drinking every night and end up in bed with people called Gerry or was it Gary – 'Miss Whitelake?' said a waiter, interrupting my reverie and gazing with distaste at my scuffed shoes and handbag which was splitting at the seams because I always shoved in an extra packet of cigarettes just to be on the safe side. 'There's a phone call for you.'

How did he know it was me? I suppose he was told to look for the hungover blonde with roots, I gloomed, dragging myself over to the telephone. Anyway, who knows I'm here? I bet it's the company; they've had me followed here and now they're going to fire me over the phone. I picked up the receiver. 'Emily, it's me,' barked Natasha, 'I can't make it, but I've got to talk to you today. I'll call you this afternoon. And look, don't tell anyone what I told you last night.' The phone went dead.

But what the hell did she tell me last night, I thought, wandering out of the café. Maybe if I gave up vodka and stuck to wine I would be able to remember things better. Maybe if I called Jack he would be able to tell me what was going on, although then again I better not because Natasha had told me not to mention it to anyone. But how could I mention it if I didn't have the faintest idea of what it was? What if Natasha was in real trouble? What if her and Cosmo's house was going to be repossessed, although that was pretty unlikely given Cosmo's private income, or her mother had succeeded in getting her committed to a drying-out clinic as she was always threatening to do, or she was pregnant, or she had lost her job as I was almost bound to do if I continued like this— 'Does Madam need any help?' enquired a voice.

I wheeled round in alarm. A stunningly beautiful woman was looking at me with the same expression of distaste the waiter had adopted. It took me a moment to work out she was a shop assistant. Oh God, I had wandered into the Ralph Lauren bit of the shop, which, along with the Donna Karan bit, I usually avoided like the plague. Give me Max Mara any day.

'Uh, no thanks, I was just looking,' I muttered. The shop assistant gave me a polite and contemptuous smile, faintly reminiscent of Camilla's, and wandered off. I sighed, and headed for the street.

2

Actually, I really was meeting someone for lunch: Catherine, a close chum from the old days at Bristol, who was now a journalist. In the calming atmosphere of the Covent Garden Brasserie, which had a couple of huge heaters on to counteract the cold, I eased myself gently into a spritzer, or rather, vice versa, shudderingly lit my first cigarette of the day, and listened as Catherine told me about a friend of hers who had sent her a portion of his novel to read, and was apparently going mad.

'You'll never guess what he did,' she confided. 'He sent me a tape of the first chapter, which he read out. Great, I thought, I can listen to it while I'm cooking – I had a few friends round for supper last night, you don't mind not being invited do you, Emily? I don't think you'd have liked them, anyway. Anyway, I turned the tape on and do you know what he'd done? He hadn't just read out the text – he'd also read out the punctuation. It was absolutely hilarious. You should have heard it. He undid her bra full stop. New paragraph, open inverted commas. Cor, what a pair, comma, close inverted commas, he said, full stop. Then he – are you listening Emily?'

'Yes,' I answered. 'Listen, have you spoken to Natasha recently?'

'She rang me yesterday afternoon,' said my friend, dragging on her cigarette. 'Said she was having some problems with Cosmo, just for a change. Apparently they had a row and she went off to stay overnight at Chris's – you know, that chap she had a fling with? – on Sunday and now Cosmo's accusing her of infidelity. Spot on, if you ask me, but not with Chris. You know she went to a party on Saturday and apparently shared a taxi back with Henry. Well, Pimlico and Holborn are not obvious destinations to share a taxi to, if you ask me, *and* Cosmo was away, staying with those friends of his in Oxford and apparently Natasha refused to go with him.' Catherine sat back and looked at me triumphantly.

I reluctantly decided not to pursue it. Problems with Cosmo and Natasha's possible infidelity were a constantly absorbing topic, but were not, I was sure, whatever it was she wanted to talk to me about. On the other hand, I could well believe she had gone off with Henry: he was a relative newcomer to our little group and as Natasha had already worked her way around most of the others, a bit of novelty would have been just her cup of tea. Also, I was a little concerned at the mention of a gathering I had not been invited to.

'Whose party?' I asked. I was relieved when Catherine mentioned a name I faintly recognized but did not know, and then felt compelled to bring the conversation round to my concern. 'You know, she was talking to me about something I can't quite remember, and I've been receiving a string of the most peculiar phone calls. She keeps ringing me up and then sort of disappearing.'

'Problems with Cosmo, if you ask me,' replied Catherine complacently. 'Nat's always been like that. Fancy another spritzer?'

About an hour later I unwillingly hauled open the huge steel doors of the building in which I worked, grimaced at the doorman, took the lift up to the third floor, and came out to see a new sign emblazoned with the firm's name hanging above reception. Klinker Dorfmann Bergin Wallis, it said, although because that was a bit of a mouthful, most people just referred to it as Klinker Dorfmann – apart, of course, from Bergin and Wallis, both of whom wildly resented any abbreviation. The other day I had overheard the two of them bitching about the chairman, Mark Klinker, who was rarely seen in the office. 'Spends the whole bloody day on the golf course, hasn't brought in any new business for years and takes precedence over our names!' Donald Bergin had snorted before noticing me and telling me off for smoking near a building that housed one of the clients. The clients had an almost deity-like role in our lives: while not actually physically worshipping them, we were supposed to give the impression that we would, if necessary, perform a human sacrifice if their interests so required. Human failings like an addiction to nicotine were not tolerated in their presence.

'Emily!' bellowed Camilla as I attempted to slink past her door. This was one of her particularly annoying habits: she usually did it when I was hungover or did not want to be noticed, and this time both were the case. And it always filled me with rage. She was supposed to be my secretary, after all, so why, I thought, did I always have to be summoned into her presence like a naughty schoolchild?

As ever, though, intimidated by the steely poise which was such a contrast to my own way of going about things, I skidded to a halt and went into her office, noticing for the first time as I did so that it was a little bigger than mine. Camilla, as usual, was on the phone, but rested the receiver against her elegant shoulder and beamed up at me. 'Just a few messages. Interbank rang and asked if they could arrange a meeting tomorrow morning between you and Buzz Copenhager' (her tone studiously avoided any hint of irony). 'Your mother rang to ask if you were going up this weekend, Natasha rang and said it was a personal call and Gerry rang and said he'd call back. I didn't know you knew Gerry, Emily.' She looked at me quizzically.

'Oh, yeah,' I answered vaguely and went off back to my office. Who the hell was Gerry? Maybe Camilla was trying to humiliate me by making up calls from strange men to get me to react, or, worse still, maybe it was a dissatisfied client whose name I had forgotten, ringing up to complain.

I sat back in my chair, looked dispiritedly at a few piles of paper and jumped as Richard Dorfmann, my boss, loomed up beside my desk. 'Ah, Emily,' he enquired, 'problems with the plumbing all sorted out?'

'Uh, yes thanks, although he said he might have to come back next week.'

A faint cloud of disapproval crossed Richard's mild features. I was obviously not the first one to try this on. 'Yes, well Emily,' he said, 'actually I was wondering if we could touch base this afternoon on the Interbank account. I was a bit concerned about a memo I got from the MD's office this morning.'

A black cloud of gloom fell upon me. I had been

expecting this for some time. My inability to get any press coverage whatsoever for our major client was matched only by my inarticulateness at meetings with their (and our) senior staff and my incompetence at dealing with anything that arose out of the meetings afterwards. I bowed humbly to fate. 'In about half an hour?' I asked. Richard nodded assent, and went off down the corridor.

Half an hour to while away before the axe fell then. I turned to my phone. It rang instantly. I snatched it up hoping that it would be Natasha and that the strange series of messages would be explained, but it was only Jack. 'Well, Emily, you seemed to be getting on pretty well with Gary last night,' he said spitefully. Jack was an old boyfriend of mine, and although neither of us had any desire to revive any smouldering flames – or at least he did not, anyway – both of us resented it intensely when the other got lucky, or, in this case, got blindingly drunk and disgraced herself publicly. Again.

'Yeah, well,' I mumbled, unwilling to continue the conversation.

'So tell me, did you do the dirty deed?' asked Jack, trying to sound as if he did not mind and was not going to gossip to the vast number of our mutual acquaintance afterwards.

'To tell you the truth,' I muttered reluctantly, 'I can't remember.'

'Can't remember!' Jack was obviously pleased as Punch, feeling, as he did, that for women once exposed to his own overwhelming sexual technique, to say nothing of enormous member, all men after him were bound to be something of a let-down. 'Come on Emily, you must remember *something*.'

'Nope,' I answered, and hastily tried to change tack before he asked any further searching questions. 'Have you spoken to Natasha recently?'

'Last night, Emily. I don't know if you were too engrossed to notice, but she was there too. She looked a bit weird, I thought.'

'Weird, why, did she say anything?' I demanded.

'No, nothing in particular, I thought it might have been a row with Cosmo. Why are you so concerned all of a sudden?'

'Oh, no reason,' I said. 'Listen. I think I may be going to lose my job.'

Jack sighed. It was a topic we had discussed quite a number of times in the past, and, close friend as he was, you could not expect him to talk about my career or lack of it absolutely every day of his life. He sighed again. 'Look, a group of us are meeting for a drink tonight. Why don't you come along, and we'll talk about it then.'

I hesitated. 'Well, I was going to have a dry night tonight.'

Jack snorted, with some degree of justification. 'Come on, Emily, you haven't had a dry night since I first met you, and that was a good five years ago. I'll see you in the Bleeding Heart at about seven. Bye.'

I put the phone down and jumped, seeing for the first time that Camilla had entered the room while I had been speaking.

'Everything okay, Emily?' she purred, smoothing a strand of immaculately coiffed hair back from her face.

I nodded coldly, gathered my bits of paper about Interbank together, and headed for Richard's office.

'Ah Emily, take a seat,' said Richard, peering over

the top of his glasses at me. He looked more like a university don wrestling with the subtler challenges of medieval literature than one of the best known names in the world of public relations. The venetian blinds in the office were drawn as usual, which gave the room a dark and mysterious feeling. A computer winked on the table beside his desk. Behind him, shelves were piled high with folders and files containing information about Klinker Dorfmann's clients. It looked more like a reading room than an office, except that on the walls, where there should have been prints and watercolours, there were awards for jobs well done. The whole thing was a shrine to making money. 'Are you listening, Emily?' demanded Richard, interrupting my train of thought.

'Yes, yes, of course.'

'Good. Now, as you know, I had a call from Tim Watson this morning, and he's a little bit concerned about some aspects of handling the account.'

I smiled weakly, and braced myself.

'He feels, you know, as I do, that the senior personnel at Interbank aren't taking full advantage of our expertise. There was some initial resistance at the thought of hiring a PR firm, although frankly how anyone could doubt the significance of inter-media communicational data combined with a profile-raising awareness campaign in these difficult days, I really do not know.'

I smiled even more weakly, and began to feel confused. So far there had been no mention of the hash I had made of last week's meeting (I had suggested the senior managers of Interbank might need a course in media training – i.e., how to lie to the press – and then had not known how much media training would cost.

'Not the sort of professionalism we expect from staff in Klinker Dorfmann Bergin Wallis,' sniffed Donald Bergin afterwards, smoothing his immaculate hair and sneaking a glance at himself in a nearby mirror.) Nor had there been mention of a recent survey of International Banking in the *Financial Times*, which had failed to contain one single reference to Interbank.

'What Tim and I both feel is that although some of the individual department heads have been making full use of the relationship, on a corporate level, we feel we could do a lot more for the whole team,' continued Richard, peering earnestly over his glasses. 'So I've asked Camilla to set up a meeting between you and Buzz Copenhager tomorrow.'

'Yes, she mentioned it,' I said. Buzz Copenhager III, who I had never met as he had only recently come over from America, was the head of corporate communications at Interbank – whatever that was. I had never really worked out how corporate communications was different from the stuff we usually did, but having been in PR for four years now, I thought it might be embarrassing to ask. Neither was I entirely sure why he was the third Buzz Copenhager – it would have been a sadistic father to have passed that name on, but I supposed they thought about these things differently in America.

'He's going to bring along a copy of next year's business plan, and I thought the two of you might have a brainstorming session tomorrow morning about any immediate action you might take. Then I thought we could touch base on Thursday, and you can tell me how the session went.' Richard sat back and ran an enthusiastic hand through his greying hair.

'Yes, of course,' I replied, thoroughly confused.

Surely I must have notched up enough misdemeanours over the last couple of weeks to merit at least a written warning, if not outright dismissal. I could not understand my boss's attitude: if I were him, I would fire me immediately. Well, far be it from me to complain.

Smiling even more weakly, I returned to my desk, and did not even mind when Camilla snubbed me in the corridor. Sitting down, I turned to my phone. It rang instantly. 'Emily, it's me,' snapped my mother irritably. 'Didn't you get my message?'

'Yes, sorry, I've been in a meeting with Richard.'

My mother gasped. She was well enough acquainted with my work situation to know what a meeting with Richard could mean. 'No, Mummy, don't worry, he didn't fire me,' I protested.

'Oh,' said my mother. 'That *is* a relief. Well done, darling. Now you must tell me, are you planning to come up this weekend? Daddy and I would love to see you, of course, but we've been asked out for dinner on Saturday night by the Berkinshaws, and if you're not coming, we'd like to go.'

I glared at the phone resentfully. Not only did my mother have far more admirers than me, she also had a considerably fuller social life. Well, not fuller perhaps, but a lot more civilized. Sometimes I wished I spent more time at chi-chi little dinner parties in Cheshire rather than in mad scrambles for food at friends' houses in Battersea. 'But I thought Jamie was coming up too and we were all going to have a family weekend,' I protested.

'I've spoken to him and he quite understands,' said my mother firmly. 'He said he and Charlotte would go and spend the weekend in the Lake District with

26

friends instead. Now we'd love to see you of course, darling, but this weekend is now a tiny bit inconvenient. Of course we'll cancel if you really want us to.'

'No, Mummy, you go,' I sighed resignedly. 'I'll probably come up in a couple of weeks instead.'

'Now darling, if you're sure,' replied my mother, greatly relieved. 'And how are things on the boyfriend front?'

'No-one special at the moment,' I said defiantly.

My mother sighed but took it well. 'Never mind. Now do give Jack my love when you see him and that's tremendous news about the job.'

She rang off, leaving me feeling thoroughly deflated. Why did my family have to consider it good news because I had managed – so far – not to get fired? And I was fed up to the back teeth at being reminded that by my age my mother was married with two children – not that she had ever seemed unduly pleased with her lot. I looked back at the phone. It rang instantly. 'Oh, hi Emily, it's me,' said Camilla. 'Just to let you know, Natasha rang again while you were in with Richard. She said she'd call back. You know, personal calls are not encouraged in the office, Emily.'

She hung up before I could think of a suitably scathing reply. I tried Natasha's office, but they said she had left early. I glanced at my watch. Only five o'clock. It was at least another hour before I could slip off, and I still had to trawl through Interbank's tedious quarterly journal to see if there was anything in it that merited a press release. I sighed, and slipped off to the loo for a surreptitious cigarette.

3

A couple of hours later, having spent much of the intervening time closeted in a small cubicle, glaring at the emerald tiling and dropping my used matches in the sanitary towel disposer, I found myself staggering down the little wooden staircase into the Bleeding Heart, stopping, as I always did, to read the touching little tale of the Bleeding Heart's legend: a medieval woman having her heart ripped out by a jealous husband. The heart, needless to say, continued to beat (and bleed) for several days afterwards. I supposed such a fate was just marginally worse than working in PR.

'Emily!' shouted Jack, as I pushed through the swing door. I looked at him and felt a slight pang. I had always been rather proud of the fact that my most serious boyfriend – or ex-boyfriend now – was really extremely good looking. Jack was very tall and slim, with broad shoulders and floppy dark blond hair which he was always having to push out of the way. He had very dark blue eyes and high cheekbones. The only imperfections were a crook in the middle of his nose, where he'd broken it as a child, a sprinkling of very light freckles and a slightly lopsided grin.

Luckily, however, Jack had always been totally unaware of his looks and was without a shred of vanity. Today he was wearing a dark charcoal grey suit, which contrasted with the lights in his hair, a red and white striped shirt and an expensive looking red tie. I made my way over to the table, noticing as I did so that Jack was sitting next to someone who looked vaguely familiar – oh dear God no, it was Gary. I smiled weakly and slid in beside my ex.

'Emily, I believe you know Gary?' asked Jack politely as he pecked me on the cheek and poured me a glass of wine. 'Oh yes, of course, you met last night.'

'Hello, how are you,' I said to Gary. More and more people were arriving at the table, including, to my intense displeasure, a rather glamorous blonde bimbo, clad, as far as I could see, almost entirely in gold jewellery. Worse still, Jack greeted her rather warmly. Perhaps he intended to get back at me for last night.

'I'm sorry I didn't get the chance to call again,' began Gary, who was rather better looking than he had seemed at seven o'clock this morning, 'but I was held up in meetings all day.' He had an agreeably swish voice, too.

'Know what you mean,' I replied glumly, wondering faintly what he was talking about. 'Where I work we have meetings before meetings to decide what we are going to say, and then meetings after meetings to analyse it all afterwards. And for the really big meetings, we have rehearsals. They put more energy into them than you would for a major new production of a stage play. The whole thing is supposed to run seamlessly – all hell breaks loose if you miss your cue. Whenever you walk down the corridor of my offices you see people behind closed doors passionately extolling to empty seats and then leaning over and winking while they rehearse their impromptu jokes. I always fluff mine.'

Gary grinned. 'I can't really see you in PR, you know.'

'Neither can my boss,' I replied, helping myself to more wine. 'He thinks my talents would be put to better use elsewhere. I only ended up in it because two chums of mine from university, George and Ian – they were there last night actually – got me the job after I'd been travelling for a year and then working in a book shop and I didn't know what else to do.' I was about to expand on my grievances, but at that point Catherine, who had arrived without my noticing and was deep in conversation with some man caught my eye.

'Ask Emily,' she insisted. 'It's true. It's absolutely hilarious. You should have heard it. I turned on the tape . . .'

I listened for a minute and then, bored, I turned back to Gary, who was by now deep in conversation with Jack and the bimbo. Jack was holding forth. 'Yes, well we were going out for about three years,' he was explaining, 'but we split up because Emily wanted to get married and I didn't. You know, the same old story.'

Gary and the bimbo looked at me sympathetically. I was getting slightly fed up. I had heard this mono-logue quite enough times in the past for my liking. 'How did you and Jack meet?' asked Gary as the bimbo began to explain to Jack how she also did not wish to get tied down.

'Through a mutual friend, Natasha, she was there last night as well,' I began. 'Nat and I were at university in Bristol together and when we all came down to London she and her then boyfriend Steve had a party which Jack came to.' Quite by chance I glanced round and there, at the door, was Natasha. 'In fact, that's her right now,' I said, abruptly standing up. 'Sorry, I must go and talk.' As usual, heads had craned to look at her. Like me, she was of medium height, but Natasha looked positively Slavonic, although in fact her family had lived in Cornwall for generations. She was very slim, with very black hair, cut in an elegant crop. She had cheekbones that stood out by about a mile, large, dark slanty eyes and an extremely full mouth, which was always emphasized by a gash of scarlet lipstick. Men took one look and drooled.

I knocked my chair over in my haste to get over to her, skidded across the floor, fell over and as I managed to get back to my feet, began, 'Nat, what on earth is going on?'

'Shhh, wait, Cosmo's right behind me,' hissed Natasha, making for our tables. I followed reluctantly. 'How's the gang?' she cried, slipping in beside Catherine.

Catherine beamed. 'Oh Natasha, I've got this great story to tell you. It's absolutely hilarious . . .'

I sighed and went back to sit next to Gary, who was now deep in conversation again with Jack and the bimbo. 'Well, after I left New Zealand last year, I spent some time in Sydney,' the bimbo was saying. 'But the guys there were, like, you know, just awful. So I thought I'd come to Europe, to, like, get to know some really interesting people.'

She beamed at Jack, who was lapping it up. Rather a low-cut top, I thought sourly. I sullenly took another slurp of wine and then accidentally caught Gary's eye. He winked. I began to rather warm to him. 'And so do you find European men more interesting?' asked Jack.

'Oh yeah,' breathed the bimbo enthusiastically, leaning forward and exposing an ample cleavage. 'Especially English men. It's like they're so enigmatic. You can never tell what they're thinking.'

Actually, it was pretty obvious from Jack's face exactly what he was thinking. I felt a sharp stab of jealousy. Gary shot me another glance. 'You know, if she jumped up and down she'd knock herself out,' he whispered. I began to warm to him a lot more. Jack and the bimbo were not paying any attention to us: Jack was in the process of explaining how warm and un-English he found antipodean women to be. 'By the way,' said Gary, clearing his throat slightly, 'I've been invited to some friends for dinner this Saturday, and I thought if you weren't busy, maybe you'd like to come. It's nothing formal, just a party in Battersea.'

'Yes, if it's okay with them,' I replied.

'Oh, it will be, they told me to bring anyone I liked. They're a very nice couple. I should warn you, though, it usually turns into a bit of a free for all at their place, they've got some very eccentric friends. Luckily one of them knows how to repair furniture, so the damage can usually be put right. Shall I call you tomorrow so we can arrange to meet?'

'Yes, do.' I sat back, feeling quite pleased, even if he was a computer programmer. At this moment ructions began on the other side of the table.

'Men,' bellowed Natasha, who was obviously in full swing. '*Men*. All they ever want to do is go out, drink nine pints, come home, beat the wife, kick the dog and have sex with the children.'

The table laughed. 'No, I mean it,' she boomed, looking quite flushed by this point. 'Take Cosmo. He's a bastard, you know.'

'Natasha, not now.' It was Cosmo, who had followed her in and was sitting beside her across the table. I quite liked Cosmo, actually; in spite of the large private income he was a fairly mild-mannered chap who worked as an assistant producer at the BBC. He was not remotely up to dealing with Natasha.

'Yes, now. Let's let all our friends hear what you think about me. Everyone, he's accusing me of sleeping with someone else.'

'Natasha, *please*.' Cosmo was beginning to look very upset, and I can't say I blamed him.

'No, let them hear it,' roared Natasha. 'He practically kicks me out of his flat, I have nowhere to go so I go and stay with Chris, and then I get accused of infidelity. *Men*.'

The words were spat out. The table was silent, even the bimbo looked taken aback. Jack, not for the first time, attempted to ease the situation. 'Who needs topping up?' he asked, getting to his feet, wine bottle in hand. Everyone relaxed and started muttering again, except Natasha.

She leant over to Cosmo. 'I've had just about enough of you,' she hissed. She straightened, and glared at me. 'Come on, Emily, let's go and find somewhere decent to drink.'

I hesitated. After this little outburst, I was fairly sure that Catherine was right and it was just Cosmo-trouble that was on her mind. Also, I was getting on quite well with Gary. Also, I was extremely reluctant to leave Jack in the clutches of the bimbo. Jack turned and caught my eye. 'Go on, Emily,' he urged, 'we were thinking of going to the Bar Madrid later, so we could meet you there if you like?'

'Okay,' I replied reluctantly. Natasha was standing

33

beside me, and looked as if she could explode again at any second. I pushed back my chair.

'See you on Saturday then,' said Gary. 'I'll give you a call tomorrow.'

I smiled at him, gathered my belongings and headed towards the door. Camilla burst through, ignored my rather feeble smile, shouted 'Gerry! How amazing!' and bounded off across the room. I sighed and followed Natasha into the little cobbled courtyard outside the Bleeding Heart.

'That was a bit much, even for you,' I complained as we headed out towards Holborn, although without much hope of a reasonable explanation. Ever since I'd first known her, Natasha had had two objectives in life: a full social life and a rich husband, and was liable to fly off the handle if the prospect of either of the two seemed to be threatened.

Natasha had completely calmed down. 'Yeah, sorry about that, but I had to talk to you,' she explained. 'When I was supposed to see you this morning, I couldn't get away because Cosmo actually came to the office and demanded to know about Chris, and I couldn't get rid of him. Occasionally he went outside to fume, which is when I tried you. And you can imagine how I've been feeling all day.'

'Well, just tell him there's nothing between you and Chris and he has to stop being so jealous,' I snapped. We were walking down Holborn now. It was cold, windy, I wanted a drink and I was feeling thoroughly fed up at being called upon to intervene between Natasha and Cosmo yet again.

'Oh I've done that, but that's not the problem, Emily. Haven't you got any advice about what I should do about Henry?'

'Henry?' I was even more irritated. Catherine was obviously right there, too. 'What about him?'

Natasha stopped walking and turned to me. 'You can't have forgotten what I told you,' she whispered, aghast.

'Well it was late, and I had had a few drinks,' I protested. 'So you had a fling with Henry and Cosmo's pissed off. To be honest, I don't really blame him.'

Natasha looked at me. 'You really can't remember, can you?' she said incredulously.

I was actually becoming quite interested. 'What was it?'

'I can't believe even you would forget something like this!' exploded Natasha furiously. 'For God's sake, Emily, this is the worst thing that has ever happened to me and you can't even remember. For God's sake.'

'Well what is it!' I asked. 'I can't help if you won't tell me.'

Natasha breathed very heavily, and looked at me. 'Would it help if you took notes?' she inquired.

'Just get on with it.'

'OK. Well, Cosmo went away on Saturday night to visit these friends of his in Oxford, and I didn't feel like going, so I went to a party.'

'Yes, I know all that, Catherine told me.'

'You didn't say anything to Catherine, did you?' erupted Natasha, stopping in the middle of the street. 'You might as well have broadcast it on the nine o'clock news. Oh, thanks a lot, Emily.'

'Of course I bloody didn't,' I retorted. 'I've told you, I can't even remember what it is. I just saw her at lunchtime and asked her if she knew what was wrong.'

Natasha glared at me and started walking again. I looked wistfully at the Cittie of York as we passed it on the right. 'We could nip in for a quick drink and you could tell me the rest of the story there,' I suggested hopefully.

'*No*, Emily. I'm not chancing you forgetting this again.'

'All right, all right. Just get on with it then. Henry's not going to tell anyone, is he?'

'That's just the point, Emily!' Natasha's voice reached a crescendo. 'He can't tell anyone! He's dead!'

'Dead!' She had my attention now. 'But Henry can't be dead. I saw him last week, and he looked fine. Natasha, what happened?'

'Well, that's what I keep trying to tell you. I don't know.' Natasha paused and looked at me dramatically.

'You must know,' I said, 'you were there.'

'Well, yes, but it's not quite as simple as that, Emily.'

'Look,' I patted her shoulder to try to calm her down, 'just tell me what happened right from the beginning.'

'Well, I was at this party,' Natasha began. 'Henry was there, and we got chatting, and you know how it is, I thought, I'm really pissed off with Cosmo, what the hell.' This was not an uncommon introduction to Natasha's stories. So far, so good, I thought.

'So he asked me for a drink back at his place, and we went, and it was the same old story.' Natasha glanced at me slightly self-consciously, and kept on talking. 'So I woke up the next morning, and I was a bit pissed off, because I didn't mean to do anything, and Henry was still asleep.'

'So everything was all right then, was it?' I asked.

'Look, Nat, you didn't kill him to keep him quiet, did you?' I wouldn't have entirely put it past her.

'Of course I didn't kill him!' shouted Natasha. We had stopped walking again, and several passers-by turned round and stared. After a struggle she began to speak calmly again. 'Will you please take this seriously, Emily? What happened was that I thought I'd slip out before he woke up because I didn't want to talk to him. So I got home, but when I'd done so, I found that by mistake I'd taken his keys instead of mine. So I had to go back to his flat, and I was getting a bit worried as Cosmo had said he might come back early.'

'Yes, well what happened then?'

'Well I knocked and there was no answer, so I let myself in, and I called, "It's Natasha, back for a quickie."'

I looked at her in disgust. 'Yeah, Emily, you're one to talk,' accused Natasha, momentarily distracted. 'What did I hear about you and Gary last night? Anyway, there was no answer, which I thought was a bit strange, so I went back into the bedroom. At first I didn't see him, he wasn't on the bed.'

'So what did you do?'

'Well, I began to think there was something wrong. So I called "Henry, it's me" again, in case he was in the bath or something, but then I saw it. Oh Emily, it was awful.'

'What?' I demanded. 'What did you see?'

'His foot,' said Natasha. Her voice had practically dropped to a whisper. 'I saw his foot stretching out from the other side of the bed. I walked around, and he was lying on the floor, his arms and legs were all over the place and there was a trickle of blood coming out of his mouth. He wasn't moving at all – he was obviously dead. I was so shocked I couldn't move for a second and then I ran out of the bedroom. And by this time I was getting really worried because Cosmo was due back and I didn't know what to do.'

I really was taking this seriously now. 'Well, what did you do?' I asked. 'Did you call for an ambulance?'

'Well no, actually.' Natasha was looking a bit uncomfortable. 'I was getting really worried that Cosmo would be back, so, well, I found my keys and I left.'

'You left!' Even I was flabbergasted. I had known Natasha a long time and, with the possible exception of Camilla, she was the most selfish person I had ever met, but I had not thought even she would sink this low. 'Natasha, you can't have just left. Couldn't you get anyone to help him?'

'I had to, Emily!' Natasha's voice had reached crescendo level again. 'Look, Cosmo would have killed me if he'd known I'd been at Henry's. And there was nothing anyone could do, he was already dead.'

'Oh, so now you're a medical expert, are you?'

'Look, I told you, he wasn't moving, there was blood and there was no sign of life at all. And anyway, I thought someone else would find him. So I went home, and I only just had time to change before Cosmo got back, so I couldn't do anything then. And then we had a really big fight because he wanted to know what I'd done while he was in Oxford, and I said, "Oh, screwed around" and he took it seriously and I had to go and stay with Chris.

'But then yesterday, I really thought I should alert someone. So I rang his work and I was going to say, when they said he hadn't come in, "Oh, well, shouldn't someone go and check up on him?" But it turned out that he'd taken the week off, so no-one thought anything was wrong. And then I called a couple of people we both know, and said how's Henry and when were they seeing him, but none of them had any plans to. And then I even rang his parents, and I was thinking of saying anonymously, "Go check up on your son", but there was no answer.'

'Yeah, well that would have been a nice surprise for them if they'd got an anonymous phone call telling them to check up on Henry, they go over and find a rotting corpse,' I said. 'Anyway, they'd probably have recognized your voice.' We had all met Henry's parents when he had held his thirtieth birthday party at his parents' rather grand house in Barnes a couple of weeks ago.

'Well, what was I supposed to do, Emily! What would you have done?'

'I think I'd have called an ambulance in the first place,' I replied.

'Yes, well that's all very well for you, but you're not living with someone who adores you.'

I looked at her resentfully. Not only was I being pulled into some horrible situation, but she was insulting my man-less state as well. Only my mother was supposed to do that. I had never really got round to having another serious relationship since Jack and I split up, although then again, neither had he, and I did not feel the need to be constantly reminded of it. 'Well, what do you want me to do about it?' I asked.

'I want you to go and visit him, so you can discover him and call the police.'

'Me? No, Natasha. Absolutely not. According to you he's been dead three days now – what sort of state is he going to be in?'

'Oh please, Emily, he can't have decomposed that

fast in this weather and it would only take a couple of minutes. Anyway, we're nearly there now.'

I looked around. She was quite right: we had just got to Holborn tube station, and Henry lived in one of those horrible little ex-council flats on Boswell Street, just to the right. 'Absolutely not,' I said.

'Oh Emily, please,' Natasha implored. 'Look at all the things I've done for you.'

'Like what?' I demanded.

'I introduced you to Jack, didn't I?'

'Only by chance,' I hissed, 'and look at how that bloody turned out.'

'Well, I never got angry that time at Bristol when you borrowed my favourite dress without asking and spilled red wine all over it.'

'Yes,' I said hotly, 'but what about that time when my parents gave me that beautiful Peugeot and you crashed it? I've never got over that car, you know.'

'Well, the insurance company paid up for it, didn't they?'

'Yes,' I snarled, 'but if you remember, my parents insisted on keeping the cash. Said I wasn't to be trusted with a set of wheels. And I'd hardly put spilling wine on a dress with totalling a car. The dry-cleaning bill was a lot less expensive.'

'Oh please, Emily, I need your help.' Natasha's eyes were filling with tears. That was the thing about her – when she turned it on, no-one, man or woman alike, had the heart to resist.

I sighed. It would be one up on Camilla after all, I bet she had never discovered a corpse. 'All right,' I conceded, 'but on one condition. You come with me.'

'Me?' Natasha looked quite as shocked as I had been. 'Emily, I can't! What would Cosmo say?'

'Look, it would be perfectly all right. You're with me, we could say we just decided to call on Henry to have a drink and then we found him. No-one would have to know you left on Sunday when he was like that. But listen, how are we going to get in?'

'Oh, that's all right, I left the door unlocked, so the neighbours could break in and find him. I suppose it will be all right if you're there.' She looked at me doubtfully.

'Come on,' I said, starting to walk, 'let's get this over with. And while we're waiting for the police, I fully intend to find something to drink there as well. Bloody hell, Natasha, I hope you appreciate this.'

We walked up Boswell Street, which seemed even narrower and darker than usual, and made our way up the foul cat piss smelling steps to Henry's flat. It was completely dark. The wind lashed at us and it had started to rain. We edged nervously along the narrow concrete walkway and crept up to the door, which was covered with bars and bolts. Someone had written 'Abandon hope all ye who enter here' on the wall beside the door. 'You go first,' whispered Natasha, positioning herself behind me.

I took hold of the doorknob, and turned. I was shaking from head to foot. The door swung slowly open, I scrunched my eyes as tightly closed as I could, and reached inside to turn the lights on. I found the switch and clicked. 'My God!' gasped Natasha behind me. I opened my eyes and looked into the flat to see – nothing. Not one single thing. Everything in the flat, the sofas, chairs, pictures, rugs, even the books on the bookshelves were all gone. There was a little kitchenette to the left that looked over the sitting-room, and apart from the sink where a tap was slowly dripping, there was nothing there either. The stove, fridge and washing machine had gone, the cupboard doors were hanging open and there was nothing inside them either, not even a mug.

'The bedroom's over there,' croaked Natasha, pointing to a passage at the back of the room. Grasping each other's hands, we walked up to the passage, and Natasha pushed open a door on the right. Nothing. No bed, no wardrobe, no chest of drawers – and above all, no Henry. We stood, staring at one another for a second – and then ran. Neither of us stopped until we had pelted downstairs and run the full length of Boswell Street, where we stopped under a street light, both gasping for breath. My desire for a drink had never been stronger.

'What are we going to do?' whimpered Natasha. She had gone quite white, and was shivering nervously. 'Who would have taken the body, Emily? What are we going to do?'

'Find Jack,' I announced firmly. 'He'll know what to do, and he said he was going to be in the Bar Madrid.'

'He won't tell Cosmo, will he?'

'Not if I ask him not to,' I said. 'Come on.' We set off up the road.

4

I was being roasted over a spit. Tongues of flame were licking my arms, my legs, my breasts – sweat was gushing off me. The flames were getting nearer and nearer my head, which was pounding and thumping, there was a roaring sound in my ears, tears were gushing down my cheeks, my body felt as if it was about to explode – when suddenly someone threw a bucket of cold water over me. I screamed.

'Are you all right?' I sat up abruptly. Someone was sitting up in bed beside me. I squinted at him in the light of a small bedside lamp which he had obviously just turned on. I had no idea who he was.

'Oh yes, fine,' I muttered. The man beamed at me. 'You looked kind of hot just now, so I pulled the duvet off you and boy, that was quite a snarl you made.'

American accent. That gave me no clue at all. I rather feebly pulled the duvet back around myself, and lay back, thoughts swirling round in my head. I had the vague feeling that rather a lot had happened last night, but for the life of me I could not remember what. The man got out of bed, displaying rather an attractively tanned physique, I thought, and put on a white towelling robe with 'BC' embroidered on the

43

pocket. 'I'm just going to take a quick shower, and then I'll put some coffee on,' he said. 'You take your time. When I'm done in the bathroom, you'll find everything you need: my wife always makes sure we're pretty well stocked up.' He winked at me.

'Uh, yes,' I murmured weakly. 'I'm really sorry but I can't quite remember your name.'

'Bernard,' he replied, putting the emphasis on the second syllable, as Americans are wont to do. 'And you never got round to telling me yours.'

'Judith,' I answered sullenly. I was thoroughly fed up with waking up with strange men, and this one seemed too cocky by half. I did not feel like telling him my real name. Left me with some pride, at least.

Bernard winked at me again, remarked, 'That was quite a night, Judith,' and went out the door.

Great, I thought. First, it was quite a night and I could not remember a damn thing about it, second, not only had I done it again but he was obnoxious and married and third, I felt terrible. I could not remember whether I had had anything to eat last night. I hoped Jack had not noticed or he might tell Gary.

Hang on, that turned a key. Why would Jack tell Gary? Because I had met them both last night. And Jack was chatting up a bimbo and then Gary asked me out to dinner on Saturday. I sat up again and, despite another pang of jealousy about Jack, began to feel quite cheerful. A date. It was ages since I had been on a date. I must remember to tell my mother. But then I had had to leave because Natasha was being her usual difficult self . . .

I fell back against the pillows. It was all coming back now. Natasha, Cosmo, Chris, Henry, poor thing, wherever the remains of him were now, the empty flat and our flight to Bar Madrid. We had grabbed a taxi and Natasha was going on incoherently and selfishly – 'What am I going to do, Emily? My life is in ruins' – and I was thinking, this can not be happening to me. And then we had got to the Bar Madrid, but the others had not arrived, so we ordered and consumed a bottle of wine pretty quickly. And then we had had another, while the conversation shifted from poor old Henry to what Natasha was going to do about Cosmo and was it not about time I got over Jack and found someone else?

I blinked. What had happened then? Oh yes, just as we were polishing off the second bottle the gang had arrived: Cosmo, Jack, Catherine and the bimbo were all there with a number of others I did not know, but I was pretty sure Gary was not among them. Thank heavens for that. And I had raced over to Jack, and begged, 'I've got to talk to you *now*,' but he for once was not being at all co-operative, had his arm around the bimbo (who was still, I seemed to recall, looking at me quite sympathetically, God knows what he had said after I left) and then introduced me to some of his banking friends, one of whom must have been Bernard. Natasha, by this time, was nose to nose with Cosmo and did not look like being disturbed.

And so more drinks were ordered, I tried and failed to talk to Jack a couple of more times and then it got distinctly blurry. I very vaguely remembered Natasha and Cosmo leaving and Natasha saying she would call me the next day, and then Jack and the bimbo leaving and Jack saying he would talk to me tomorrow, and although the details were now sketchy to put it mildly, I could guess the rest. I had a few more drinks to cheer myself up, Bernard decided to escort me home and one thing had led to another. Apparently it was enjoyable, according to him.

I heard the shower being turned off in the next room, and Bernard himself appeared at this moment, dripping wet and clad in a very skimpy towel. He was tall and blond, but whereas Jack, who was also tall and blond had the very English floppy hair and high cheek-boned look, Bernard was more stocky and muscular. Probably all those years at college playing American football. 'Bathroom's free!' he smiled brightly, and disappeared again.

I looked at the clock on the bedside table and shuddered. It was only just after half past six. The bed was extremely comfortable: it was vast and seemed to have at least three hundred pillows scattered around. The large room, which had dark plush curtains hanging at the windows, was filled with antique furniture and had some quite nice watercolours on the walls. In one corner there was a table stacked with some highly unusual gold and wooden bowls. The room was also extremely warm. That was the nice thing about Americans: unlike the English, they had understood and embraced the concept of central heating.

Still, I thought blearily, dragging myself out of bed and into the very well-equipped black and steel bathroom, which was just next door, I had better get a move on. I had a meeting with someone or other that morning, which I seemed to remember was quite important and I had better prepare myself properly just for once. And there was this whole appalling business with Natasha: I must get hold of Jack as soon as possible and ask him what to do. I caught sight of myself in the mirror, which was rather offputtingly placed along the wall beside the loo and looked away hastily: my eye make-up was halfway down my cheeks, my hair was sticking straight up on end and my tummy seemed to have grown during the night. Heaven knows how, as I was sure I had not eaten anything for at least five years. Must remember to do some exercise some day, I thought, stomachs creep up on you unexpectedly.

After finishing in the bathroom, where I had a bath and made liberal use of Bernard's wife's make-up, I staggered downstairs. Bernard, by now dressed in a dark blue suit, loafers and Hermes tie, was standing in the kitchen gulping down the remains of a cup of coffee. 'Look, I'm really sorry, Judith, but I'm going to have to go,' he declared, pouring me out a cup. 'I've got an important meeting on this morning, but you just take your time, have some coffee, and just shut the door when you leave. Don't worry about locking it, my cleaner is due in just over an hour.' He beamed at me again and picked up a Burberry's raincoat and a very smart burgundy briefcase.

'Oh, right,' I replied weakly. 'Can you tell me where we are?'

'Turn right when you leave the house, walk up to the end of the road and you'll be on the Old Brompton Road. Bye, Judith, last night was great.'

With that he was gone. I briefly considered asking Jack about him, but, due to the Gary situation, decided not to for the moment at least. I sighed, poured myself another cup of coffee and looked around the room. The kitchen, which was large and gleaming, was as well equipped as the bathroom. It had a few rather peculiar-looking tribal heads dotted around the shelves.

I went to investigate the sitting-room: it was absolutely huge, with an enormous Adam-style fireplace at one end, topped by a large mirror. The silver frame was made in the shape of two swans extending their necks and twining round one another at the top. There were a couple of vast cream sofas and chairs and some more good antique furniture dotted around. But with the exception of some more tribal looking figures – large ones were keeping guard by the door and smaller ones were nestling on the shelves – the place did not seem to have been lived in that long, it had a slightly rented feel to it. On the other hand, Bernard, whoever he was, was obviously not short of a penny or two. Shame he was married.

I went out into the hall and examined myself in the mirror. I was a bit pale and had dark circles under my eyes, but on the whole I did not look too bad, thanks to Bernard's wife's make-up. The only trouble was, I was still wearing yesterday's clothes, and I did not think I had time to go home and change as it was already quarter past seven and I was supposed to be making an early start, not that I could entirely remember why. I sniffed my shirt hesitantly. Not too bad. I sprayed a bit more scent on just to be on the safe side, put on my coat, found my briefcase and made for the door.

It took me ages to find a taxi. My bank balance said I should go by public transport, but it was a foul morning, rainy and windy, and I did not feel like the walk to the tube. I felt thoroughly depressed as I pushed open the huge steel doors leading up to Klinker Dorfmann Bergin Wallis. The doorman winked at me, in a way that was horribly reminiscent of Bernard, and I took myself up to the office. The reception area was still dark: the receptionist did not arrive until 8.30 and so there was no much-needed coffee. As I walked up the hall, steaming gently from the rain on my coat, I noticed a light from Richard's office: he looked up from his desk as I peered in. His awards for PR well done gleamed on the wall beside him. 'Emily!' he exclaimed in astonishment. 'This is a bit early for you, isn't it? Come in to prepare for your meeting with Buzz? Do you know, I found yesterday Buzz isn't really his name? It's just one of those damn silly American nicknames – apparently, he's called something quite normal really.'

'Buzz?' I asked blankly, walking into his office and dripping on the carpet. I knew there was some reason I had come in early, but could not quite place it.

'Buzz Copenhager III? BC to his staff? Interbank? The meeting wasn't cancelled, was it?'

'No, no,' I replied. The most awful thought had just occurred to me, produced by a sudden memory of a towelling robe. 'Tell me, what's Buzz like?'

'Oh, nice chap, although not really my sort,' opined Richard. 'American. Bit of a ladies' man, so I'm told, although he does have a most delightful wife. She's a specialist in African art; they're supposed to be putting together quite a collection.'

By now I was feeling quite ill. Although on the one hand I could not believe fate would have played quite such a lousy trick on me, on the other, I did not want to take any chances. 'Richard, can I have a word?' I asked.

Richard, who was just settling down to his papers again, looked up. 'Yes, Emily?'

I slid further into the room. 'Look, Richard, you know I'm very committed to working on the Interbank account,' I began.

'Yes.' Richard's normally calm features had begun to harden.

'But I just thought,' I whispered miserably, looking down at the carpet, 'perhaps I'm not senior enough to handle the meeting with Buzz Copenhager. I thought maybe someone else should do it.'

There was silence for a moment. Then Richard said, 'Sit down, Emily.'

I did so.

'Now look, Emily,' he began, 'personally I've always liked you, and I'm happy to have you working for our firm. But not all the board members think like that. Donald, for example, isn't at all happy about what he sees as your lack of commitment, and just the other day he was telling me about a meeting you hadn't been at all prepared for.'

'Donald Bergin,' I burst out, 'is a self-opinionated arrogant git whose most important consideration in life is making sure his tie matches his handkerchief. What he's really got against me is that I'm a woman and I smoke.'

'I don't like your smoking either if it comes to that, and I will not have you talking about members of the board in that way,' said Richard heatedly. He nearly raised his voice. 'And I'm not at all happy about your attitude either, Emily, if you're going to speak to me in that tone of voice. Now, I've told you I'm trying to help you, but I am absolutely not going to do so unless I see a little more co-operation from you. Understood?'

'Yes, sorry,' I muttered.

'Now look, I told Donald, against his better judgement, that I wanted you to meet Buzz Copenhager. If you are now going to stand there and tell me you are not prepared to do so, I think you should think seriously about your future in this firm.'

I had been expecting this for some time, but not quite like this. 'Yes, look, I'm sorry,' I said hastily. 'I was just a bit nervous. But I did come in early to prepare, after all.'

'Yes, well it makes a nice change,' replied Richard.

'Coffee anyone?' tinkled a voice. I whirled round. Camilla was standing in the doorway clutching two steaming mugs, hair gleaming, immaculately dressed, pearls just right and a very understanding smile on her face. I wondered how long she had been there.

'I didn't want to interrupt,' she explained to Richard, gliding in and presenting him with a mug, 'but I knew you had a lot on today, and I thought this might help.' Richard melted. Camilla beamed at him, sipped from the second mug and turned to me. 'There's some more coffee in the machine, Emily,' she announced coolly. 'Come in early to gen up on Interbank?'

I nodded ungraciously. 'It's a bit early for you, though, isn't it?' I snapped.

'Oh no, I always get in around now. It's the best time of the day. Hope it goes well with Interbank. I do envy you, getting to have so much contact with the clients. And I believe Buzz is very charming.'

She beamed again, and made for the door. I followed her, went to get a cup of coffee and made my way to my desk.

The next couple of hours were a nightmare. On the one hand there was Natasha and Henry: on the other there was the terrible prospect of the Interbank meeting looming up and me being neither prepared nor a stranger to one of the most important people in

Interbank involved with the account. I tried to ring Jack, who always got in very early, but he was locked away in a series of meetings. Jamie, as usual, was incarcerated with a sick Labrador. There was no point in trying to ring Natasha or anyone else for hours yet. I tried to bury myself in a three-foot-high bundle of Interbank documents, got increasingly irritated by the surprise my early appearance commanded as my colleagues appeared one by one and sloped off to the loos for more and more cigarettes.

Eventually, 10 rolled round. The meeting was at 10.30. I was about to go to the loo for one last cigarette when my phone rang. I grabbed it immediately. 'Emily, it's Jack,' came the voice down the phone, sounding, I thought, a little strained. 'I gather you called.'

'Yes, look, I've got to talk to you as soon as possible,' I replied. 'Are you free at lunchtime?'

'I suppose so. Where shall we meet? El Vino's, 12.30?'

'That's fine,' I said, greatly relieved. 'Listen, Jack, who were those people I was talking to in the Bar Madrid?'

'Oh, just a few friends of mine in the City,' he replied. 'We bumped into them in the Bleeding Heart and I said to come along. I thought you might know one of them, actually, Buzz Copenhager? I hadn't met him before but apparently he's over from the States for a few years with Interbank, and I thought that was one of your accounts. God, Emily, why did you let me go off with that awful woman?'

He hung up. On the one hand I felt extremely gleeful (the night obviously had not gone as well as he was hoping): on the other I felt paralysed with terror.

My worst fears had just been confirmed. What on earth was I going to say to Buzz?

Richard loomed up beside my desk. 'Isn't it time you were off, Emily?' he asked. 'I thought the meeting was at half past ten, and I do *not* think it would look good if you were late. Do try to remember they're paying us a retainer of £7,000 a month.'

'Yes, I'm just going,' I replied, hastily pulling my papers together and ramming them into my increasingly decrepit briefcase.

Richard looked at it in distaste. 'Don't you think it's about time you got a new one?' he asked. 'Now remember, Emily, adding value to the relationship is what it's all about. Even if you don't have any immediate suggestions, tell him the whole team is looking forward to a really exciting and important opportunity in making the best use of the business plan. Suggest to him some research we can carry out, either about Interbank's business profile or about some specific aspects of the business plan. And Emily, *don't smoke*.'

'I wasn't going to!' I burst out angrily. 'I never smoke in meetings. Anyway, Buzz smokes too.'

'I didn't know you'd met him before,' said Richard sharply. 'When was this?'

'Oh, I haven't,' I stuttered hastily. 'I was just asking a few people about him.'

'Getting in early and then checking up on the client before you meet him?' asked Richard incredulously. 'You are turning over a new leaf. I'm impressed.'

I smiled weakly, and made for the door.

Getting there was awful. First I could not find a taxi. Then when one finally stopped, it was non-smoking, and I had to get another. Then the traffic was completely jammed between Chancery Lane, where I worked, and Cheapside, where Interbank's office was based. I spent the time nervously chain-smoking, combing my hair, spraying on more scent and touching up Buzz's wife's blusher.

Eventually the taxi drew up beside the huge steel doors that housed Interbank's London office. I got out of the car. My hands were shaking so badly I dropped my purse as I was trying to pay the driver. Coins went everywhere. I scrabbled about in the gutter trying to collect them, in the process got my hands extremely grimy and then forgot to ask the taxi driver for a receipt before he drove off in disgust.

I pushed my way through the huge steel doors. Whereas the doors in the building where I worked were lightly coloured wood, with large gold door knobs, these were real Sixties monstrosities, with huge sheets of glass and nasty steel bars going from top to bottom. I got to the reception desk where the doorman looked at me dismissively. 'Um, I'm here to see Buzz Copenhager at 10.30,' I explained, noticing with dismay that the clock on the wall behind the desk showed that it was now twenty to eleven.

'Name?' inquired the doorman.

'Emily Whitelake.'

The doorman picked up a phone and punched a few buttons. 'Emily Whitelake here for Mr Copenhager.'

A voice said something. The doorman put down the phone. 'Take the lift to the fifth floor, and someone will meet you there.'

My knees were shaking so badly I almost had trouble getting to the lift. I collapsed inside, gave one despairing glance into the mirror and slumped against the wall.

The lift doors opened. An extremely smart-looking

woman was waiting for me. Dressed in a dark grey, conservative skirt that reached just below the knee, and an ivory silk blouse, it looked as if her hair had on about three bottles of hair spray to make sure every wisp stayed in place. 'Miss Whitelake?' she enquired warmly.

I stretched out my hand, noticing as I did so that it was still covered with grime from the street outside.

The woman noticed it too. She grasped it rather gingerly. 'I'm so sorry I'm late,' I explained weakly. 'The traffic getting here was terrible.'

'Oh, don't worry, Buzz is very relaxed about tardiness,' said the woman. Like many Interbank employees, she was American. 'Perhaps you'd like to freshen up before your meeting begins?'

'Oh, thanks, I dropped my purse outside,' I offered by way of explanation.

The woman smiled, took my coat and ushered me into the ladies' loo. I looked at myself. Perspiration had broken out on my nose and upper lip. Despite the number of times I had combed it, my hair was sticking straight up on end again. I washed the dirt off my hands, tried to calm my hair down and stepped outside. The shaky feeling in my knees was getting worse.

'Step right this way,' invited the immaculately groomed woman. She ushered me up the corridor, opened the door, said, 'Miss Whitelake is here to see you, Buzz,' and left me to my fate.

I stepped inside the door. Buzz, or was it Bernard, was standing behind his desk at the other end of the room, with arm outstretched and a big grin on his face. Both vanished instantly when he saw me.

'Judith!' he exclaimed. 'What are you doing here?' I

could see the terrible thought that this might be some kind of *Fatal Attraction* scenario entering his mind.

'I'm not Judith,' I said miserably. 'I'm Emily Whitelake.'

'Yes, but . . . ?' He was obviously at a complete loss for words.

'I'm sorry, when you asked my name this morning, for some reason I didn't feel like telling you my real one,' I explained lamely. 'I'm really Emily Whitelake. I really had no idea who you were. I do hope this isn't going to affect our professional relationship.'

'Our professional relationship!' shouted Buzz. 'I think you should know one thing, Judith, I mean Emily, or whatever your real name is, I do not mix business and pleasure.'

'Well, you told me your name was Bernard,' I said resentfully.

'It *is* Bernard!' shouted Buzz. 'Buzz is what everyone calls me but frankly I do not give my nickname to complete strangers who I do not expect to meet again!'

'Yes, well I'm sorry, I really didn't know.'

There was a noise behind me. The well-coiffed woman, who was obviously of the Camilla school of secretaryship, had entered the room with a tray of coffee and was looking at both of us with undisguised astonishment.

'Just put the tray on the table,' commanded Buzz, getting control of himself. The woman obeyed and left the room. Buzz moved over to the tray. 'I seem to have spent the whole morning offering you coffee,' he snapped without a trace of humour. 'Well, sit down. Since you finally managed to make it here, I suppose we had better get on. But let me make one thing perfectly clear. If anyone else either in the bank or in your firm hears about what happened last night, I'm having Richard take you off the account. Understood?'

'Whatever you say,' I replied. I was beginning to dislike Buzz Copenhager III pretty intensely. I could see he might have been a little bit shocked to see me, but I thought this was taking things a bit far.

Buzz placed a cup of coffee in front of me, sat down and drew two enormous documents towards us. 'This is next year's business plan,' he informed me coldly. 'It came in this morning.'

'Yes, I just wanted to say what an exciting and important opportunity all of us at Klinker Dorfmann think that working alongside the plan is going to be,' I said.

Buzz looked at me. 'Cut the crap, Emily, and let's get on with it.' He rolled up his sleeves and opened the document.

5

About an hour and a half later, after what had been one of the worst meetings in my soon to be short-lived career in PR, I staggered out onto Cheapside, hailed a cab, ordered it to go to El Vino's and slumped back in despair. Buzz had not been kidding when he told me he didn't like mixing business and pleasure. He treated me with cold disdain throughout the meeting, with the effect that I became not only more nervous and miserable, but I entirely forgot everything I had ever known about Interbank – and that was not a lot.

Time and again I asked him who a name that had just been mentioned was, only to be told that it was the chairman, chief executive or managing director. Time and again he mentioned some kind of business the bank was doing or one of its departments was involved in, only for it to become horribly apparent that I did not have the faintest idea what he was talking about.

At one point I suggested that we could do some research into the firm's capital market business, only to be informed that we had done precisely that research nine months ago. At another point I suggested that the firm's employees should be assembled in small groups to meet the bank's managing director when he came over from America next month, just to be told that not only had Buzz thought of that already, but the meetings had already been arranged and I had received a personal invitation to one of them over a week ago. Which I had accepted. At the end of the meeting, he did not even bother to shake my hand, told me that he would be speaking to Richard tomorrow, and turned back to his work.

I had never been more in need of a drink or Jack than I was at that moment. When I finally got to El Vino's, he was there already, sitting in the back with a bottle of white wine. He was looking more than usually handsome: his blond hair was falling forward slightly over his forehead, and he had taken his jacket off so I could see the outline of broad shoulders and slim waist. I was so relieved I nearly burst into tears.

Jack, however, was obviously in a filthy temper, and did not notice the state I was in. His dark blue eyes were looking almost black.

'Wotcha,' he said, pecking me briefly and pouring out a second glass of wine. 'Emily, don't you ever let me do something like that again. You're supposed to be concerned about my well-being, why the hell did you let me go off with that godawful woman?'

'What on earth happened?' I asked, lighting a cigarette and cheering up instantly.

'Well, first we went back to her place, which was a pokey little hell-hole off Earls Court Road. She didn't have the common decency to offer me a drink or anything, she offered me a cup of *tea*.' Jack sat back and looked at me.

'I bet it was herbal,' I murmured sympathetically.

'It was, actually,' spluttered Jack. 'Anyway, I got the

disgusting stuff down, and you know what she did then? She started reading me her poetry!'

I burst out laughing. Jack's idea of literature was an in-flight Jeffrey Archer novel on one of his many business trips, and even then he was more likely to be chatting up one of the stewardesses. I was beginning to feel considerably better.

'It's not funny!' shouted Jack. 'And it got worse from there. After hours of this drivel, which was sadly lacking, I might add, in any literary merit at all – the cold frost reminds me of my lover's cold heart sort of thing – we finally got to the bedroom. At last some action, I thought. And we were just getting down to it when you know what she asked me to do?'

'What?' I could hardly wait.

'Recite one of her bloody sonnets as we were having sex,' said Jack coldly.

I was laughing so hard now that I could barely answer. 'Well it serves you bloody well right,' I said. 'These New Zealand women are much warmer and more in touch with their feelings than the English, you know. I heard you telling her so last night. Anyway, what did you do?'

'Made my excuses and left, as your friends in the journalistic profession would put it,' snarled Jack. 'I informed her that due to an unfortunate incident with my English master at a time when we were studying the Romantic Poets, any prolonged exposure to the sonnet form renders me temporarily impotent. Honestly, you never did anything like that and you read English at university.'

'So you went home without doing anything?' I demanded gleefully.

'I certainly did. Scarper, Jack, I told myself, while

scarpering is still an option. God, what a night.' He grinned at me and began to relax.

'Where did you meet her?' I asked.

'She's a temp at the bank, but not for much longer if I have anything to do with it. Anyway, how are you? You seemed to be getting on very well with the City boys when I left.'

'God, Jack, you could have told me,' I said. 'I'm probably going to lose my job because of those bloody City boys.'

Jack pushed his hair back and sighed. He obviously thought this was going to be another one of those crisis about my career lunches. 'Look, why don't you get out of PR altogether?' he asked. 'You hate it, you're miserable there and anyway you're far too good for them. Go into banking or industry or do something creative.'

'No, no, it's not that,' I began, but Jack was getting into full flow. I had embarked on my career in PR shortly after we started to go out together, and he had always thought the corporate lifestyle was a bad idea for me. The only reason he worked in banking, he often told me, was so that he could make a lot of money, have a place in town and in the country and enjoy himself in his spare time.

'Your problem,' he informed me, 'is that you have a problem with sucking up to people in a position of authority, which means you don't get promoted and then you get bored. On the other hand,' he held up a finger to silence me as I tried to interrupt, 'you let your bloody family influence you and so you try to follow a mainstream career path. Just because your father's a doctor doesn't mean you need to be a professional type too. And although your mother's a perfectly nice woman, you know very well the only thing she cares about is getting a suitable son-in-law, so you feel as though you've let her down too. The only sensible one of the lot of you is your brother.'

'Well, thank you for that helping of amateur psychology, but I really mean it,' I protested. 'Something awful has happened that has nothing to do with whether I should be in PR or not. I went off with Buzz Copenhager, the Interbank chap, last night. Except I didn't know he was the Interbank chap, I gave him a false name and anyway I thought he was called Bernard and then I had a meeting with him this morning.'

Jack began to look concerned. 'What happened?' he asked.

'He shouted at me when I got there, and then he was a complete pig for the rest of the meeting.'

'Yes, well, I only met him last night myself, but he does strike me as one of those humourless Americans who might not see the funny side of this. Why on earth did you think he was called Bernard?'

'Oh, he told me he was,' I said. 'Actually, he is, Buzz is just a nickname.'

'So you both gave one another false names?'

'Uh, yes, I suppose so,' I replied fretfully. 'Anyway, that's not the point. He made me so nervous that I forgot everything I was supposed to know — including that I'd been invited to meet the MD, by the way — and at the end of the meeting he said he was going to call Richard tomorrow.'

Jack put his hand on my arm. I tingled slightly. 'Look,' he advised, 'even if he is going to be difficult, he's not going to want to make last night public. He's got more to lose than you, you know. Remember, he is married and it's not going to look too good for him if Interbank finds out that he's out in bars screwing around all night. And it will look a lot worse if they find out that it's with one of their very own PR firm's account managers.'

'Consultant,' I muttered.

'What?'

'Consultant. We got a memo last week saying that all account executives, managers and directors are now to be known as consultants.'

'How bloody ridiculous,' snorted Jack. 'Time was, my angel, when you had to spend eight years at medical school and then another twenty at some hospital in the back of beyond before you could become a consultant. Anyway, I really really wouldn't worry. The whole thing does not exactly show him in a very good light.'

'No, I know,' I sighed. 'Anyway, that's not what I really wanted to talk to you about. Something awful has happened.'

'Something else awful?' asked Jack. 'What a full life you lead. No wonder you hate your job, it must leave you so little time to cultivate crises all over the place.'

'No, I really mean it,' I protested. 'It's not me, it's Natasha. It's terrible.'

'Not another row with Cosmo, is it?' asked Jack sharply. 'If so, count me out. I am not getting involved, Emily. Natasha is more than capable of getting her hands on that trust fund by herself.'

'No, no, it's not that.' I repeated to Jack what Natasha had told me.

'She did what?' said Jack blankly when I had finished. 'She woke up and found him dead so she went off back to Cosmo without telling anyone?'

'Well, she didn't know he was dead then,' I said irritably. I felt it was my duty to defend my friend. 'It was only when she went back to get the right set of keys she realized that he had, um' – I paused briefly before completing the sentence, it was on the whole a little difficult to explain – 'er, sadly expired in the course of the night. And anyway, that still doesn't explain why the flat was completely empty when we went back last night.'

'So that makes it all right?' Jack was still staring at me in wonderment. 'Is there nothing that woman won't do to keep that house in Pimlico?'

'Honestly, Jack, it's not like that,' I said untruthfully. 'Natasha just operates in a slightly different way from most people. Whereas you or I might have called a doctor, Natasha, uh, just . . .' I trailed off. Come to think about it, I could not really land on any reasonable explanation for Nat's behaviour. You had to know her as well as I did to understand. 'Well anyway, she was trying to protect poor Cosmo's feelings,' I finished lamely.

'I do think most people would have had the common decency to call an ambulance,' said Jack censoriously. 'Anyway, there must be some logical explanation for this. People do not just die and then vanish, and take all their personal possessions with them.'

'Well, what could have happened then?'

'I don't know. Maybe someone came in and called a doctor, and then maybe burglars broke in after that. There are dozens of possible explanations.'

'Well, what are we going to do?'

'We?' asked Jack.

'Oh please. I don't know what to do, and now I've

got this awful Buzz Copenhager thing as well. Please help.'

Jack looked at me with a combination of irritation and affection. 'Oh, all right,' he sighed. 'But only if you cook dinner for me next week.'

'You're an angel,' I said.

'An idiot, more like. Look Emily, I've got to get back to work, but I'll call you tomorrow when I've thought about it. And don't worry about Buzz Copenhager. All talk and no trousers from what you've told me.' He winked at me, gathered his possessions and disappeared.

I followed him out and glanced at my watch. It was still only 1.30, and no-one got back before two. I had not had breakfast, I was hungry, and I wanted something to go with the half-bottle of wine I had consumed. There was a Burger King on Holborn close to where I worked.

Ten minutes later, I wearily pushed my way through the crowd queuing up behind me, and perched precariously at a small table. I spilled my fries (small) out on to the tray, unwrapped my Burger King Double Whopper to cool down and took *Cash*, by Melvin Arthouse, one of Britain's brightest young novelists, out of my briefcase to read as I partook of my meal.

I grasped the book firmly in my left hand, and grabbed the burger in my right. 'Right, fucker, now hear me out,' I read. 'Go to where the scumbags go, the weirdos go, the rehab junkies go and die with them.' I took a bite of hamburger. I only managed to get a bit of bun and a few shreds of lettuce in my mouth: some meat plopped on the tray, I smeared ketchup round my mouth and a tomato shot onto the floor.

Thoroughly exasperated, I put the burger down, grabbed a few chips and read on. 'You're a real sick case,' I read. 'It sucks. But the streets suck!' I attempted to grasp the hamburger again. By this time the two slabs of meat were sliding around all over the place: I had to put *Cash* down and take a firm grasp with both hands. I bit, and after wiping my hands and mouth, all of which were now covered in mucousy reddish-coloured substance, I picked up the book once more. I was irritated to see that now there was a ring stain on the upper left hand corner of the left page, where the waitress had neglected to wipe the table.

I clenched the book with my left hand and took a handful of chips with the right. Then I attempted to turn the page. A greasy smear appeared where my fingers had touched the book. I sighed, wiped my fingers on the increasingly tatty napkin, and grabbed the burger once again. Just as I managed to lever it to my mouth, a great big blob of red slime plopped onto the page of my book. I cursed, bit, got some more burger on my coat, put the burger down, picked up the remains of the napkin and wiped the book. The red smear spread across the page. I put the book down, wiped my hands and mouth, went to get a new napkin and gingerly picked the book up again. The Coke stain had spread further across the page. I sighed, gathered the remains of burger, fries, napkin and book, put them all on the tray, took it to the rubbish bin and tipped it all down into the container.

I sighed again, wrenched open the door, stepped onto the street and bumped straight into Camilla, carrying a very large Harvey Nichols bag. 'Business lunch?' she asked sweetly.

A few minutes later I was back in my office. I sighed

wearily, sat down and looked at my phone. It rang instantly. 'Hi, Emily, it's Nigel,' came the unwelcome tones of my next door neighbour. 'How's it going?'

Nigel? I blinked at the phone. Why was he calling me at work? 'What's wrong, has there been a break-in?' I demanded unceremoniously.

'No, no, Emily, I was just ringing to make sure you're still on for this evening.'

Still on for this evening? What on earth was he talking about? I blinked at the phone again, and then it all came rushing back to me. Last Sunday, at the same time as Natasha had been leaving Henry all on his own and sick and dying, I had been lying at home nursing a hangover of quite gargantuan proportions. While I had been in this weak and malleable state, Nigel had appeared at my door and invited me to a dinner party he was having on Wednesday. Normally I avoided Nigel's little gatherings like the plague (he was a social worker and so were all his friends) but this time round I had not been quick enough to come up with an excuse. 'Oh yes, this evening,' I said feebly. 'Of course, what time am I expected?'

'About eight. Listen Emily, you're okay with vegetarian food, aren't you?'

I hated bean sprouts with a passion, but it seemed rude to say so. 'Yes, fine.'

'See you at eight then. *Ciao.*'

He hung up. If there was anything I hated more than bean sprouts it was people who used irritating Italian expressions when they came from Birmingham. On top of that I hated people who bludgeoned me into dinner parties when I was feeling too ill to refuse to go, and on top of that I hated Nigel. This was not turning out to be my week.

I supposed I should ring Natasha and tell her Jack was going to help us, but I felt too miserable and lethargic. Working in PR is destroying me, I thought. I looked at the various piles of paper littering my desk, but I was too fed up to do anything about them. On top of one pile was my invitation to meet Interbank's MD. Why am I not a writer? I thought in despair. I turned to my computer and glared at it. The screen blinked back at me. Write something, Emily, anything, I told myself. I lifted my fingers to the keyboard and began to type.

Christmas is coming and I am getting fat
Time to embark on the F-plan di-at
If I can't lose a whole stone half a stone will do
Ready for my winter break trekking in Peru.

I stopped and sighed. I had better not tell Jack that I had started writing poetry too. And if doggerel was the best I could manage, I had better stick with the day job, and fat chance there was of me trekking in Peru if I did not do something about my overdraft. Could life possibly get any worse?

'Emily,' tinkled a voice. Camilla had loomed up behind me and was reading my screen. 'What a sweet little poem,' she said. 'By the way, Emily, you've still got a bit of ketchup at the side of your mouth.'

I rubbed my lips and glared at her. 'What is it?' I said.

Camilla smiled at me sympathetically. 'Just coming round to remind everyone that their self-assessment forms have to be in by this evening, and I thought you might need a bit of extra time to work on yours. Oh, I bumped into Gerry last night, and he seems very taken with you. Funny.'

She smiled sympathetically again and moved on, leaving me fuming with impotent rage. I did not appreciate remarks about those self-assessment forms ('What do you consider to be your strengths in PR?' read one question, followed even more ominously by, 'What has been your single greatest achievement over the last year?' That one was easy – not getting fired – but I thought I had better dream up an alternative answer.) And who was Gerry? I was becoming increasingly convinced that he was a figment of Camilla's imagination, made up specifically to torment me. And if he did exist, what was he doing in the locker room at school?

I sighed and turned back to the piles of papers. On the top was a pitch document for Borings, a small, insignificant but extremely blue-blooded merchant bank we were trying to talk into signing up with us. 'They won't be able to pay us much,' Donald Bergin had said, as he tried to persuade his fellow board members to negotiate a special discounted rate, 'but just think of the prestige in having them as a client' – which, roughly translated, meant that he was looking forward to frequent lunches with Sir Ronald Boring in the House of Lords.

Pitch documents were a combination of boasts and lies to try to convince the potential client of how wonderful we were. 'Setting objectives,' I read. 'In the years ahead, the business objectives will be:

– to re-establish Borings as a major performer in the international capital markets;

– to establish Borings as a truly international authority in the derivatives market.'

There were pages more of this drivel, explaining how we were going to target new clients, journalists, interested third parties (i.e., our clients who were lawyers and accountants so we could make even more money from them too) and containing the results of a little 'pilot research study' we had done to examine the level of awareness of Borings in the press and the public. The results of the study proved conclusively that absolutely no-one had ever heard of them.

The document contained a number of appendices boasting about the amount of press coverage we had obtained (or, to put it more accurately, my colleagues had obtained) for an accountancy firm. About thirty-five articles, mainly reproduced from such esteemed organs as *Accounting for Success*, were all included. There was a further appendix, filled with self-important biographies of the Klinker Dorfmann staff who hoped to work on the Borings account. I turned to mine.

'Emily Whitelake has extensive experience of the banking and financial sector,' I read. 'After graduating from Bristol University with an honours degree in English Literature, Emily spent some time gaining experience from travelling around the world' – actually the only things I had gained from my year off were a very nasty tummy bug, an extensive photograph album and the unwanted attention of several thousand men who took an unnatural interest in my blonde hair, but there you are – 'after which she joined Klinker Dorfmann as an account executive.' This bit glossed over the several years I had spent starting and not completing an MA, plus missing out my career as an assistant in a bookshop.

'Rapidly promoted to account director,' I read on. My rapid promotion had actually only happened about six months ago, and that was only because Ian and George put in a good word with Richard, when he was a bit tipsy after lunch. They had made him sign the letter before he sobered up, and he had regretted it from that day to this. I read further, learning about myself that I had worked for lots of interesting clients (two of whom had had me taken off their accounts, although we had not put that bit in), that I enjoyed the cinema and reading, and that I was single and lived in West London. I pushed the document away in disgust.

The afternoon dragged on. The worst thing about working at Klinker Dorfmann was that it was like flying: a combination of sheer terror and total boredom. On the one hand, I was scared sick of doing something wrong (Donald Bergin's attitude was becoming markedly cooler), and on the other, I simply did not know how to pass the time. All around me my colleagues were writing press releases based on some spurious research that would be forgotten ten minutes after it was sent out and spending more time than would have been merited on a Beethoven quartet arguing about whether the headlines should be written in bold capital letters or just plain capital letters. Some anarchic souls even favoured underlining the important bits, although that was considered a bit *de trop* for Klinker Dorfmann.

Elsewhere in the building other colleagues were rehearsing impromptu jokes, holding meetings to decide on the agenda of forthcoming meetings or working out tricky questions that might be asked at their clients' impending press conferences. George and Ian, the only two colleagues I got on really well with, were out winning new business.

I filled in my self-assessment form (strength: commitment to client needs, greatest achievement: a sentence mentioning Interbank in the *Independent* last

May, placed there by a journalist friend who knew I was desperate) and tried to do my bit to help Natasha by ringing Henry's workplace and his parents. As expected, his workplace told me that he had the week off, and they did not think he was going away. There was no reply from his parents. I eventually tried ringing Natasha, but her boss told me that she was off sick with the flu. There was no answer at her flat.

I tried Jamie, who still lived in Bristol, where he had been at university a couple of years before me, but he was incarcerated with a dog with learning difficulties (apparently it would sit when told to fetch and run when told to sit, according to his receptionist. Sounded like my kind of dog, according to Jack's analysis). I even considered ringing my mother, but decided that hearing about her social life and latest admirers would depress me still further. Between times I made an increasing number of trips to the loo, staying to smoke two cigarettes at a time rather than one. By the end of the afternoon the cubicle was so smoky you could hardly see the loo seat. All the while there was no communication from Interbank, and no word from Richard, who was away visiting a client.

Catherine rang, pretending to be concerned about the effect on my morale of Jack's behaviour last night, but obviously dying to find out what had happened between the two of them. I curtly informed her that Jack was going through a short bout of temporary impotence and so there was no chance of him mis-behaving. The only bright spot of the whole afternoon was when Gary rang about dinner on Saturday: we arranged to meet at 7.30 in a little pub called The Woodman on Battersea High Street before going on to his friends from there.

By five o'clock I was feeling so bored and restless that only the knowledge of my forthcoming Harvey Nichols bill (I had recently spent some serious quality time with my Harvey Nichols charge card) stopped me from printing out my resignation letter on the spot. Months ago I had put a resignation letter onto my computer to be used in case of emergency, and had protected it from prying eyes with a secret password: 'Bollocks'. I was just wondering when I could slope off when the phone rang. I grabbed it. 'Emily, it's me. I've got to see you right away,' shouted Natasha down the phone.

'How's the flu?' I asked.

'What? Look Emily, don't be a pain. I've had a terrible fight with Cosmo and I think he's going to walk out. And Emily, *I've seen a ghost*!'

By this time I was becoming seriously annoyed. 'Look Natasha, don't be so bloody ridiculous,' I began. 'I have quite enough problems without you coming on with this superstitious crap. I've seen Jack and he's said he'll help us and I can't do anything . . .'

'Meet me at six in the Atlantic Bar,' interrupted Natasha who obviously had not been listening to a word that I had been saying. 'I've got to go. See you.' She banged down the phone.

What could I do? I signed my self-assessment form, sealed it in an envelope and took it to Camilla. 'Yah,' she was saying into the phone. 'We're all meeting for drinks at eight and I've got this fabulous new dress that Mummy bought me . . . Yah?' she enquired as I approached. I handed her my self-assessment form. Camilla took it, ripped open the envelope and began reading it. 'Thanks, Emily,' she said dismissively.

'But that's for Richard,' I protested.

'I deal with all his correspondence while he's away,' said Camilla. She peered at the answers in amusement. Further work strengths: attention to detail, I saw her reading. Unfortunately I had spelt attention with only two tees. 'Thanks, Emily,' she said again, and returned to her conversation. 'It's from Azagury, and I said, "Mummy, you can't possibly spend that much . . ." ' she continued. I backed away and went off down the hall. 'Listen, I've just been given something really funny,' I heard her say as I went into my office.

Not that I really cared anymore. Although I was, as ever, the first to start packing up, I cleared my desk by sweeping all spare papers into a seventh pile, switched off my screen and headed off down the hall.

6

The Atlantic, as ever, was packed. Media types and parties up to visit from Essex were crammed around the tables, and a warm haze of alcohol fumes and cigarette smoke greeted me as I pushed my way through the large swing doors. Maybe I should apply for a job here as a waitress, I thought, it would be a lot more fun and probably more financially rewarding than Klinker Dorfmann. I blinked in the low light and then fought my way through the scrum to the back, where Natasha was anxiously sipping a glass of kir and feverishly smoking a Marlboro. Whatever her other problems, she seemed to have found the time to go to the hairdresser: her sleek black hair had been trimmed into an even chicer style than before, and she was wearing a very tight-fitting red dress. A group of men at a neighbouring table were looking at her admiringly. I made a mental note to have my roots done.

'Waiter!' bellowed Natasha when she saw me, 'another kir! God, I'm glad you're here, Emily, I've had the most dreadful day.'

'Well, mine's not been that great either,' I snarled. 'I'm almost certain to lose my job and I can't stay long, I'm going out to dinner.'

Natasha looked at me with disdain. 'Look, can't you stop thinking about yourself just for a minute?' she enquired. 'My life is in ruins, Cosmo's threatening to leave and now I'm being haunted.'

'Why any self-respecting ghost would want to stay around you for more than two minutes I really cannot imagine,' I said coldly. 'You'd probably ask it to arbitrate in your fights with Cosmo, to say nothing of satisfying your carnal needs when there was no-one else around.'

Natasha ignored this. 'Listen,' she breathed, 'this is spooky. Last night Cosmo started challenging me again about what happened over the weekend. So I told him that actually I'd had several lovers while he was away, and he got so mad that he walked out. So I was really pissed off, and I didn't know where he was, and I didn't know what to do. So this morning I had to call in sick, and I went off to his office to see if he was there. And just as I was crossing Shepherd's Bush Green, *I saw it!*'

She paused and looked at me dramatically. 'Saw what?' I inquired.

'Saw the ghost! Henry's ghost!'

'Nat, don't be so bloody ridiculous,' I said, signalling to the waiter for two more kirs. 'You saw someone who looked like Henry, and because you feel guilty, as so you bloody well should, you thought it was actually him.'

'No no, it really was him,' said Natasha. 'He was going round in a taxi, and when I saw him he turned round and stared at me. And it was really weird: he looked really white – not like a normal person. What am I going to do if he starts following me around and decomposing? That's what happened in *An American Werewolf in London*, you know.'

76

The whole thing was getting out of hand. 'Natasha, for God's sake pull yourself together,' I said. 'Since when do ghosts go around in taxis? If it really was Henry, then he's not dead and he's probably too pissed off with you to get in touch. And anyway, he's not American.'

'No, he is dead,' said Natasha solemnly. 'Look.' She pulled a tatty newspaper cutting from her handbag. 'It's from today's *Telegraph*,' she whispered.

I took the piece of paper. 'Body found in mysterious circumstances,' read the headline. 'Police yesterday discovered a body in an alley near Bevan House in London's Holborn district. The body is that of a young man in his early thirties, who is thought to have been dead for a few days. There may have been a drugs connection, but the police are releasing no further details until relatives have been contacted.'

I handed the cutting back to Natasha, feeling distinctly uneasy. 'Look,' I said uncomfortably, 'don't you really think you should go to the police? If it is Henry and they find out you were with him, you're going to be in the most awful trouble.'

'And if I tell them the truth then Cosmo will find out and that will be the end of that. I can't, Emily, I really can't. What am I going to do?'

'Well, at least the police have found the body,' I said. 'At least we know where it is. If you really can't tell them, you're just going to have to sit tight and wait and see what happens.'

'But I might need an alibi!' shrieked Natasha. 'Look, Emily, can I say I was with you?'

'No, you can't,' I said bluntly. 'Loads of people could have seen you leaving with Henry, and loads of people saw me in the Market Bar as I was at a party there. If you start lying you'll make it much worse. If they find out, you'll just have to say that you went back to Henry's for a drink, but that you went home and he seemed fine then.'

'I guess so,' said Natasha unhappily. 'What a mess. But what am I going to do about this ghost?'

'I really doubt it was Henry,' I responded soothingly. 'Maybe he has a cousin or something that looks like him. I really wouldn't worry if I were you.'

Natasha sighed and stubbed out yet another Marlboro. 'Okay, I'll leave it for now. I better go, I'm meeting Cosmo. I finally got hold of him at his office, and we said we'd have dinner to talk about why our relationship is going wrong.'

'Good idea. Try not to drink too much. I better go too, I'm having dinner at Nigel's.'

'Nigel's?' Natasha looked at me quizzically. 'What's got into you Emily, I thought you said that social workers were even more miserable creatures than accountants. And Nigel's a real creep, you know: he tried to touch me up at that party you had in September.'

'Yeah, I know, he tries to grope everyone,' I said sadly. 'But I accepted the invitation when I was hung-over. I'll call you tomorrow.'

Our little drink had taken longer than I thought, and by the time I had been to a cashpoint, found a place that sold my cigarettes (at about three times the price of anywhere else in London, Piccadilly Circus was such a rip-off) and tumbled into a taxi, it was well after eight o'clock. Then the taxi got jammed in the traffic, which took another half-hour, and I had to stop it en route at an off-licence to get a bottle of wine. And yet again I managed to scatter the contents of my handbag when I got out. I really must get one with a better clasp, I thought.

Eventually I made it into the building. It felt odd going out to dinner in my own house. I dragged myself upstairs and banged on the door. It was wrenched open almost immediately. 'Emily,' said Nigel, giving me a wet peck on the cheek, 'where have you been? You're the last to arrive. You haven't been out drinking already, have you?'

'No, no,' I said, hoping my breath didn't smell of kir, 'I was just really late leaving the office. We have a series of important client meetings coming up.'

'But I rang half an hour ago, and they said you'd been gone for hours.'

'Oh, they must have meant someone else.' I slid into the flat and looked around me. A row of social workers looked up disapprovingly. Almost to a person they were dressed in jeans and sweaters: Nigel was the one exception and he was wearing a tracksuit. I pulled my brightly striped skirt, which was a good five inches above the knee, as far down as it would go.

'Would you like a drink?' asked Nigel politely.

'And how,' I said.

Nigel poured me a glass and proffered the bottle round. A social worker seated nearby covered her glass. 'I think I'll wait till dinner,' she said. I sat down. Nigel's flat was decorated in the high Habitat style of a few years ago and obviously had been neither touched nor cleaned since then: everything was stripped pine, with a few ethnic-looking rugs thrown over the sofas and the dingy grey carpet. A couple of naff posters hung on the wall. I sat on a sofa covered by a rug that looked as if it had been used as a doormat until recently.

'So Emily,' began a straggly-looking worker with long dark greasy hair and no make-up, 'we were just discussing the problems of sexual stereotyping that still exist in society today.'

I smiled uneasily.

'The fact that so many women still feel it necessary to wear short skirts and make-up, dye their hair and pander to our patriarchal-dominated commercial society just sickens me,' said the worker smugly, looking pointedly at my legs and drinking something from a cup that looked horribly like tea.

I took a large slurp of wine. 'Oh yes, I entirely agree,' I said.

The worker looked at me gravely.

'But I do think people should make a bit of an effort,' I went on. 'After all, you expect men to make an effort too. You don't expect them not to wash or shave just because that would be pandering to a commercial society.'

'But Emily,' interposed another worker, this one wearing a beard, 'I just, like, think you're being too judgemental. I have a beard and it's an expression of inner security, it's like, hey, I'm not ashamed to present myself as a man in his natural state. Why should I shave just because men's toiletry manufacturers want me to smear my face with something that's been tested on animals. Should a rabbit suffer just so I could smell good? Don't you feel that you're letting women down everywhere by allowing yourself to be judged on your physical appearance rather than your innate abilities?'

I briefly wondered if Richard thought I had any innate abilities and much as I sympathized with animal rights I wished slightly that the rabbit had been prepared to make the ultimate sacrifice. There was rather an unpleasant odour wafting from the beard. 'Well anyway, in my job I've got to look smart, and that goes for the men too,' I said.

'Oh really,' asked the beard politely, 'and what is it that you do?'

Everyone looked at me expectantly. I looked down. 'I work in PR,' I muttered. There was a brief silence.

Nigel broke it and a cheap-looking glass by leaping up. 'A dirty job, but someone's got to do it!' he cried. 'Dinner's ready!'

Dinner was ghastly. I had not believed that anyone really still ate nut cutlets, but there they were, dried and brown and tasteless. They were accompanied by horrible stir-fried vegetables, the main component of which was bean sprouts, and a dreadful salad which consisted largely of kidney beans. The only way to get the stuff down was to gulp large quantities of wine, which I did, uneasily noticing that my glass was being refilled a lot faster than other people's.

Still, who cared? I was beginning to enjoy myself. The social workers were quite sweet, really, and I had not noticed it before, but Nigel was really quite attractive – if you did not mind pock-marked skin inter-marked with lines and the fact that he never washed his hair, that is. By the end of the evening, I was feeling really quite convivial. I had a very long discussion with a worker about how I had read literature at university and used to be really arty until I sold out to the commercial world. 'I remember a time,' I informed her solemnly, 'when reading a play by Shakespeare was the most important thing in my life.' The beard joined in at this bit and made various snide remarks about how working in PR paid better than reading Shakespeare, or, indeed, doing something socially worthwhile such as being a social worker.

Then I got on to how unhappy I had been as a child, and how my difficult relationship with my mother had made me feel insecure about my looks and abilities. I ended by earnestly explaining to her that I had never been able to speak as openly to anyone before, and I felt we were to become really good friends. And then Nigel was being very sweet: he kept refilling my glass, and sympathizing about how rotten it must be at work, and putting his arm around me in a very friendly way. Why had I not realized how nice he was before? I wondered. And then there was a blur of people moving round all over the place, and then I suddenly realized that I was the only one left. 'I must go,' I muttered, trying to stand up.

'OK,' said Nigel, beaming at me. 'Just one for the road?'

7

I lay in bed with a sense of deep foreboding. My eyes were tightly shut, and I had knotted myself into a little ball. I was not sure where I was, but I was absolutely certain I did not want to be there. There was a funny smell in the room and the sheets felt rather clammy. I could sense the presence of someone else, and did not even dare to speculate as to who it might be. Oh, Emily, I groaned to myself, how could you have got yourself into this position again? Emily, Emily, Emily . . .

'Emily!' shouted a voice right beside my ear. I sat up with a start. It was pitch-black, and the room looked strangely familiar, but I could not work out where I was. I looked around wildly, and almost reeled back in shock. Nigel was lying beside me, concave and spotty chest displayed in its full glory, and, worse still, he stretched out an arm in an attempt to put it around me. I leapt back. 'Oh, Emily, don't be like that,' he crooned.

I jumped out of bed, and began dressing feverishly. We were in his bedroom, which was why it had seemed so familiar: it was the same shape and size of my own, just next door. Unlike mine, everything felt

83

rather greasy to the touch. 'Come back to bed, Emily,' whispered Nigel, in what I assume he took to be a seductive and caressing tone.

'I can't, I've got to get to work,' I whimpered.

'But Emily, it's only six o'clock. I woke you because it sounded like you were having a nightmare. Oh, Emily, I've wanted this to happen for such a long time.'

And as luck would have it, just for once I did remember what had happened. The thought was so appalling I tried to banish it instantly, but without success. 'Come back to bed,' whispered Nigel again.

I fought back rising revulsion and panic, and tried to think about what to do. This required drastic and immediate action. I sat down on the bed, and tried to dodge Nigel's outstretched hands.

'Look Nigel, you know I'm very fond of you,' I began.

'Oh, and I am of you.'

I tried to stay calm. 'And last night was really wonderful,' I lied.

'Oh, it was.'

'But Nigel,' I said desperately, 'we're friends, and I don't want anything to get in the way of our friendship. Last night was brilliant, but I really don't think it should happen again.'

'Why not? Emily, I want to be much more than just good friends,' said Nigel, throwing the covers aside and lunging at me.

I leapt up from the bed and thought desperately. 'Oh, so do I,' I said, 'but I just don't think it would work. And then we'd split up and be furious with each other and it would totally ruin the friendship.' I dodged again as Nigel leapt round the bed in an attempt to embrace me: luckily he tripped over his running shoes and went sprawling on the floor. I pirouetted neatly over the body and made for the door.

'Wait, Emily,' cried Nigel as I fled into the hall, 'don't go!'

It was unlike me to do a runner, especially this early in the morning, but one had to be cruel to be kind. 'I'll call you later,' I cried, 'I've really got to go to work.' I raced down the hall, fumbled madly with my keys, let myself into my own flat and slammed the door behind me. I leaned panting against the wall. Silence. Nigel had obviously and mercifully decided to give it a rest. I went into the sitting-room, dumped my bag and coat and looked at the phone. It rang instantly. Six o'clock in the morning? Who on earth? Oh no, I thought, but it was too late, I had already picked up the receiver.

'Emily, it's me,' whispered Nigel. 'I understand why you had to go. It was a shock to me too and I think you need some time to come to terms with it. But it was wonderful, and I really think we're going to be happy together. I'll call you later.' He hung up.

I slumped onto the sofa with my head, which was pounding quite badly, in my hands. Just when it seemed things could not get any worse, I thought. And Richard was back today, and Buzz was going to call him. And Henry was haunting Natasha. And I was going to lose my job.

I lay down on the sofa, and closed my eyes. I will just rest for a minute, I thought, and then a bath – a moment later a siren went off in my ear. I jerked upright, appalled to see that it was cold grey daylight outside, where a moment ago it had been pitch-black.

The siren turned out to be the telephone, lying beside me. I grabbed it.

'Emily?' drawled Camilla's voice.

What did she want at this hour? 'Yes,' I snapped.

'Emily, you've overslept. It's nine o'clock.'

I looked at my watch. 'Oh no.'

'Richard thought you might have had an early morning meeting, but I looked in your diary and there was nothing there,' said Camilla. 'I'll tell him you're on your way in.'

She hung up before I had a chance to say anything. That lousy bitch, I thought. That *lousy bitch*. But there was nothing for it. I sighed and headed for the bathroom.

Just over an hour later, having bathed and dressed in record time, I struggled to open the vast double doors of Klinker Dorfmann Bergin Wallace and staggered inside and to the lifts. A few stones lighter, I got out. There was an ominous hush in the place. The receptionist avoided my gaze as I went in, and most of the other offices seemed empty. Not, however, Camilla's. 'Emily!' she bellowed with a voice like a trumpet as I attempted to slink past, 'glad to see you've made it in at last! There have been a few phone calls.'

'What,' I snarled.

'Interbank rang, Buzz wants to come in for a meeting with you and Richard this afternoon. Lucky it wasn't this morning.' She gave a tinkling little laugh. 'Natasha called and so did someone called Nigel. He said he wants to speak to you urgently. I do hope you're not being unfaithful to Gerry.' She gave another little laugh and handed over the pile of messages.

'When is this afternoon's meeting?' I demanded.

'Four o'clock. Try not to sleep in!'

I looked in cold fury at her Agnes B-clad shoulder – she had already turned away – and stomped off to my office. I didn't know what made me the angriest: her sneaking on me to Richard, those nasty little digs or the fact that she was wearing yet another piece of new clothing. I was beginning to doubt whether I had ever seen her in the same thing twice. I took off my coat, turned on my computer, and turned to my telephone. It rang instantly. 'Emily, it's me,' cooed Nigel. 'Why haven't you returned my call?'

'I've only just got in,' I hissed. 'Look Nigel, what is it, I've got a lot on.'

'More's the pity,' said Nigel repulsively. 'I was just wondering if you're free for lunch.'

'I'm really sorry, but I'm seeing a client,' I said firmly and untruthfully. 'Another time perhaps.'

'What about dinner tonight?'

'Nigel, look, I can't,' I said desperately. 'I'll call you later and talk about it, OK?'

'But Emily,' I heard him say as I put the phone down. I felt like a bit of a cow, but this really had to be nipped in the bud, and fast.

Also, I wanted to talk to Jack. I dialled his number. 'Jack Melbourne,' a voice said.

'Listen, Jack, it's me,' I said. 'I just thought I should tell you what happened last night.' I filled him in on the details about the ghost and the newspaper cutting.

'Look, Emily, I've got some news about last night too,' said Jack, 'but first I want to make a few phone calls. I'll ring you later and tell you about it.' He hung up. I put the phone down, and it rang again instantly.

'Ah, Emily,' said Richard, 'more problems with the plumbing?'

'I'm really sorry, but I overslept,' I said.

'So I gathered. Perhaps when you've got your thoughts together you could debrief me about Interbank?'

'Yes, whenever you like.'

'Perhaps you could pop along in about half an hour,' said Richard, hanging up.

I put my head, which felt as if it was about to fall off, in my hands. There really was nothing more that could go wrong now. I slumped back and looked at my phone. It rang instantly. 'Emily, it's me,' said Camilla. 'I forgot to tell you your bank manager called earlier and said to ring him urgently. He said he must speak to you today.'

She rang off. Fear gripped me. The call must have been about my overdraft level. I had been paying for everything by cheque recently, in the hopes that they would not be cashed before my salary came in. But there had been quite a few dinners out recently, to say nothing of the new dress I bought on Saturday to cheer myself up – I could stand it no longer. I ran off to the loo for a cigarette.

Half an hour later, the whole of which I had spent entombed in the little emerald cubicle (a snotty colleague had put up a no smoking sign, which I completely ignored), I tottered into Richard's office. He was clicking intensely at his word processor, and looked more like a don than ever. 'Ah Emily,' he said, giving me a surprisingly warm smile considering his manner earlier, 'come in and sit down. I do hope you got on well, I tried to ring you last night to find out, but apparently, you'd already left for the evening. Now, where's the business plan?'

'The business plan?' I asked blankly.

'The Interbank business plan,' said Richard, a note of irritation creeping into his voice. 'Have you left it at your desk?'

The business plan. In all the recent palaver, I had totally forgotten the actual reason that I had had a meeting with Buzz, and now, I realized, I had totally forgotten the business plan too. For all I knew, it was still in Buzz's office in Interbank.

'Oh, well I didn't actually take it away with me,' I whispered weakly, looking at the floor.

'Didn't take it away?' said Richard grimly. 'You mean you met one of our most important clients to discuss what use we could make of their business plan, and you forgot to bring it back with you?'

I nodded. I felt so close to tears that I thought I better not risk speaking. 'This is too much!' shouted Richard leaping to his feet. 'I have given you every chance I can, Emily – and this was a big one – I have supported you in the face of everything Donald's told me and you repay it like this! What more do you want from me? What are you doing here? We've given you the best training available, we've put you on the best accounts, we've given you the best secretary in the firm, and this is what you do in return! This is too much!'

'But I—' I began. I could hardly speak. I had never heard Richard shout before – indeed, I had a feeling no-one had, and I really did not know what to say. Begging for mercy was the only option I could think of, and Richard did not look as if he was going to grant it.

'Don't even try to say anything, because there is really nothing you can say,' Richard resumed in a hoarse voice. 'I think if you even try to make an excuse, I am going to say something I might regret. I very strongly suggest you start thinking about other career options, because the way you're going, there are not going to be many options for you here. I cannot believe you forgot that damn report!'

'Is this what you are looking for?' tinkled a voice.

We both whirled round. Camilla was standing in the doorway, bearing a huge file with Interbank's name and dreadful corporate logo (a gambolling lamb, the bank that likes to say baa I thought sourly) stamped all over it.

'Where did you get that?' I demanded.

'Oh, I had to get something from your desk last night after you'd gone, and I didn't see the plan, so I had an awful feeling that you might have forgotten it,' purred Camilla. 'I sent a bike round this morning to collect it.' She beamed at Richard.

'Well, I must say, Camilla, you've notched up a few points there,' said Richard. He was gaping at her in open-mouthed awe.

'Well, you could have given it to me!' I burst out. Upset had turned into sheer unadulterated fury. If Richard had not been there, I think I would have hit her.

'I meant to, but then you were in so late,' said Camilla coolly. She laid the file down on the table, smiled at Richard and floated out of the room. Richard looked down at the plan, and then back at me. He breathed heavily.

'All right,' he said eventually. 'Through behaviour which has gone quite beyond the call of duty from another member of staff, you've been rescued from this one. I hope you realize quite how much you are indebted to Camilla. But I will not have this happening again, do you understand, Emily? One more mistake, and I'm giving you your marching orders.'

'Yes,' I said. 'Thank you.'

There was another long pause, and then Richard pulled the plan towards him. He began flicking through the pages. 'And Buzz,' he said, 'how did you get on with him?'

'Oh fine,' I said.

Richard gave me a long, hard look. 'Come on,' he said, 'we better start going through this.'

More than an hour later I reeled out of Richard's office. I could hardly bear to think of the number of points that he raised that I had totally missed at yesterday's meeting. Richard was obviously regretting sending me, and was even more obviously trying to work out how he could undo the damage. Miraculously, I had no meetings scheduled until Buzz was due to arrive: I didn't think I could have coped with them. I arrived back at my desk, and looked at the phone. It rang instantly. 'Emily, it's me,' said Jack. 'Look, this Henry thing is very weird.'

Henry? It took me a second to remember. 'Why?' I asked.

'Well look, I've rung his office, and they said he was on holiday. Then I rang a few mates of his, and no-one knew anything about him taking time off. Then I even rang the police and asked them for the name of the man they found dead, and they wouldn't tell me, even when I said I was concerned about a friend going missing: they just asked for the friend's name and hung up when I wouldn't give it. But then, Emily, this is the weirdest thing. You said his flat was completely empty?'

'Yes.'

'Well, it isn't any more. I went round last night to have a look myself. No-one was there, but the door was locked, and when I looked through the window, the place was full of furniture. It all looked perfectly normal. You are sure you went to the right flat, aren't you, Emily?'

'Of course I'm sure!' I cried. 'Anyway, Natasha was with me, so she'd have noticed if we'd gone to the wrong place. Look, I think we should go back there tonight.'

'If you really want to,' said Jack. 'But you know, you and Natasha are going to get into terrible trouble if it turns out that something has happened and you didn't tell the police about it.'

'I know,' I said, 'but it's Natasha. She won't hear of it. Look, do you want me to get her to come along tonight?'

'It might be an idea,' said Jack, 'but tell her not to start on the histrionics, because if she does I'm leaving. Why don't we meet in the Cittie of York at about 7.30?'

'OK, see you there,' I said and put the phone down. It rang instantly.

'Guess who?' cooed Nigel.

I resisted the temptation to slam the phone down. 'Look Nigel,' I said. 'I'm really busy. Can't we talk some other time?'

'If you want to, Emily,' said Nigel, 'but I just rang to say that if you're not free for dinner tonight what about tomorrow?'

This really was it. Something had to be done. 'Look Nigel,' I began.

'Yes?'

'Look, I really like you as a friend but it can't be any more than that.'

'You said that before, but Emily, you were just in shock. Come out tomorrow and you'll see how nice it is.'

It was brutal, but I had to do it. 'I can't,' I said. 'If you really want to know, I've met someone else.'

There was a pause and then Nigel said, 'What?'

'I've met someone else,' I said. 'I'm seeing him on Saturday.'

'Well dump him!' shouted Nigel. 'I don't believe it, Emily. After last night, as well! How could you have done that if you met someone else?'

'I was pissed,' I said bluntly.

'No, I don't believe it!' Nigel roared. 'You might have had a few drinks but you weren't that bad. I've got to see you, Emily.'

'No!' By that time I was shouting myself. 'Look Nigel, just accept it, it was a one-off thing. It's not going to happen again and I just want to be friends, all right?'

'No, it's not all right!' bellowed Nigel. 'I've got to see you and I'm going to!' He slammed the phone down. I replaced the receiver and jumped as there was a sound behind me.

'That sounded complicated,' said Camilla, who had obviously been eavesdropping for ages. 'Hope Gerry doesn't find out!'

I had had about enough of this. 'Look Camilla, who is Gerry?' I asked.

'You know Gerry,' said Camilla, peering at me with

genuine astonishment. 'You met him the other night. When I bumped into him, he said he was taking you out on Saturday.'

I gaped at her. 'You mean Gary,' I said.

'Yah, Gerry,' said Camilla. 'Oh, of course, I forgot, it's only the old crowd that call him Gerry. We've all known him since we were children but the parents were a bit, you know, nouveau, so they called him Gary. That might be why he went into computers. Anyway, Mummy quite rightly didn't want her children's set to include someone called Gary, so she suggested we call him Gerry instead. Said it would help his social standing. I can't understand why he didn't stay with it, but he went back to Gary as soon as he left home. I still can't bring myself to say it, actually.'

'Oh,' I said. I paused and then I couldn't stand it any longer. 'Listen Camilla, what was he doing in the locker room at school?'

Camilla hesitated. She was obviously torn between the urge to gossip and the desire to appear superior. The urge won out. 'Well,' she began in a confidential whisper, 'he . . .'

The phone rang. 'Ignore it,' I said. But the bloody thing had obviously brought Camilla back to her senses: she was not going to gossip to me.

'Oh, I'll tell you another time,' she said vaguely, and drifted out again.

I sighed and picked up the phone. 'Emily?' said a voice.

'Yes,' I said.

'Emily, it's . . .' The phone went dead. I began to shake. I knew that voice, but it could not be him. It could not possibly be him. I was really beginning to think he was dead and the police had found his body. Or alternatively, there was a completely reasonable explanation as to why he was missing, and so why would he ring and hang up on me? My hands were shaking slightly. I did not believe in ghosts, but was it possible that they haunted the friends of people who left without calling an ambulance?

I nearly jumped out of my skin as the phone rang again. 'Emily, it's me,' barked Natasha. 'Any progress?'

'Well sort of. Natasha, a really weird thing just happened.'

'What!' shrieked Natasha. 'He's not haunting you too, is he?'

'Of course not,' I retorted. 'No, it's just that Jack went to his flat last night and it's fully furnished.'

'*What?* It can't be,' said Natasha.

'Well it was, and listen. We're going there again tonight, and you've got to come too.'

'No!' It was beginning to seem as if everyone who rang me had to speak in tones that would have registered on the Richter scale. 'No, Emily, I can't!'

'Well, you've got to,' I snapped. 'Jack will be there so it will be perfectly all right, and he wants to make sure we went to the right flat.'

'Of course we did!'

'I know,' I said patiently, 'but look, Natasha, I think if Jack is trying to help the least you could do is come along.'

There was a long pause. 'Well,' she said eventually.

'We're meeting in the Cittie of York at 7.30,' I said. 'I'll see you there.' I hung up and looked at my watch. Nearly one o'clock. I wondered if any of my colleagues felt like a drink: I had an idea I was going to need one if Buzz was coming in this afternoon. I turned round to see who else was in the office, glancing at my phone as I did so. It rang instantly.

'Miss Whitelake?' said a voice.

'Yes,' I said cautiously.

'Miss Whitelake, this is Mr Lanson from the Fleet Street branch. Didn't you get my message earlier?'

I stared at my phone in horror. It was my bank manager. 'Um yes,' I began desperately, 'I'm really sorry but I've been in a meeting all morning.'

'Be that as it may, Miss Whitelake, I need to speak to you. Do you realize that you have exceeded your overdraft limit by several hundred pounds? And we raised the limit just two months ago.'

'Oh no,' I said weakly. 'I had no idea I had. Look, I'm getting paid at the end of next week, won't that cover it?'

'Unless you have had a fairly substantial pay rise, no, I'm sorry, but it won't,' said the loathsome Lanson. 'Miss Whitelake, we have been very supportive of your various financial mishaps in the past, but I'm afraid we cannot let this happen again. We will be writing to you to call in the overdraft.'

'To what?' I said. Events seemed to be moving so fast that I really had not the faintest idea what he was talking about.

'Call in the overdraft, Miss Whitelake. We will be asking you to pay it back.'

'But I can't!' I cried. I had no idea what my overdraft was, but I knew it was a jolly sight more than I could pay back in a month of Sundays on my current salary, and what was I going to do about my Harvey Nichols bill?

'I'm afraid you are going to have to, Miss

Whitelake. Surely you have some financial resources?'

I supposed this meant savings. 'Nope,' I said.

'Then can't you call on your parents for help? I believe your father is a doctor, surely he will be able to provide assistance.'

My blood ran cold at what my father would do if he found out the full extent of my overdraft. 'No, I can't,' I said.

'Well, we do not wish to be unreasonable,' said the creep, 'so we will give you some time to resolve your position, say a month? You will be receiving a letter from us clarifying the position, and in the meantime perhaps you would be so good as to give the matter some consideration. We look forward to learning precisely how you intend to repay the debt.'

He rang off. I leaned back in my chair and shut my eyes. What am I going to do? I thought. I could try tapping Jamie for funds – the owners of neurotic dogs paid awfully well – but I had done that only a couple of weeks ago and, patient a soul as he was, I did not want to push it. My father was out of the question. This time it really can't get any worse, I thought, as I leaned back a bit too far and overbalanced.

'Oh, do be careful, Emily,' tinkled a voice. I scrambled inelegantly to my feet, cursing as a ladder shot up my tights and glared at Camilla. Did she not spend any time in her own office?

'What the hell is it now?' I snarled.

'Temper, temper,' said Camilla. 'I just came in to let you know that George and Ian have gone to the Printer's Devil, and asked if you wanted to go along. It would make a nice change from Burger King, anyway.'

She floated off. Who was I to complain? I felt

touched and rather grateful that any of my colleagues were speaking to me at all after the last few days and if ever, in a lifetime of needing drinks, I needed one, that time was now. I grabbed my coat and bag and shot off to the pub.

8

The Printer's Devil was absolutely packed. I fought my way through the scrum to George and Ian, who were halfway through their pints and discussing some new and highly profitable bit of business they had brought into the firm. I had never had a conversation like that in my life. 'Hullo, Em,' said George breaking off, 'we thought you'd never get here. I know you're not a drinking woman, but can I tempt you to a glass of wine?'

'Oh, just the one,' I said, slumping into a chair beside them.

George beamed at me and began elbowing people out of his way to get to the bar. As an ex-rugby player, he was rather good at it. Ian smiled at me equally sympathetically and slurped at his pint. 'Rough few days?' he said.

'You could put it that way,' I said. 'Do you think I have a future outside PR?'

'Not sure you've got much of a future inside it,' said Ian, roared with laughter and then caught sight of my face. 'No honestly, Em, just joking,' he said hastily.

George returned with my drink. 'There you are,' he said cheerily. 'Get that down you. Has Ian told you that we've just pulled in the contract for redesigning Tellwort Kansen's annual report? Megabucks!'

I had known George and Ian for a long time, in fact we had all been at Bristol together, where the two of them had pretended to study geography and had actually divided their time between the rugby pitch and the various bars around town. I could trust them. 'Just what is the secret of doing well in PR?' I asked. 'Where am I going wrong?'

George slapped me on the knee. 'Two things,' he said. 'First, put any original ideas totally out of your head, agree blindly with everything the client says and give the impression that he or she is the most important thing in your life. Secondly, concentrate on the money. Simple, a child could do it.'

'Don't forget wining them, dining them and then charging it all to their account,' added Ian.

'Yes, and if it's a man, you have to suck up to them and make some fat old slob think he's incredibly attractive,' George went on. 'That's why women are employed in PR, you know. I've often thought Camilla would be very good at the job.' They both roared with laughter.

'No, seriously Emily, just make them feel needed,' said Ian. 'Anyway, that's enough about the office. How's Natasha?'

'Oh, her normal neurotic self,' I began, shifting slightly and happening to look round. I froze. It could not be him. I leaped to my feet and screamed 'Henry!' But whoever it was – he had his face half turned away and I couldn't really see it – did not hear and moved, after which he disappeared into the crowd. 'I'll be right back,' I panted to the boys, who were looking at me with frank astonishment, and started shoving my way viciously to where the figure had been. No Henry.

I made my way outside and looked wildly down the street. No-one who even faintly resembled him. I began to shake. Natasha could not possibly be right, could she? At least she had Cosmo to protect her if there were marauding spirits about the place. I made my way back into the pub, and sat down, trembling all over. 'Emily, what on earth is going on?' said George who was looking at me with some concern. 'You look like you've seen a ghost. Are you all right?'

'Yes fine,' I said. I gulped at my wine. 'Just a rough couple of days, that's all.'

'You know, you should go easy on that stuff,' said Ian, looking at my glass and finishing off his pint with a gulp. 'Anyone fancy another drink?'

About an hour later I pushed my way wearily through the huge doors, which seemed to get heavier as the days went by. George and Ian had gone off to a client meeting ('Nothing to say to him, but we like to keep the old boy happy by turning up once a week,' murmured George confidentially as they clambered into a taxi), leaving me to go back and face Camilla, Buzz, Richard and the music on my own. There was still an hour and a half before Buzz was due: how on earth was I going to fill my time? I shrugged despairingly and did the usual: I headed off to the loo.

The next hour and a half were the longest I had ever spent. I could not actually stay in the emerald-tiled cubicle for the whole time, so I emerged occasionally to wash my hands, comb my hair, read the no smoking sign – whoever had put it up had now underlined it several times – and retire back into my little hidey-hole. I heard others come and go as if I was in a dream.

I am different from them, I thought sadly, they have a life and a career and probably love and happiness and what do I have? No career, no money and a bunch of psychotics for friends who went around murdering people in their sleep and then lying about it afterwards. And ex-boyfriends, who insisted on rehashing the unhappy tale of our lost relationship in front of ludicrous antipodean harpies. And the only men who wanted me were horrendously ugly social workers who thought we could make beautiful music together or dubious computer programmers or horrible American bankers who threatened what was left of my job security. And my mother disapproved of me because I was not married and my father disapproved of me because I was not a doctor. All I have left is Jamie, I thought sadly, and there was a limit to what even his patience could bear. I was getting so maudlin that I was rather beginning to enjoy myself, when suddenly the loo door flew open and a horribly familiar voice shouted 'I don't believe it!'

I froze. I didn't know what to do with my cigarette: if I dropped it into the loo it would fizzle and make a sound, and if I did not, smoke pouring out from under the door would give my presence away. Eventually I mashed it against the wall and held my breath.

'I just don't believe it,' shouted Camilla again. 'Hasn't she seen that sign? If she wants to have a cigarette she can go outside, or bring in some business so she can leave the office and smoke.' There was a sympathetic murmur from some acolyte, who had obviously been brought in to hear further tales of Camilla's glories.

'I'm going to report it to Richard,' said Camilla. 'This is just too much.'

The door banged behind them. I crept out of the loo, waited until I was sure they were out of the way, and then belted back to my office before a lynch mob came to get me.

But I need not have worried – about Camilla at least. Richard had far better things to think about, like where the hell was I? In my sorrowful state, I had forgotten to check my watch, and had unfortunately rather overshot: Buzz had been waiting in reception for ten minutes, and Richard was going berserk in his office, as Camilla informed me when she came scuttling back to my desk. 'I'd get in there fast if I were you,' she said.

For once I thought she might have a point. I gathered up my note pad and shot off to Richard's office. 'Where the hell have you been? Look, never mind, let's go and meet him,' he shouted, gathering up Interbank's business plan and heading for the door.

Together, we trotted at speed up to reception. 'Ah, Buzz, how nice to see you,' gasped Richard, trying to get his breath back. He looked like an increasingly loony don who had just finished some major piece of research: he dragged his hand wildly through his hair and then held it out to Buzz, who shook it rather warily. 'And you know Emily, of course,' boomed Richard, shoving me forward. I held out my hand, which Buzz, who had turned round to pick up his briefcase, ignored. Richard shot him rather an astonished glance, and then said, 'Well, well, let's get started. The meeting room's just up here, Buzz.' We trooped off.

Initially it was all quite civilized. We plonked ourselves around a large oval-shaped table, Camilla, murmuring efficiently, brought in some coffee, Buzz smiled up at her and Richard got started. 'It's a great plan,' he said, thumping the enormous document in front of him. 'Emily and I touched base this morning and we think there are some really interesting and exciting opportunities to raise Interbank's profile in this country. Isn't that right, Emily?'

'Um, yes,' I said. Buzz shot me a filthy look and said nothing.

'Initially, we want to concentrate on raising your profile in the press,' said Richard, self-importantly. 'We think it's important to establish a programme of journalist lunches right away to make them more receptive to publicizing the research that you will be putting out later in the year.'

'Yes, I think I suggested that myself when I met Miss Whitelake yesterday,' said Buzz coolly.

'Absolutely,' said Richard heartily. 'Well, Emily will get on to it right away: we'll get together an initial list of journalists, OK it with you and get the ball rolling. Now I think the next thing to do is to maximise the publicity potential of the MD's visit next month. We wondered if it would be possible to bring forward the publication of "Stars, Stripes and Stripping Assets" to coincide with his trip. I know it would be too late to use a Thanksgiving Day theme to launch it, but with Christmas, turkey and fun for all the family on the way, there's a great opportunity to focus on the American Christmas – and the US approach to festive business. Christmas is a bad time for business journalists – they'll jump at the chance of a new angle when a major piece of research is being released.'

Buzz actually looked quite interested. 'Well, that's an interesting thought, Richard,' he said. 'I know that the research and analysis has been finished: it would just be a case of pushing the design element of the report through and putting pressure on the printers. You have a design department, don't you? Maybe some of your staff could give us a hand.'

Pound signs twinkled in Richard's eyes. 'Buzz, we do,' he said. 'Our chief design consultant, Derek Jeffries, is highly experienced in dealing with corporate literature such as yours. Emily, will you touch base with Derek after this meeting so he can get some initial ideas going?'

'Oh, sure,' I said. Fat, arrogant and extremely unpleasant, Derek was kept away from the clients as much as possible, due to a general feeling that he would drive the lot of them away if they ever met him, but he was extremely good at his job – if you counted draining money away from a lot of brainless bankers as being good at a job.

'And now, Buzz,' continued Richard, who was obviously beginning to think that the whole thing was going swimmingly, 'we come to the most exciting opportunity of all. All of us at Klinker Dorfmann think . . .' The phone in the corner rang. Richard stopped, blinked at it, said, 'Excuse me,' and walked over to pick it up. 'Richard Dorfmann,' he said and paused. Then he turned round with a rather funny expression on his face. 'It's for you, Emily,' he said. His voice was ominously calm.

I had been pretending to take notes: I dropped my doodles, said, 'Oh,' and walked over to the phone.

Richard handed me the receiver. 'Make it fast, will you,' he said softly, and headed back to Buzz.

I put the receiver to my ear. 'Emily Whitelake,' I said.

'Emily, it's for you. Said it was very urgent,' said Camilla. The phone clicked as she put the call through.

'Emily Whitelake,' I said again.

'Thank God you're there!' screamed Natasha. 'I'm not going to that place tonight, I tell you, it's haunted!'

Oh no, I thought, this was all I needed. 'Look, Natasha,' I hissed, 'I can't talk now, I'm in a very important meeting.'

'Don't be so bloody selfish!' yelled Natasha. 'He's haunting me! I just went outside to get some fags and I saw him again, right across the street! I stared at him and then he began to walk and he vanished! *Right into thin air!*'

'What do you mean vanished,' I said sharply. 'People don't just vanish.'

'Well, a crowd of people walked past and when they'd gone by, he'd gone! Just gone!'

'Look, it probably wasn't even him,' I said soothingly.

'It was! Emily, what am I going to do!' The murmuring at the table behind me was getting louder.

'Emily,' said Richard loudly, 'perhaps you could continue your call later?'

'Yes, of course,' I said hastily. I turned back to the phone. 'Look Natasha, I really can't talk now,' I hissed. 'I promise I'll call you back right after the meeting, but I've got to go now.' I hung up before she could say another word and walked back to the table. 'Sorry about that,' I said. The two men watched as I sat down, Richard with controlled irritation, Buzz with cold fury.

'Right, well as I was saying,' said Richard. 'Buzz, we think your decision to open a new range of offices in the tiger economies in the Far East one of the most exciting ventures Interbank has embarked on. It is extremely important for thrusting American banks to ingratiate themselves, I mean integrate themselves with the likes of Korea and Malaysia. We would like to suggest a whole programme of seminars held by the most senior Interbank personnel running through into the spring, as well as involvement in a conference we have just been notified will be coming up in April. It's called "East meets West: how to bank best". Some of the most important figures in the industry will be there, Buzz, and I really think you should be represented.'

'Well, that's a very interesting idea,' said Buzz. 'We've been holding a series of internal discussions in Interbank about how to make the best use of the growing economies in the Far East—'

The door burst open. 'Emily!' shouted Nigel from the doorway. Behind him was the panic-stricken receptionist, chanting 'You really can't go in there.' Nigel ignored her, hurtled into the room, attempted to embrace me as I sat in the chair, failed when I ducked and then stood in front of me with his arms stretched wide. 'Emily!' he shouted again. 'We've got to talk!'

Both men had leapt up from their seats. 'What the hell?' said Buzz.

'Emily, who is this man?' shouted Richard.

'I'm her lover,' shouted Nigel even more loudly, 'and I must talk to her!'

Everyone else was shouting, so I thought I might as well join in. 'No you are not!' I yelled, leaping to my feet. 'How dare you burst in here! This is a very important meeting, get out now!'

'How can you treat me like this after last night!' cried Nigel. Camilla had appeared from somewhere behind him and looked as if she could hardly control her joy. I saw Richard's face: he had turned bright red and looked as if he was about to explode.

'Emily, get this man out,' he hissed through clenched teeth.

I grabbed Nigel by the arm and began to propel him towards the door. 'I'm not going anywhere!' he shouted.

'Look, just come with me, I'll go with you,' I snarled. I got him out into the hallway, slammed the door behind me and shoved him into another meeting room opposite which, thankfully, was empty.

'I mean, just what—' I said, '—just what do you think you're doing?' I was so angry I could hardly speak. I had made some damn silly mistakes in my time, I had done some damn silly things, but I had never burst into someone else's meeting – and I had certainly never been burst in upon before.

'Oh, I'm sorry, Emily,' said Nigel, who seemed to have calmed down completely, 'but I just had to talk to you.'

'No you didn't,' I snarled. 'I made my feelings quite clear over the phone. I told you, I do not want anything more between us and after this I don't even want to be friends. How dare you do this to me! Do you realize I am probably going to lose my job over this?'

'Well, if you do, I'll support you,' said Nigel.

This was the last straw. 'No you won't!' I shouted. 'I would rather starve on the streets than live in your smelly crummy little flat and see your smelly crummy little face every day! You are physically disgusting and I hate you! I only agreed to come to your rotten little dinner party because I had a hangover and I would never in a million years have gone to bed with you unless I was completely out of my head, which I was last night. If you had any decency at all you wouldn't have taken advantage of me in that position, but you probably couldn't even spell decency, let alone know what it means. I've got so many problems I couldn't even begin to list them and now you barge in here making me look like a complete idiot in front of my boss and our most important client and you seem to expect me to set up house with you when you have finished off what remains of my career and made me a laughing stock in front of the whole firm. I hate you!'

Nigel did precisely what could be expected of him under the circumstances: he burst into tears. I was feeling so cold with fury that I did not care at all, and would have happily turned him out onto the street in his present condition if only I could have got him out of the office, but, as ever, the situation was taken out of my hands. The door burst open, and Camilla appeared, bearing a tray of coffee. 'I thought things might be a little tense in here, and that you'd probably need some coffee,' she purred happily, putting the tray down on the table. Camilla never brought me coffee, it was obviously just an excuse to find out what was going on. 'Why, you poor thing,' she crooned, 'what has she been saying to you?'

Nigel looked up and melted. Tears vanished, he blew his nose and straightened his measly little shoulders. 'Oh nothing, just a lover's tiff,' he said.

'No, it bloody wasn't, we are not lovers!' I shouted.

'Keep your voice down, Emily, the whole building can hear you,' said Camilla, gliding over and shutting the door. She went back over to Nigel, who was sipping his coffee with what he obviously considered to be a strong and resolute expression on his face. To me he looked like a drowned rat. 'Now what's wrong,' she cooed.

'Well,' said Nigel falteringly, 'we spent last night together and now she says she doesn't want anything to do with me.'

'Well, you know, Emily has quite a lot of men friends,' said Camilla happily, sitting down and taking his hand. 'I suppose it was inevitable that some of them would read a bit more into it and get the wrong impression.'

I could hardly take this any longer: I went to the window and glared outside.

Nigel sniffed and took a gulp of coffee. Camilla went on with calming the situation down. 'You know, she's really not right for you,' she said. 'You need someone a lot more stable who can look after you.'

Turning from the window I saw Nigel looking hopefully in Camilla's direction. Camilla saw it too, and hastily backtracked. 'You know, someone who works in your kind of field and understands what you do,' she purred. 'Not someone who works in a vicious business like ours and who never has time to think about other people – as I'm sure you do, Nigel.'

Nigel sniffed again. 'You know, you're probably right,' he said. 'Emily just wouldn't be able to fulfil the needs of a man like me.'

'Ha!' I said and turned back to the window. They both ignored me.

'Now,' said Camilla, 'would you like some more coffee or do you feel strong enough to go?'

Nigel stood up and straightened his revoltingly shiny tie. Just for once he was wearing a suit, but it looked as if it had been bought at least ten years ago and not cleaned once since then. 'I think I should go,' he said in a manly voice. 'Thanks for the talk, Camilla. See you around, Emily.'

'No you bloody won't!' I shouted as he went out the door.

Camilla stood up and looked at me. 'You know, I think I handled that rather well,' she said.

'Oh yeah?' I said. 'I would have been perfectly capable of getting rid of him if you hadn't butted in. Oh and thanks a lot for the character reference. "Emily has a lot of men friends." '

'Well, you do,' said Camilla coolly. 'And you didn't seem to be doing a lot to get rid of him when I came in, just a lot of screaming and shouting. Anyway, Richard asked me to come in and sort things out, and I really wouldn't go back into that meeting if I were you. You should have heard what Buzz said after you left.' She swept out.

I followed, exhausted. I could not have gone back to the meeting anyway: the room opposite was empty, they had obviously finished ages ago. I went back to my desk and put my head in my hands. In the background, I could hear Richard calling for Camilla to come into his office. I could take it no more. I headed off to the loo for another cigarette.

9

'You just wouldn't have believed it,' I said to Jack. We were sitting on green, leather-bound chairs in one of the little enclosed confessional-like cubicles in the Cittie of York waiting for Natasha (I had managed to gather the strength to ring her back: needless to say, she was neither in her office nor at home, but I left several messages insisting she meet us tonight) and I was draining a much-needed glass of wine. An orange lamp winked on the wall beside us, casting a glow over a nineteenth-century cartoon from the original *Vanity Fair*. Jack was being extraordinarily decent about the whole ghastly story, he even managed not to laugh when I told him about Nigel bursting into the meeting.

'Well, I always told you he was a creep,' he said. 'Serves you right for living next door to a social worker. You know, though, Emily, you should really cool it with the amorous adventures, seems to me that they're causing a little more trouble than they're worth.'

'All right, all right,' I said, 'but you're hardly one to talk. It wasn't me that was asked to recite verse in Earls Court. Anyway, they don't all turn out so badly, Gary is taking me out on Saturday night, you know.'

'And I hope the evening goes very well, although personally I do not think he's the right man for you,' said Jack coolly.

'Well, introduce me to someone who is then,' I snapped.

'The only person I've ever met who is remotely able to understand you is me,' said Jack.

It was an unhelpful remark, but there was something in it. Jack and I had fitted together very well: we came from similar backgrounds, although he was brought up in London and I came from Chester, and by a coincidence both our fathers were doctors. There was, however, the small matter of our break-up several years ago. 'I don't think so,' I said firmly. 'The time has come for me to extend my wings and I think Gary's a jolly nice chap. His only fault is that he seems to have known Camilla as a child, but we all have our little failings.'

'And he's called Gary,' said Jack spitefully. 'No, no, sorry, I don't mean it,' he added hastily as I opened my mouth to retaliate. His dark blue eyes glittered mischievously. 'Honestly, Gary's a great name. We can't all be called Jack. I'll tell you though, Em, there's something about him I can't quite put my finger on. Nothing bad, but I sometimes think there's a bit more to him than meets the eye.'

'Well what?' I demanded.

'Don't know,' said Jack. 'I'll tell you if it comes to me. Anyway, what are we going to do about this Henry thing? These unconfirmed sightings are very strange.'

'And unconfirmed phone calls.' I told him about how the phone had gone dead when I was sure it had been Henry's voice.

'You know, there is something weird about all this,' said Jack, gathering together the glasses. 'We are definitely going to have to check it out. Another drink, Em?'

As he made his way over to the bar, I saw Natasha struggling through the door. Obviously enjoying herself hugely, she had dressed for the full dramatic potential of the situation: clinging black dress, black shiny tights, black high heels and a black cloak which she swirled around her as she walked in. Her black hair and pale skin were set off by a gash of scarlet-woman lipstick and some very dramatic pieces of silver jewellery which must have cost a fortune. No wonder she did not want to lose Cosmo. He might only work for the BBC, but he did have a private income. I looked down at my own battered mini-suit, tights which I suddenly realized still had a run in them from lunchtime and scuffed shoes, and tried to put the thought of my Harvey Nichols bill out of my mind.

'I don't know why I agreed to this,' she hissed, sliding onto a chair beside me. 'I know something awful's going to happen: ghosts can be very mal-evolent, you know.'

'Oh, don't talk such rubbish,' I snapped.

'It's not rubbish!' cried Natasha. 'I heard of some-one once who was alone in a graveyard at the dead of night . . . Oh hi, Jack. Vodka and tonic, please.'

Jack dumped the glasses, pecked her briefly and went back to the bar.

'Anyway,' she continued. 'He was alone in this graveyard—'

'Natasha, do shut up.' I was feeling pretty nervous myself and the last thing I needed were tales of ghosties and ghoulies. 'Look, we'll all have a drink, and then we'll just go along to the flat and see what's going on. Anyway, Jack's with us, nothing too awful can happen.'

'Oh, I don't know,' said Natasha darkly. 'Thanks, Jack.' She took her vodka and tonic and began to sip.

'So,' said Jack sympathetically, 'I hear you're having quite a time of it.'

'Oh, it's just too awful,' said Natasha, directing the full force of her very dark eyes on him. 'I mean, I feel so responsible. I keep thinking, there must have been something that I could have done to save him.' I watched irritably: I knew only too well the effect Natasha could have on men when she chose.

Not on Jack, though. 'Well, you could have called an ambulance at the start,' he said heartily, 'but never mind about that now. I'm sure we'll get the whole thing sorted out.'

'Oh, but I couldn't,' breathed Natasha. 'Hasn't Emily told you about how Cosmo's been treating me? You know' (her voice trembled) 'I keep thinking, maybe he's going to turn *violent*.'

Jack controlled a snort with some difficulty, and I could see why. It was far more likely that it would be Natasha that got funny ideas with the carving knife than poor meek-mannered old Cosmo. Still, he behaved remarkably well. 'I'm sure you have nothing to worry about, but we'll sort it all out. Come on girls, drink up. We might as well get this over with.'

All three of us drained our glasses, gathered our coats (Natasha swirled very dramatically when she put her cloak on) and headed for the door. It was a dark, rainy, cold November night and I shivered as we began making our way up Holborn.

None of us said anything on the way there. Even

Jack was looking a bit nervous, and as we turned the corner and headed to Boswell Street, Natasha put her arm through mine and hung on. We got to the building. The stairs seemed even darker than usual and obviously provided lavatory facilities for every cat in London, and a few other species of animal as well. We walked up to the flat. It was dark inside, but when we pressed our noses to the window, it did indeed look perfectly normal: the room was filled with furniture. The only thing was, it was not Henry's furniture. The huge sofa which used to be just under the window had gone: instead there were a couple of smaller sofas and a dining-table which had not been there before, in the background.

Natasha had obviously reached the same conclusion. 'That stuff's not his,' she announced matter-of-factly.

'Well, whose is it then?' asked Jack.

'It's mine, as a matter of fact,' said a voice. We whirled round. A middle-aged man, who even in the dark I could see was extremely well tanned, was standing behind us and looking suspicious, to put it mildly. 'Can I help you?' he asked.

'Yes,' said Jack stepping forward. 'We're looking for Henry Campion, he lives here.'

'No he doesn't, I do,' said the man.

There was a short silence. Natasha broke it. 'But he does!' she burst out, stepping forward. 'I was here with him at the weekend!'

'Were you?' asked the man, producing a set of keys from his pocket. 'I'm glad to see Henry's got such good taste in women. Would you like to come inside?'

We all nodded. He unlocked the door, rubbed the piece of graffiti on the wall beside it and frowned.

'Must get that seen to,' he muttered, ushering us in and switching the lights on. The place looked a jolly sight better than it did when Henry lived there: the furniture was expensive and, somehow, foreign looking, the bookshelves on either side of the fireplace were filled with weighty-looking tomes rather than the paperback drivel that Henry kept, framed photographs of faraway places and chi-chi little watercolours were all over the walls and, to my utter joy, there was a drinks cabinet that looked even more impressive than the one Henry kept. The man saw me looking at it. 'Drink, anyone?' he asked.

'Yes please,' said Natasha and I simultaneously. Jack looked a little more cautious.

'That's very kind of you, but we don't even know who you are,' he said.

'My name is Edward Dickinson and I'm a friend of Henry's,' said the man. He went over to the cabinet, took out glasses and bottles and turned round. 'Gin and tonic all right with everyone?' he asked.

'Yes please,' said Natasha and I simultaneously.

'Look,' said Jack who was not responding to this hospitality as well as I thought he should, 'where is Henry?'

'Well, I'm not absolutely certain, I haven't seen him myself,' said the man, sloshing liquid into glasses. 'I haven't got any lemon, I'm afraid, but I did remember to freeze some ice. You see, I've been in Brazil for about a year now and I only got back yesterday. I haven't had time to look him up.'

'But what's happened?' asked Natasha. 'Why are you here now?'

'Well, why shouldn't I be?' said Edward, looking at us blankly.

'Because it's Henry's flat!' cried Natasha. 'I told you, I was here with him just a few days ago! What have you done with him?'

'Are you feeling all right?' said Edward looking at her with some concern. 'Sit down and have a drink.' He produced some ice from a little fridge under the drinks cabinet, clinked the ice into the glasses and began to hand them round. 'I haven't done anything with Henry. I told you, I haven't seen him myself since I got back. He didn't live here permanently, you know, he was just looking after the place for me when I was away. It actually belongs to me. Didn't he tell you that?'

Natasha was looking too flabbergasted to speak. Jack obviously felt he should step in. 'We knew he was just renting the place, but we didn't know who the owner was or anything,' he said. 'You see, the three of us have known one another for years, but we all only got to know Henry quite recently, through another friend, Catherine. I think she met him at a party last year. Do you know her?'

'I can't say that I do, but as I mentioned, I've been away for a year,' said Edward. He walked over to the fireplace and lit a cigarette. 'To be honest, it hadn't even occurred to me there was any reason to worry about Henry. About a month ago I wrote that I was coming back and needed the flat again, which was just as we'd arranged I would do. Everything was perfectly in order when I got back, the only thing I was a bit annoyed about was that he had left the doors unlocked, which really isn't safe in this area. There was a murder round here the other day.'

'What murder?' said Jack sharply.

'I'm not exactly sure, it happened before I got back,'

said Edward, 'but I believe it involved a row about drugs. That's what the man in the shop opposite told me, anyway. It happened near this very building. I'm really going to have to think about moving.'

We all exchanged glances. Whatever had happened to Henry, this explained the mysterious body, at least. 'Anyway,' said Edward, 'I've told you about as much as I can, now it's your turn. Why do you think that something's wrong?'

'Well,' said Jack, 'we're a bit worried about Henry. He seems to have disappeared.'

Ignoring an anguished glance from Natasha, he told Edward the full story of the last week. When he had finished, Edward gave Natasha rather a funny look. 'I really think you should have called an ambulance,' he said.

'I know I should!' cried Natasha. 'But it's too late to do anything about that now. Do you think he's dead?'

'Well, I hope not,' said Edward. He was looking at her very oddly. 'But now you come to mention it, it is very odd that he didn't even leave me a note with a forwarding address. I wouldn't mind getting in touch with him, we still have bills to sort out and so on, to say nothing of forwarding his post. Also, I'd quite like to meet up for a drink. You say you didn't know him that well, I don't suppose any of you would have been able to get in touch with his parents?'

'Well yes, I did try actually,' said Natasha. 'We all went to a party at their place a little while ago so I had the number, but there was no answer.'

'Why don't I try again now,' said Edward. He walked over to the phone, dialled and hung on in silence. We all exchanged glances. 'No,' said Edward finally, dropping the receiver, 'no answer. Look, though, I'm sure it's all right. One of us would have heard if something was wrong.'

'Then why hasn't he been in touch!' shrieked Natasha.

'Maybe he was angry with you,' said Jack icily.

There was a short silence, and then Edward stood up. 'I'm sorry to be inhospitable,' he said, 'but I'm having dinner with my publisher tonight. I'm certain there's nothing to worry about, but I'll give you all my phone number in case something turns up. Oh no, you'll already have it, it's Henry's old one. Also, I'm having a return to England party a week on Saturday: you are all invited if you're free. You know, I'm really surprised Henry didn't mention me, I've known him for years.'

'Actually,' said Natasha in a very small voice, 'he did.'

'What!' said Jack. He'd been uncharacteristically quiet while all this was going on and I could see his opinion of Natasha was shooting downhill faster than you could say 'mine's another'.

'I'd completely forgotten,' said Natasha miserably, 'he told me last week that a friend of his was coming back from South America. But I cut him off before he could tell me any more because I wanted to talk to him about what I should do about Cosmo. Actually, Emily, I have the strangest feeling I might have mentioned it to you that night when you forgot everything.'

Jack shot her a look of sheer disgust. I was actually beginning to feel quite sorry for her and I was a bit embarrassed that I seemed to have forgotten yet another crucial piece of information. 'Look, never mind,' I said, 'as long as he's all right. I'm sure we'll be able to track him down.' We all stood up and began putting our coats on. Natasha must have been upset, she even forgot to twirl.

'He'll turn up,' said Edward. 'If he gets in touch, I'll tell him to give you all a call.' He began ushering us towards the door. 'I've enjoyed meeting you,' he said, opening the door, 'even if the circumstances are a little unusual. Don't forget the party, I hope you can make it.' He shut the door behind us.

Jack waited until we got to the bottom of the stairs and then turned to Natasha. It might have been dark all around us, but his face was a whole lot blacker. Before he could say a word, Natasha leapt in. 'I know,' she said. 'Please just don't say anything. I feel absolutely terrible, and I feel even worse that I dragged you into this. I promise I will make it up to you, but right now, I really need to go and talk to Cosmo. I'm really sorry. I'll call you tomorrow, Em.' She ran up the road. She must have been feeling contrite: she only ever called me by my nickname when she was feeling really bad. Jack and I watched her hail a taxi, give it instructions and leap in. It sped off up the road.

Jack turned to me and shrugged. 'O what a tangled web we weave,' he said. 'You know, that chap seemed very upfront, but it's a bit odd, turning up from nowhere like that. I wish we could find Henry, it is a bit worrying he hasn't been in touch with anyone.'

'What do you think's happened to him?' I said anxiously.

'Don't know, but there is at least one possibility: he has very reasonably taken a week off to move, punctuated by the odd break for a drink in a pub,' said Jack. 'Come on, Emily, don't worry about it. It'll all be OK.' We began to walk up the road.

'What are we going to do now?' I asked.

'I don't know about you,' said Jack looking at his watch, 'but I'm absolutely starving. Dinner?' I nodded. Jack hailed a taxi, shoved me in and said, 'Where to?'

'Anywhere,' I said.

Jack leant forward, said something to the driver and sat back. 'Tell you one thing, though, Natasha is going to have some explaining to do to someone,' he said thoughtfully. We drove off.

10

I could not work out whether I was awake or asleep. I kept trying to open my eyes, but every time I did so I seemed to tumble further and further into a mass of pillows. Wherever I was – and it seemed very familiar, even though I knew it was not my own bed – felt incredibly comfortable. I knew that as long as I stayed here there would be no hostile American bankers or PR harridans or psychotic friends or missing bodies or suspicious foreign travellers to deal with. This is the life for you, Emily, I thought, warm and comfortable, and you can stay asleep for ever. I rolled over and someone put their arms around me.

I sat up sharply. It was pitch-black, but I vaguely recognized the surroundings although I was not absolutely sure where I was. I seemed to be holding someone's hand. I blinked, and as I got used to the darkness, I saw it was Jack. He was looking at me affectionately. 'I wouldn't have woken you, but you were talking in your sleep,' he said.

'Oh, thank heavens it's you,' I said, curling up against him. To my relief, he was wearing boxer shorts.

'Well, who did you think it was going to be?' said

Jack, stroking my hair. 'By the time I got you back here you didn't look in much of a state to go man hunting.'

'I don't go man hunting,' I said haughtily, 'they hunt me. What time is it anyway?'

Jack looked at the clock beside the bed. 'Just after six,' he said. 'We don't have to get up for a while.'

I dozed off against him. This was not actually an unusual occurrence. Jack and I frequently shared a bed when we had been out on the tiles together and – usually at least – nothing happened. This appeared to be one of those occasions. 'Jack,' I said eventually, 'are you going to go to Edward's party?'

'I should think so. You should go too, you could meet some interesting new people. You know, the type that don't leave sick people on their own because they're worried about losing access to a very substantial trust fund.'

'Oh, I know,' I said, 'but she's all right really. She's been very decent to me at times.'

'I know and you two go back a long way,' said Jack. 'Anyway, I suppose we should both be grateful to her, she did introduce us, after all.'

'Mm,' I said. 'Listen Jack, can I ask you something?'

'Anything, my darling.'

'Did we get up to anything naughty last night?'

'Honestly Emily, it's lucky I know you as well as I do, or I would be pretty insulted. I would hope that you would be able to remember something about it if we had. No, we got straight into bed and you passed out pronto.'

'Maybe I should calm down my lifestyle,' I said sadly.

'No, you can't do that,' said Jack hugging me. 'I know you, you're made for mischief.'

'Do you think so?' I asked, highly flattered. I sat up in bed. I was wearing one of Jack's T-shirts, and for once my head was not throbbing too badly. It must have been because I had had quite a lot to eat last night. Jack and I had gone to 192, a fashionable modern restaurant near where he lived, and spent the evening spotting Notting Hill trendies. 'I wish I was one of them,' I had told him. 'Well you could be if you did something creative and gave up that dreadful job,' he had said. I wished I had not remembered that. With all the drama of last night, Klinker Dorfmann had gone right out of my head and I knew, without any doubt at all, that today was judgement day.

Jack was clambering out of bed. 'Unfortunately, I think I had better get moving,' he said. 'I'll bring you a coffee.'

Funny really, it was a bit of a rerun of waking up with Buzz. Jack brought me a cup of coffee, offered me the full services of his bathroom, which I already knew very well anyway, and left before I did to go off to the City. But this time, thankfully, there was no wife's make-up, no mirror by the loo, no African artefacts and no complication. After he had gone, I took my time getting ready. I was going to have to turn up to the office wearing the same clothes as the day before for the second time in a week, but bugger it, I thought, it is rather too late for that to matter now. I did, however, spend some time on my hair and make-up: if I am going to get the sack, I thought, I'm going out in style.

At about 8.30, I staggered through the huge heavy doors of the building, received a wink from the doorman with a sad smile and made my way up to the office. The receptionist ignored me as I went in.

Donald Bergin shot past without saying anything and a couple of people avoided my eye as I went up the hall. Camilla, unusually, was nowhere to be seen. I sat down at my desk. There was a note from George: 'Not sure about Ian, but I'm free for lunch. Where are you taking me?' I switched on my computer and looked at the phone. It rang instantly. 'Emily, it's Richard,' he said in rather a quiet voice. 'I think we need to have a little chat.'

'Shall I come along now?' I asked.

'I think that would be for the best.' The phone went dead. I dragged myself from my chair, and headed off to Richard's office. The door was closed when I got there. I knocked. 'Come in,' said a voice. I opened the door. Richard was sitting at his desk. Beside him was Camilla. She got up when I came in, nodded briefly in my direction and went out, closing the door behind her.

'Sit down, Emily,' said Richard. He did not look or sound angry, if anything he was looking sympathetic. I sat down opposite him.

'Now Emily,' he said, 'this is very difficult for me to say, but I'm sure you will think it's for the best.' He sighed and looked down at his hands. 'I'm taking you off the Interbank account,' he said eventually, having cleared his throat several times. 'I had a talk with Buzz after you left the meeting, and, I'm afraid, he said that although he was extremely happy for the agency to continue working with Interbank, he did not want you working with him. I don't know why, but I'm afraid he seems to have taken a bit of a dislike to you. I don't think it's entirely fair, I know you've done a lot of work on the account in the past, but recently it has just not been working out. I'm very sorry, Emily.'

I looked down, 'Well, I can't say I wasn't expecting this,' I began. 'Who's taking over the running of the account?'

Richard looked down again and muttered something.

'*What?*' I said.

'Camilla,' said Richard more loudly.

'Camilla!' I said. 'But she's just a secretary!'

'Was,' said Richard. 'She was promoted last night. Donald has been pressing for some time for her to be made into a consultant, and we all think she has just the management skills to handle an account like Interbank. I've known for some time that she's wanted to play a more integral part in the firm, and she's more than up to it. Just because she didn't go to university doesn't mean she can't do the job, Emily, and she'll be taking over the running of your other accounts too.'

'But what about Buzz,' I burst out, 'is he going to like working with an ex-secretary?'

'He seemed delighted with the idea when I mentioned it to him last night.'

'Well, what about me?' I asked. 'What's going to happen to me?'

'We've been thinking about that,' said Richard unhappily. He seemed to be enjoying this no more than I was. 'We do need someone else in the design department, working with Derek. We're getting in an increasing number of design projects, and we need someone to be able to liaise between him and the printers, as well as keeping track of deadlines, supplies, making sure the systems are running smoothly . . .' He trailed off.

I sat for a moment. 'You must be joking,' I said.

'No Emily, I'm very sorry, but I'm not. I know you've been with us for a few years, but we simply cannot have incidents like the one yesterday happening again. We'd become a laughing stock.'

'But that was a one-off!' I said. 'You know that's never happened before. Oh Richard, you really can't expect me to be Derek's assistant.'

'But there have been other problems,' said Richard. 'Look Emily, we just haven't seen the commitment from you that we need. Your time-keeping is dreadful, your work has been shoddy and you just don't seem to have an understanding of client affairs. And there are problems with other members of staff too. There have been several complaints about you smoking in the ladies' lavatory and we've all noticed that you never come along on corporate outings.'

'But I don't like bowling,' I said.

'That's not the point, Emily, and you know it's not. We like to create a warm family atmosphere and you just don't seem to want to join in. I've heard that you've been complaining about having to attend the firm's Christmas party for children next month. And you know that Derek's going to be dressing up as Father Christmas.'

'He'll probably give the children nightmares. What do George and Ian say about this?'

'George and Ian haven't been consulted,' said Richard firmly. 'They are both highly valued members of staff, but they're not on the board. Ultimately it is up to us who stays and who goes.'

'But what about Mark?' I burst out. 'He hasn't been in the office more than twice this year and it's November!'

'The chairman is a different matter,' said Richard.

'He has contacts, Emily, he can open doors for us.'

'But Richard, I can't work with Derek,' I said miserably.

Richard looked down. 'There is another option,' he said quietly.

I knew what it was but even so it was a blow hearing it. 'Go on,' I said.

Richard sighed. 'Emily, you're just not right for the firm,' he said. 'And to be honest, I don't think PR's the right field for you. But you have been here a while, and we want to be generous, in fact, we're prepared to be very generous.'

My ears pricked up. 'How generous?' I asked.

'Well, first of all, we'd want you to resign. But then we'd be prepared to make you an *ex gratia* payment of one year's salary. That is far more than we are required to do by the terms of your contract, and far more than we'd be required to do in a court of law. And it would give you some time to think about what you really wanted to do.'

I was thinking fast. A year's salary was not to be sneezed at. If I got it in a lump sum, I would be able to pay off my overdraft, all my credit card bills, and, more importantly still, my Harvey Nichols bill, take a little holiday, maybe buy some new clothes and still have enough to live on for quite a while. No point in hanging about. 'All right,' I said.

Richard relaxed visibly. 'I'm very glad you see it that way,' he said. 'I'm very sad it's got to end like this, but I think you will be much happier in a different career altogether. Now, if you go and type out a letter of resignation, I'll have the cheque made up. And Emily, I'm not trying to throw you out of the building, but I really think it would be for the best if you left today.'

'That's fine,' I said. The heavy weight that had been hanging over me for, well, years now, seemed miraculously to have lifted.

'Come back in half an hour,' said Richard as I opened the door, 'everything will be ready.'

I began to make my way back up the corridor. Camilla appeared at the door of her office. 'Look Emily, I'm really sorry,' she began.

'Fuck off,' I said, and continued on my way, happier than ever. I had been wanting to say that for a very long time. I clicked up my resignation letter on my computer. 'Please type in password,' said the computer. 'B-o-l-l-o-c-k-s', I typed. The letter flashed up in front of me. 'Dear Richard, it is with the deepest regret that I am tendering my resignation,' I read. 'Yours sincerely.' It was insincere but to the point. I typed in the correct date, pressed the print button and sat back as it went to the printer on the other side of the room. Then I looked at the phone. It rang instantly. 'Emily Whitelake,' I said.

'Emily, it's me,' barked my mother. 'Just ringing to see how you are.'

'I've been resigned,' I said.

'*What?*' said my mother. I explained to her what had happened. 'Oh Emily, I am sorry,' she said.

'Well I'm not, Mummy. I absolutely loathed it here and now I've got a few months' leeway to find a decent job. Honestly, I wish it had happened years ago.'

'Well, if you're sure, darling,' said my mother. 'Now Emily, I was just ringing because you said you might be coming up in a few weeks. The thing is, Daddy and I have been invited to stay with the McCauleys. They've got a lovely little chalet in Austria, near Innsbruck, and I thought I should check when you wanted to come and stay. They want us to go out there the week after next.'

I looked at the phone resentfully. My parents' civilized social life was rearing its ugly head again. 'Don't worry, Mummy, you go,' I said resignedly. 'I want to be around here to start sorting things out for the future and I'm coming up at Christmas anyway. I assume you'll be back by then?'

'Of course we will, weeks before then,' cried my mother, greatly relieved. 'And how's the boyfriend situation?'

'Actually, I've got a date with someone tomorrow night.'

'*What?*' cried my mother joyfully. 'What's his name and what does he do?'

'He's called Gary and he's a computer programmer.'

'Oh,' said my mother. 'Well never mind, darling. Now do give my love to Jack when you see him, and that's tremendous news about the resignation, darling.'

She rang off. I was in too good a mood to be deflated. I wandered over to the printer to collect my letter, and then went back to my desk. I looked around. No-one was there. Slowly and methodically I erased every single programme on my computer which contained details going back over the years on the Interbank account as well as my other account work, general letter headings, fax headings and details of all the past billings I'd had to do. That will give them something to do, finding out exactly what they should bill the clients for, I thought happily.

Then I emptied my desk, which was extremely simple; I put everything on it and in it into three surrounding rubbish bins. The only thing I kept was a framed picture of Jack and me taken a few years ago at a friend's wedding, which I stuffed into my briefcase. Then clutching my letter, I went back to Richard's office. 'Ah Emily, come in,' he said. It was a bit like an exchange of hostages: he held out the cheque, I held out the letter and we both grabbed simultaneously. I inspected the details, so did Richard, everything was in order. Richard held out his hand. 'I'm truly sorry, Emily, and I hope we'll meet again,' he said.

'Oh, so do I,' I said untruthfully. I wandered back to my desk and called George on the internal extension. 'That's a really sweet offer about lunch,' I said, 'but I've got a few other things to do, like going to the bank. You know I've been resigned?'

'Well, I did hear something,' George admitted. 'Look Em, are you going to be all right?'

'More than all right,' I said. 'And I hope you're going to keep in touch.'

'Of course we are, we go back a long way,' said George. 'If we can't do it today, Ian and I are taking you out to lunch next week. I'll give you a ring on Monday and we can arrange something.' He rang off.

There was a noise behind me. Camilla was standing there, looking serious and committed. 'Emily, even if we don't get on, I think we should be professional about this,' she said. 'I'm sorry about what's happened, but, like Richard, I think it's for the best. Now, I thought you could show me around the Interbank files, as well as the other clients you've been dealing with.'

'It's all in there,' I said gesturing at the rubbish bins. 'If you can't find anything, don't call me at home because I don't have anything to do with treacherous two-faced little bitches. I'm sure you'll be great at the job, Camilla.' I swept out of the office, just for once managing not to trip over anything and remembering to grab my coat and bag and headed off up the street in the direction of the nearest bank.

11

The afternoon was sheer joy. I banked the cheque, went home and spent an afternoon sending off fully paid bills. Then I had a long bath, and came back into my small sitting-room draped in a towel. I looked with pleasure at the books that lined one wall (all right, so most of them belonged to my parents but it looked impressive) and made a mental note to replace the tatty rug on the floor I'd bought in a jumble sale for a tenner and replace it with a decent little Turkish number that I intended to pick up in the next Harvey Nichols sale. After all, I could afford it now.

I tidied the whole place which was quite simple: all the clothes on the floor and the chairs went into the laundry basket, all the books went back onto the shelves and all the old papers went into the rubbish. My desk was now clear because I had paid off all the bills covering it: I filled up the space by plonking down the picture of Jack and me that I had taken from the office. I could not resist stroking the picture of Jack: handsome at the best of times, he was wearing morning dress in the photograph, was tanned from a holiday we had taken driving around Italy, and looked wonderful.

Then I turned on the television: they were showing a repeat of last Sunday's Left Bank Programme, a late night art show. It was featuring a modern American artist called Johann Krapp (I would have changed the name if it were me) who had recently married a French pornographic film star who went by the name of La Tittiolation. He was comparing a picture he had painted of him fondling La T's bum to the roof of the Sistine Chapel. 'Just as Adam reaches out to God, I am reaching out to touch La Tittiolation's ass,' he said. 'This is one of the most spiritual of my works.'

Bored, I turned off the television and looked around me. My eye alighted on the phone. It rang instantly. 'Emily, it's me,' said Jack. 'I rang your office but they said you'd resigned. What on earth's happened?'

'Well actually, I didn't have a great deal of choice in the matter,' I said. I told him the whole story.

'Well, you know, I honestly think it's for the best,' said Jack. 'Especially if they've given you all that dosh. Listen, Emily, I was just ringing to say that I still can't find Henry. Have you or Natasha heard anything?'

'Oh no,' I said. 'But I thought you said there was nothing to worry about.'

'Well yes, I thought so originally,' responded Jack. 'But I was thinking about it today, and it really is very odd. People do usually tell their friends when they're moving, and Henry doesn't seem to have mentioned it to anyone. I've been asking a few mates of mine and no-one knows anything about it.'

'Look,' I said, 'why don't we wait until Monday? He's supposed to be back in work then, and if he doesn't show up, then we'll know if something's wrong.'

'Maybe.' I could hear Jack inhaling on a cigarette

over the phone. 'Look, why don't you just call Catherine and see if she's heard anything about it? She was the one who met him first, after all, she might know who else to call.'

'OK, will do,' I said. 'I was thinking about consulting her on the job front anyway, she's always full of good ideas.'

'Good. Now listen, Emily, are you doing anything tonight?'

'I thought I'd have a dry night in,' I said.

'Don't be ridiculous,' said Jack. 'A group of us are meeting for drinks at Balls Brothers on Cheapside. See you there at about seven?'

'See you there,' I said, hanging up. I was glad I was going out: I wanted to celebrate my freedom. And for once I would have enough money to pay for my round: I had found time in the middle of bill paying to ring up the loathsome Lanson and inform him that I had just deposited a very substantial cheque. After the initial sharp intake of disbelieving breath, he had agreed to allow me to use my cash card. I wandered into my tiny little bedroom to get ready.

Balls Brothers was packed. The relief of coming in to a warm crowded dimly lit bar was enormous after the bitter cold outside, and the light was glinting off the dark brown polished wood of the bar's interior. I pushed my way over to Jack, who was surrounded by his City chums. 'Hello, my darling, and congratulations,' he said kissing me. 'Gentlemen, raise your glasses to this lucky woman. This morning she was freed from the chains of possibly the worst job in the world.'

'Oh really, what was that?' asked a banker.

'I worked in PR,' I admitted.

'PR, eh? Rather you than me. I'm Alexander, by the way,' said the banker. 'Call me Alex.'

'Emily,' I said, shaking his hand. 'Actually I had to deal with the likes of you most of the time, I worked mainly on financial accounts.'

'Oh really, what sort of clients?' asked Alex.

'Well, mainly banks and things,' I said.

'Really, what a coincidence,' said Alex. 'My flatmate—' At this point we were interrupted by Jack, who had just returned from the bar with a glass of champagne for me. 'Now don't start trying to chat up Emily, she's with me tonight,' he said putting his arm around me. 'And also, she does have a date tomorrow night.'

'Lucky man,' said Alex raising his glass to me. I was beginning to warm to him considerably. Although I was looking forward to my date with Gary, it was always nice to have a back-up list and Alexander – I preferred it to Alex, nice name – was rather good looking: tall, dark and wiry.

Jack was also in a sunny mood. 'TGIF,' he said happily. 'You would not believe the week I've had, complicated, I might add, by Emily's little adventures.'

'Really? What were they?' asked Alexander.

I personally felt we should not be discussing the intricate details of the last few days with third parties, even if he was a friend of Jack's, but my ex obviously felt otherwise. 'Well, first Em had rather a complicated week at work and became involved in a whole series of amorous adventures,' he began and received such a hostile glare from me that he hastily changed track. 'But far more interestingly, we've got caught up with a missing body,' he went on.

Alexander drained his glass and stuck it out to a chum for a refill. 'Missing bodies?' he said incredulously. 'You don't strike me as the private eye type, Jack.'

'Anything to help Em,' said Jack grinning at me, and proceeded to relate to Alexander the whole story.

By the time he had finished, Alexander was looking at us in frank astonishment. 'So this woman actually left a man she thought was seriously ill and then he goes and disappears? What kind of a woman would do that?'

'Oh, you don't know Natasha,' I replied darkly. 'I wouldn't be surprised if she'd done away with him herself except now she claims she's being haunted by him.'

'Haunted?' You could tell Alexander was beginning to wonder what kind of lunatics Jack spent his time with.

'Well, so she says,' I began, but Jack cut in, obviously concerned that his reputation as a serious banker was about to be harmed beyond all repair.

'Yes, well, Emily's friends tend to have very active imaginations. But it is odd that Henry's gone missing. Which reminds me, Em, did you manage to call Catherine?'

'Oh bugger, I forgot. I'll try tomorrow.'

Alexander looked at us with a glint in his eye. 'I think it's this Edward bloke. Turns up out of the blue, claims a long-standing friendship that no-one else knows about and doesn't seem that concerned that his tenant's gone missing. I say we go check it out.'

'What?' I said. Balls Brothers was bright and warm and a very attractive alternative to the freezing cold outside. Anyway, I wanted to celebrate my freedom and I did not call one or was it two glasses of champagne much of a celebration. 'I honestly think you're both making a fuss about nothing,' I said. 'And anyway, none of us have known him for that long. It's possible he's got stacks of friends we don't know about.'

'No harm in going to have a look,' said Alexander.

Jack hesitated. He was obviously quite keen on the idea but, manly pride reasserting itself, was loath to allow someone else to seize the initiative. 'I think Em's right, you know. Someone, somewhere would have noticed if he was really missing – his parents or someone like that. Anyway, we should be helping Emily to celebrate.'

Alexander looked rather disappointed but took it like a man. 'In that case we need more champagne,' he said and fought his way back to the bar.

'He's nice,' I said, looking after Alexander.

'He's all right,' responded Jack rather coldly. 'I hardly know him, actually, we just met up because we did a deal with his bank last week.'

'Yes, but it's nice of him to take an interest in people he doesn't even know. Maybe we should go and check up on Edward again?'

'You know,' said Jack, putting his arm around me again, rather possessively I thought, 'we're all becoming a wee bit hysterical. Now what say you and I have another drink here and then go off for dinner at— oh my God.'

I followed his eyes and gasped. 'Good Lord,' I said. A couple had just come through the door, and with a fair bit of billing and cooing were taking their coats off and examining the wine list. 'She is a seriously fast worker,' I whispered. 'What's Cosmo going to make of this?'

The couple, obviously aware of our penetrating gaze, looked in our direction and froze – or at least one of them did. 'Oh my God!' shrieked Natasha and began pulling her cloak back on. Totally recovered from the night before, she was now sporting her virginal and innocent look: a cream woollen skirt and sweater which set off her black hair, brown suede boots and a cream woollen wrap. Edward was wearing black trousers, a black polo neck sweater and a very dark jacket. They made an extremely handsome couple.

I made a beeline for them: I wanted to find out what was happening. 'Leaving so soon?' I panted, skidding up to them. 'Why don't you join us for a drink?'

Natasha cast an anguished glance at Edward, but having been discovered, he obviously thought they might as well make the best of it. 'Yes, that would be lovely,' he said. 'Natasha, why don't we stay?'

Natasha shot a venomous look at me. 'Oh do,' I said mercilessly, 'Jack will be so pleased to see both of you. Is Cosmo working tonight, Natasha?'

'No, actually,' said Natasha through clenched teeth, 'we've had a bit of a disagreement and we are no longer on speaking terms.'

'So you're young, free and single?' I asked.

'Only for tonight,' said Natasha viciously, lowering her voice and hissing at me, 'and we're going to talk things over tomorrow.' Her black eyes were shooting sparks in my direction.

By this time we had been joined by Jack and Alexander, who had produced another bottle of champagne. 'Alexander, isn't this a coincidence?' I cried happily. 'This is Natasha and this is Edward, my friends that I was telling you about earlier.'

Alexander took the situation in at a glance, but was kind enough to restrict himself to a 'Oh how nice to meet you, I've heard so much about you.'

Natasha grimaced and shook his hand. Jack, unwilling to be left out of the fun, obviously felt it was his turn to make a contribution. 'And Edward, how are you?' he asked. 'Heard anything from Henry yet?'

'No, unfortunately I haven't,' replied Edward quietly. He had a certain innate dignity that calmed us all down a bit. 'But then again, I've been very busy; I've been working all day sorting out photographs and so on. It was quite a relief to take a break when Natasha rang.'

I raised my eyebrows and looked at Natasha. She obviously felt some kind of explanation was called for. 'Yes, well I gave Edward a call to see if he'd heard anything. And we decided to meet up for a drink,' she added lamely.

'Tell me,' I said lowering my voice and hissing at her, 'was this before or after you and Cosmo had your little disagreement?'

No answer was necessary and neither did I get one. Natasha shot me yet another poisonous glance and then, deciding she had wasted enough time already, began directing the full force of her attention at Edward. 'You know, Edward's got some of the most amazing pictures,' she breathed, gazing at him intensely. 'I went round to see them before we came here, and they're just so poetic. You obviously have a real artist's eye, Edward.'

I could have sworn that Edward blushed. He might have been older than the rest of us, but he most certainly was not wiser. 'Yes, well,' he shrugged self-deprecatingly, 'it's just something I picked up. Of course I've always been very interested in the visual arts – especially when it comes to beauty.'

He and Natasha gazed deep into one another's eyes. Oh, puleeze, I thought. Jack obviously could not take much more of this either. 'Look,' he said to Alexander, 'Emily and I were thinking of going out to dinner—'

'Yes, I'd love to come,' said Alexander, beaming at me.

The look of irritation on Jack's face increased briefly, but he took it well. 'Come on then, both of you,' he said, and we began struggling into our coats.

'Oh, you're not going already, are you? What a shame,' said Natasha insincerely. She and Edward watched with ill-concealed relief as we headed for the door. 'Bye, Emily, I'll ring you tomorrow,' she bellowed as we went out into the cold.

'So what did you think?' I asked Alexander once we were outside, as Jack scouted for a cab.

'Well, she's very attractive but what's she doing with the man who killed her boyfriend?' asked Alexander.

'No, no, Cosmo's her boyfriend,' I explained. 'And they've just had a row. It's Henry, the chap that she had a fling with that's gone missing.'

'Emily, will you stop talking such utter rubbish,' said Jack. 'My sympathies are entirely with Edward now that I can see she's got her claws into him. Poor bloke won't know what's hit him. Oh, hell, what's that?' A shrill sound had gone off inside his jacket. Jack pulled a bleeper out, and frowned at it, trying to read the message in the dark. 'It says call your parents urgently,' he said eventually. 'Can you two just hang on while I see what it's about?'

He vanished into a phone box and we saw him dialling. It was too cold to make much conversation: we both just hopped from foot to foot and made desultory remarks about whether it would start snowing and how nice it would be to be on a hot beach. After a couple of minutes Jack reappeared. 'I am really sorry, but I've got to go,' he said. 'I've just been talking to my father. My mother's broken her leg, she slipped while she was up a ladder. No, no,' he said as we both started to clamour, 'she's perfectly all right, it's nothing serious, the doctor said it was a very clean break. But my father said he'd like me to go along to the hospital and I really couldn't say no. Are you two going to be all right?'

'Yes, of course. I'll take Emily out to dinner,' said Alexander gallantly.

For some reason this did not seem to make Jack's mood any better, but there was nothing he could do. We saw him off into one cab and hailed another ourselves. 'Now, where would you like to go?' asked Alexander, clambering in.

'What about Joe Allen?' I said. 'That's always bright and cheerful.'

'Sure thing,' said Alexander. We drove off up the road.

12

'Look,' said Henry, 'it's perfectly obvious where I've been. I took a cab to Mars and then I circled a few planets. The weather's quite changeable up there: Venus was a bit too hot for my liking. The stars look amazing close to, though. And then the driver got lost and we left the Milky Way altogether. It was a bit of a pain, I didn't have a change of clothing on me.'

'But Henry, why didn't you ring? Everyone's been so worried,' I said.

'No time,' said Henry. 'When I returned to Earth I transmuted into a porpoise. The uncharted depths of the sea are even more fascinating than outer space. You should try it, Emily, give you a chance to get over Jack. But then again, you don't like roughing it, do you? There are no four-star hotels five fathoms deep. I must go, a radar wave going straight to my brain says the world is in terrible danger and only I can save it. Toodle-oo.' He vanished.

'Whaa,' I said.

'Bloody radio,' said a voice.

'What?' I said blinking and opening my eyes. Where had Henry gone? He could not just have vanished into thin air.

'I said bloody radio,' repeated the voice. 'Sorry about that, I forgot to turn the alarm off. As if anyone would care about exploring the oceans first thing on Saturday morning. And all that stuff about inner space being even more fascinating than outer space. So clichéd.'

'The radio?' I blinked and sat bolt upright. The figure lying beside me rolled over and turned on a bedside lamp. 'Yes, the radio, it was the *Today* programme, didn't you hear it just now?' asked Alexander.

'Oh God,' I said lying back. Then that seemed a bit ungracious, so I rolled over and said, 'Oh yes, I must have done. I was having the most peculiar dream. So Henry still hasn't turned up.'

'Your missing friend?' asked Alexander. 'Well, not as of last night. Shall I turn the light off? It's only just after seven and it's Saturday so we don't have to get up for hours.'

'Yes do,' I said gratefully. I wanted to try to remember what had happened last night. I shut my eyes and buried my aching head against the pillow. I had been in Balls Brothers drinking with Jack and Alexander – oh no, I thought, what on earth is Jack going to say now? And then we were going to force Edward to confess to the murder of Henry, only to be confronted by Edward himself accompanied by the fast-working Natasha. And then there was Gary, who I was supposed to be seeing tonight and Nigel – I groaned. 'Oh no,' I said.

'Are you sure you're all right?' asked Alexander turning over and putting his arms around me.

'Yes, yes, just deeply hungover,' I said. I put all these disagreeable thoughts out of my mind and we both nodded off after that until I woke with a start about an hour later. Alexander was still fast asleep. I became aware of a serious and urgent need for the lavatory. 'Alexander,' I whispered, 'where's your loo?'

'Second on the left down the hall,' muttered Alexander sleepily. 'Mind you don't take the first on the left – that's my flatmate's room and she doesn't take kindly to being woken up at the weekend.'

He nodded off again. I pushed the heavy duvet aside – did no-one use sheets and blankets anymore? – crawled out of bed and wrapped myself in a man's shirt that was lying on the floor. Then I opened the door carefully and peered out. I had no idea where we were.

The hall had an array of bookcases on the right. They were mainly filled with austere looking tomes, but here and there were dotted the odd extremely expensive looking ornament or painting. Someone had also left some jewellery on one of the shelves, which looked strangely familiar although I could not quite place it. Beyond the bookshelves was a staircase. We were obviously on the first floor.

I crept down the hall and scuttled into the bathroom. I was, I had to admit, becoming rather used to waking up in strange places but it was unnerving when someone else lived there as well. The bathroom, which was large and old-fashioned – mahogany loo seat, scratched gold taps, that sort of thing – was filled with both men's and women's apparatus. I supposed the women's things, which all looked extremely expensive, must belong to Alexander's flatmate.

I performed a few ablutions, cleaned my teeth with a finger and dragged a comb through my hair. The roots always seemed to show up more strongly first thing in the morning, I thought, sighing, although at least I could afford to have them touched up now. My eye make-up was, as ever, halfway down my cheeks. I wiped it off, wrapped the shirt around myself more tightly, turned round, opened the door and screamed.

At first I thought I was still asleep and having another nightmare, but no, it really was Buzz, wrapped in a small towel and on the verge of coming into the bathroom. He was still looking blond, tanned and all-American handsome but he had gone quite white. He even seemed as taken aback as I was. 'Emily?' he squawked. 'What the hell are you doing here?'

At the sounds of the commotion, two sets of bedroom doors burst open. Alexander appeared in one, also clad in a towel, and looking tousled. 'What's going on?' he demanded. 'Emily? Are you all right?'

But my attention was riveted by the other bedroom door. I really must be dreaming, I thought. But no, it really was her. Camilla, looking a damn sight less polished than she usually did, and also wearing a towel (just how many towels do they keep in this place, I wondered briefly), was standing and staring at me with her mouth open.

My mind was not working very fast, and for a moment I just stood gawping at her. But it gradually began to dawn on me that for the very first time in my dealings with Camilla I had one up on her. 'Hello Camilla, how's the new account going?' I asked brightly.

'What are you doing here, Emily?' Camilla demanded abruptly. Caught *in flagrante delicto* she

147

might have been, but the woman had lost none of her charm. 'Who let you in?'

'I did actually,' said Alexander stepping forward. 'I gather you two know one another.'

'Camilla was my secretary,' I said coldly. I felt I wanted to assert some seniority over her and fast.

'With the emphasis on *was*,' snapped Camilla. 'I'd like to remind you that I have now taken over your job.'

'Yes, and I think I'm beginning to see how,' I said, looking at Buzz who had gone strangely quiet. 'I thought you didn't like mixing business with pleasure, Buzz.'

'Well, usually he doesn't but I'm an exception,' butted in Camilla. It looked as if it was beginning to dawn on her that she might be in a slightly difficult situation. 'I wouldn't expect you to understand this, Emily, with the number of men you hang around with, but Buzz and I are very involved. We have been seeing one another regularly for a number of weeks now.'

'Weeks!' I exclaimed, turning to Buzz. 'Did I hear Camilla say weeks?'

Buzz had gone even whiter. 'Yes, well I'm sure you understand the situation, Emily,' he said heavily. 'Look, why don't we all get dressed and talk together over a nice cup of coffee.'

With that the two of them disappeared back into Camilla's bedroom. I could hear her saying just before the door shut, 'Why did Emily say you don't like mixing business and pleasure, Buzz?' I burst out laughing. Alexander was snickering too as we went back into his room. 'Look, I'm really sorry,' he said. 'I had no idea you knew her. I know you said last night that you used to work in financial PR but I had no idea it was the same firm.'

'Oh, that's OK, this has given me a whole new insight into Camilla's character,' I said, happily beginning to pull on my clothes. I put on knickers and tights before discarding the shirt and then completed the operation with my back to him. Had my modesty to think about, after all. 'How do you know her?' I asked.

'Oh, we go back a long way,' said Alexander. 'I was at school with one of her brothers. She can be a bit of a pain, to be honest, but it's convenient sharing as we're both out all the time. It's her flat, actually. I used to work in the States and I only got back three months ago which is when I moved in here. It's funny she never mentioned your name but then again she does have nicknames for everyone at the office and she always uses them.' He stopped abruptly.

'Go on,' I said.

'Oh no, Emily, I don't think she had one for you,' said Alexander unhappily.

I finished buttoning my shirt. 'Go on, I promise not to hold it against you.'

'Well,' said Alexander reluctantly, 'I assume this must be you because I know she only worked for one woman. She said she hated working for women, by the way.'

'I bet she did. Now go on, what was it?'

'BWA,' said Alexander.

'BWA?' I repeated.

'Blonde with attitude,' said Alexander.

I burst out laughing again. 'Actually, I find that highly flattering. Now what does she call Richard?'

'Richard?'

'Richard Dorfmann. Chap who runs the firm. He used to be my boss. She was also his secretary.'

'Oh, she just used to call him Gramps,' said Alexander. 'Shall we go down and greet the love-birds?' He was now dressed in jeans and a lumberjack shirt. He looked delightful, but I felt slightly guilty about Gary. And Jack.

'In a sec,' I said, sitting down on the bed. 'I just want to get a few things straight. You say you were at school with her brother?'

'Yes, why?'

'You don't by any chance know a chap called Gary Redcliffe, do you?' I asked.

'Gerry? Yes. He's an old mate of mine, although I haven't seen him for ages,' said Alexander. 'I was at school with him too. He got into dreadful trouble because of an incident in the locker room, although I'm sure that was only a one-off. Camilla knows him as well. How on earth did you come across him?'

I gulped and for the very first time in my life, decided honesty was the best policy. 'Well actually, he's the chap I've got a date with tonight,' I said looking down.

Alexander sat down beside me and took my hand. 'Don't worry about it,' he said. 'None of us are angels. I won't breathe a word, I promise, although to be absolutely honest with you, I am not able to vouch for my flatmate.'

'Well, she's hardly one to talk,' I burst out. 'Did you know Buzz's married?' It was on the tip of my tongue to inform Alexander that Buzz was not only unfaithful to his wife but he was also not exactly doing the honourable thing by his girlfriend. Luckily I thought better of it.

'Well, I had wondered,' admitted Alexander. 'They very rarely spend a night together but I thought that might be because it was early days in their relationship. How do you know him, anyway?'

'He just happens to be one of Klinker Dorfmann's major clients, or at least his firm is,' I said spitefully. 'Makes it look a bit of a coincidence that Camilla got the account, doesn't it? How long has it been going on?'

'About a month, I think, although I wouldn't vouch for it,' said Alexander.

A month, I thought. Buzz's only been in the country just over a month. Camilla must have got her slimy little hooks into him practically the minute he got off the plane. 'Well, anyway,' I said, 'let's go downstairs.'

By the time we got into the kitchen, Camilla and Buzz were fussing around with the coffee and were the embodiment of sweetness and light. They seemed to have realized that they were going to have to rely on a certain amount of discretion on my part. I drew up a chair and sat down at the table in the middle of the room. 'So,' I said to Buzz by way of opening the conversation, 'is your wife out of town at the moment?'

There was a clatter at the sink as Camilla dropped the cafetière. 'Look, Emily, I know you'll understand,' said Buzz, coming over, sitting down, laying a hand on my arm and regarding me with an expression that could only be described as pleading, 'but my marriage broke down a long time ago. We just stay together for the sake of appearances. She knows I have other friends.'

'Really? That's not the impression I got the other morning.'

There was another clatter at the sink as Camilla

whirled round. 'What do you mean, the other morning?' she demanded.

'The other morning, when I went to the meeting at Interbank,' I explained. 'I noticed a photograph on Buzz's desk. I assumed it was his wife.'

'Yes, well that's just there for appearances as well,' responded Buzz uncomfortably. There was a brief silence.

'Now look Emily,' Camilla burst out, having poured out some coffee for me with extremely bad grace, 'this is obviously an awkward situation. But we don't work together anymore so let's all just have a coffee and forget about it.' She drew up a chair and sat down. I was irritated to see that Camilla's designer wardrobe was not confined to the office: she was wearing black leather trousers and a dark grey sweater that I knew without any shadow of a doubt was cashmere. She had also had time to comb her smooth brown hair and dab on a bit of make-up.

'What, you mean you don't want Gramps to know?' I asked.

Camilla shot a look of pure hatred in Alexander's direction. 'I'm sorry, I'm sorry, it just slipped out,' he protested.

Camilla took a deep breath and turned back to me. 'No, if truth be told, I don't want Gramps – I mean Richard – to know until Buzz and I have sorted it all out.'

'Oh yes of course,' I said. 'Successful PR is as much about what you keep out of the papers as what you get in. Isn't that what everyone says?'

'Now look, Emily, please be reasonable.'

'Like you were when you took my job?' I asked.

'That was just one of those things, Emily,' said

Camilla, reverting to serious and professional. 'It was nothing personal. And it was bound to happen sooner or later.'

She had got me there but I was not going to show it. 'Oh was it,' I answered, standing up and pushing back my chair. 'Well, it's been a lovely morning everyone, but if you'll excuse me, I've really got to go. And I will have to think carefully about what to do with my newly acquired information. Buzz. Camilla.' I turned formally to each of them. Neither said a word: Buzz looked down at his hands and Camilla slammed out of her chair and marched over to the kitchen sink, where she stood with her back to me. I followed Alexander out into the hall and to the front door. 'Well, you certainly told them,' said Alexander, leaning over and kissing me on the cheek. 'Look, Emily, I know you have a date with a friend of mine tonight, but if you can forgive my choice of flatmate, I'd really like to meet up again.'

'Yes,' I said, surprised, 'I'd love to.' I scribbled my number down and went out into the street.

I had been so determined to make a dramatic exit that it had not occurred to me to ask where we were. I turned a few street corners and eventually worked out from the postcode that I was in Clapham. South of the river was something of a mystery to me, so I went on walking for some time before I found a main road. There did not seem to be a tube station or bus stop for miles round, so I settled on a park bench to wait for a taxi. I had forgotten that most taxi drivers had a pretty similar attitude to south London as my own, and so it was a good half-hour before one came along. I kept warm by chain-smoking and stroking a cat which had appeared from nowhere until finally a cab turned up. 'Olympia, please,' I said, leaping in.

As we began to jolt our way back towards civilization, I sat back and mused on recent events. This really did explain a lot. Even I had to admit grudgingly that Camilla was an efficient secretary, but until recently she had shown absolutely no signs of real ambition. Camilla was one of those girls who came from the Home Counties, got an A-level or two if they were exceptionally bright and worked as a secretary or ran a catering firm until Lord Right came along. Until a couple of months ago, she had worked for Mark Klinker, Richard and Donald, but when my previous secretary left in September to emigrate to Australia, it was widely accepted that Mark no longer really needed her and she was assigned to me.

No-one had been more against this than Camilla herself, and ever since then my career had plummeted downhill. My rather tousled appearance was in sharp contrast to Camilla's sleek looks, and my chaotic way of life could not have been more different from Camilla's ordered manner of going about things. Klinker Dorfmann was a very conservative firm: it liked women to drink in extreme moderation, not smoke and go to bed early and alone if they were single. Camilla fitted the corporate bill (or at least I had thought she did) and I did not.

I had also suspected for some time that she was actively trying to do me down – sneaking to Richard when I came in late was just one example – although it had never occurred to me that she was actually after my job. When she met Buzz, they must have planned the whole thing between them. No wonder he was so shocked when he found out who I was the other morning.

The taxi turned into my road. What with the early

morning get-together, my little walk and the wait for the cab, time was getting on. Glancing at my watch as we pulled up outside my house, I was surprised to see that it was nearly twelve. I felt rather tired and wanted a bath and a nap.

Getting out of the cab, I paid, asked the cabby for a receipt – force of habit, there was nowhere I could use it now – collected my mail and raced upstairs. I was humming slightly as I turned my key in the lock. I seemed to have forgotten to put the mortice on. Shall I go shopping this afternoon? I wondered. I had paid off my Harvey Nichols card in full and was rather looking forward to running up another bill, although I had a nasty feeling the cheque wouldn't have cleared yet. Or shall I— 'Emily!' shouted a voice as I pushed the door open.

My first thought was it must be burglars. I slammed the door shut and was halfway down the stairs when the door was wrenched open again. 'Emily!' shouted the voice again. 'Don't go! It's me! Nigel!'

I stopped running – heaven knows why – and peered up. There indeed, was Nigel, resplendent in dark purple tracksuit trousers and a droopy orange T-shirt with figures prancing round the front. He was staging his usual weekend dirty protest, he had not shaved and dark stubble intermingled with the spots and lines on his chin. It looked as if he'd not had time to wash for a week or two either. 'Emily!' he cried again. 'We've got to talk!'

That was about the last thing I wanted to do but neither did I want the neighbours to hear whatever little gem Nigel was about to come out with now. I sped furiously up the stairs and followed him into my sitting-room. It looked as if Nigel had been in residence for a while: there was a cup of coffee on the side table, the television was on and Nigel's disgusting running shoes were making their presence felt in the middle of the floor.

'What the hell do you want?' I burst out ungraciously, marching over to the television and switching it off. 'I thought I told you that I never wanted to see you again. And how did you get in here?'

'The keys you gave me in case of emergency,' said Nigel solemnly. 'And I think it is an emergency, you know, Emily. Don't worry. I'm not going to talk about Us. I just want to help you to sort out what's in your head right now.'

'What is in my head,' I snarled, stalking into the kitchen, a tiny little box of a room just off the sitting-room, 'is a hangover and the need for some coffee and a bath.'

'Don't try to avoid the issue,' insisted Nigel, following me into the cramped space, 'you know I think you're in a period of denial right now.'

'A period of what?' I demanded, spooning ground coffee into the percolator.

'Denial. It's like you don't want to come to terms with what's really the real you. I think you should, like, get to know your inner self. All this drinking and manizing is just a way of denying what's really wrong with your life.' He attempted to put an arm around me.

'Well, it beats the hell out of talking to people like you about it,' I said, swerving sharply to avoid him. 'Shouldn't you be out sending teenage delinquents on holiday or something?'

'It's Saturday and even social workers need a rest

sometime,' said Nigel piously. 'And I think it's really sad, Emily, that you feel the need to mock our rehabilitation programmes like that. Why are you doing that? Is there something in your life you feel you need to punish yourself for and there's an inner anger when you think other people are escaping punishment as well? You know, you have a right to verbalize your feelings.'

I had had as much of this waffle as I could take. 'The only thing I feel I need to punish myself for,' I replied, breathing heavily, 'is my complete idiocy in giving you a set of keys and the only sort of anger I am going to verbalize will be at you if you go on spouting this rubbish. Can I have my keys back now, please?'

Nigel very deliberately walked over to the sofa, picked them up and put them in his trouser pocket. 'Come and get them,' he said archly.

'Don't be repulsive,' I said furiously. 'Give me my keys.'

'Emily, I would, but I know you're going to need me,' said Nigel walking back into the centre of the room and tripping over his running shoes. He bent to pick them up and then gazed at me with an expression of nauseating sincerity. 'Sometimes, you know, we all need a friend. And when you recognize that, I'll be there for you, Emily.'

With that he was gone. 'How dare he!' I screamed at a bemused-looking plant on the window sill, poured myself a cup of coffee and stalked back into the sitting-room. I sat down on the sofa and realized that I had not yet opened my mail. There was a garish-coloured envelope, addressed to Miss 'Witlak', which told me I had won at least £25,000. I binned it instantly. Then there were a couple of bill-like envelopes, which

I also binned as I never paid anything until the reminder came in. There was one last letter which I was more curious about: it was obviously personal and the handwriting looked vaguely familiar, although I couldn't quite place it. I ripped open the expensive-looking envelope and scanned the letter's contents. 'Dear Emily,' it began:

> I am really so sorry that you decided to leave so suddenly – we are all so sad to see you go and wish you every possible luck in your future career, whatever that may be.
>
> I was extremely upset not to have had the chance to thank you for all your hard work while you were here, especially on the Interbank account. I hope that our paths cross again in future and that one way or another we can keep in touch.
>
> With best wishes, Donald

I chucked the letter onto the floor and snorted in disgust. Not for one moment did I credit this to altruistic motives on Donald Bergin's part. These PR types were so two-faced and hypocritical, the only thing he was likely to be worried about was whether I told all their clients' secrets to my chums on the papers – or Klinker Dorfmann's rival firms, of course. And the only way I wanted to cross paths with Donald Bergin was if I happened to be driving a large and extremely powerful steamroller and he was on foot. Arsehole.

Reading all that oozing insincerity quite exhausted me. I will just doze for a second or two, I thought, leaning back, when suddenly a siren went off in my ear. Leaping up, I realized it was the phone. 'Emily Whitelake,' I said automatically.

'Oh, thank God you're there,' shouted Natasha.

'Emily, I've got to talk to you now. Don't go anywhere. I'm coming right over.' She slammed the phone down. Oh what now, I thought grouchily, and headed off to take a quick bath before she arrived.

I was just pulling my jeans on (I only wore them when I was feeling slim and what with one thing and another I had not had a great deal to eat over the past week) when the doorbell rang. I buzzed the intercom switch to let her in and went into the kitchen to put on some more coffee. I was just switching the machine on when I was viciously attacked by something small and furry that was lunging at my ankles. 'What on earth?' I said, looking down. There seemed to be two kittens on the floor, one black with a little white stripe on its chin and the other piebald. In the background, Natasha, still wearing the same clothes as the night before, was busily setting down a litter tray, a cat basket and a couple of feeding bowls.

'Natasha, what the hell do you think you're doing?' I demanded.

'Do you have some scissors, Emily?' asked Natasha, taking no notice of me. She came into the kitchen, grabbed a knife, said, 'This will do,' and started sawing at a huge bagful of cat litter. 'Got to get them into the litter tray right away so they'll know where it is,' she explained.

'Hang on a minute, wait,' I protested, grabbing ineffectually at the knife. 'What are you doing? You can't leave them here.'

'Well, I can hardly take them home with me, can I?' said Natasha, looking at me as if she was talking to a five-year-old. 'What would Cosmo say? They were a present from Edward.'

'What?' I said.

'Well, it was soooo sweet,' said Natasha, glancing at me self-consciously and filling the litter tray. It seemed to go down well with the kittens: they bounced into the middle of it, spraying litter all over the floor. I had to admit they were very cute.

'You see,' she went on, accepting a cup of coffee and obviously feeling that more of an explanation was needed, 'when I was still asleep he went out and got them. They belonged to the man in the shop opposite, or at least their mother does, and he's been trying to get rid of them for ages. Edward thought they'd be company for me now Cosmo's moved out.'

'I thought you said you couldn't let Cosmo see them,' I said suspiciously.

'Well, that's the thing,' said Natasha, lighting a cigarette. 'I seem to have given Edward the impression that Cosmo's moved out permanently but actually it was only for the night. We had a row, you see.'

'So you said,' I snapped, shooing the kittens. Having spread litter all over the floor, they had bounced onto one of the sitting-room chairs and were testing the strength of their claws on the cushions. 'What was it about this time?'

'Well, I just suggested that he have his trust fund paid into a joint account as he pays all my credit card bills anyway, but he refused!' said Natasha indignantly. 'Would you believe it! Said I was costing him enough as it is and then I called him a miserly jerk and he called me a greedy grasping good-time girl and it just escalated from there.'

'A greedy grasping good-time girl?'

'Yes, a greedy grasping good-time girl.'

'Good alliteration,' I said. 'What happened then?'

'Well, I thought I'm not staying in on a Friday night and I called a few people but no-one was there so then I called Edward. You know the rest.'

'Didn't you feel the teensiest bit bad about going off with the man who rented a flat to someone you left alone and dying when you're still living with someone else?' I inquired.

'Oh, stop being so moralistic, Emily,' snapped Natasha. 'And what about you? I suppose it was great behaviour going off with one of Jack's friends.'

'How did you know about that?' I demanded. I was beginning to feel that I could not blow my nose in peace without the rest of the world passing comment.

'We were watching you from the window,' said Natasha. 'What happened, anyway?'

'Oh, well, it's a bit complicated,' I said. 'And he's not really a friend of Jack's, just a work acquaintance.' I told her the whole story, including bumping into Camilla and Buzz that morning.

'But that's fantastic!' burst out Natasha when I had finished. 'Revengeville Arizona! What are you going to do about it?'

'Well I don't know that I'm going to do anything, actually. I'm not quite the vengeful old cow you are.'

'Oh well, whatever you say,' said Natasha. 'But anyway, what am I going to do now? I think Edward might be falling in love with me.'

'Well it's completely your own fault,' I burst out. 'You know, one day, Natasha, Cosmo is going to find out about your extra-curricular activities and there's going to be all hell to pay. There'll be a fat chance of trust funds being paid into joint bank accounts then.'

'Oh, don't talk such rubbish,' snapped Natasha. 'I can't help it if I'm too attractive for my own good.

Anyway, I really must be going. Cosmo will be wondering where I am. I'll just say I stayed with you.' She stubbed out her cigarette and began twirling her cloak.

'Hang on a minute. What am I going to do about the kittens?'

'Keep them, of course, they'll be good company for you since you live alone,' said Natasha. 'By the way, Emily, you still haven't heard anything from Henry, have you?'

'No, I was going to say something to you about that,' I said anxiously. 'Jack still thinks it's very odd, you know. He suggested I give Catherine a call to see if she's heard anything. I'll do it in a minute.'

'Yes, I was thinking about it on my way over here,' mused Natasha. 'I think it's odd too. You know, Edward didn't even mention him last night and they're supposed to be good friends. Well, I'm sure it will sort itself out. And if you do call Catherine, for God's sake, keep my name out of it.' She disappeared, slamming the door behind her. I collapsed onto the sofa and began picking at the arm covers. It had once been a deep red with scarlet and orange storks flying across it, but it was turning slightly mud-coloured. Must get a new cover, I thought. I can afford it now. I looked in exhaustion at the phone. It rang instantly. 'Emily, it's me,' barked my mother. 'I'm just ringing about Christmas. Now what exactly are your plans?'

I glared at the receiver in disbelief. 'Mummy, surely you're not going to tell me you've got other arrangements at Christmas?' I demanded.

'Of course I'm not, darling!' cried my mother. 'Daddy and I can't wait to see you at Christmas. The only thing is there might be a problem about Boxing

Day. We've been invited to lunch at the Petersons and I feel a tiny bit awkward asking if you and Jamie can be fitted in too – you know, their dining-room is a bit small and both the sons are married anyway, so there's really no point. Would you and Jamie mind terribly if we went along without you?'

'No Mummy, you go,' I said wearily. 'I can't speak for Jamie, but I'm sure he won't mind.'

'Now darling, if you're sure,' said my mother, failing to keep the relief out of her voice. 'And how is everything, I suppose it's a bit on the quiet side now that you're no longer working?'

'Extremely quiet,' I said defiantly. If there was one person I was not filling in about the night before, it was my mother. 'I've just been assessing the opportunities open to me.'

'Well, I'm awfully glad there are some,' my mother replied abstractedly. I could almost see her glancing at her watch. 'Now I must dash, darling, I'm due at the hairdresser's. Good luck with the date tonight.' She hung up before I could raise any objections, not that I was really up to it.

I was about to replace the receiver, when I realized I still hadn't rung Catherine. Sighing, I dialled her number. The phone went on ringing for so long that I was on the verge of giving up, when suddenly someone snatched it up. There was a shriek over the line, the unmistakable sound of a man and a woman giggling, and I could just make out Catherine saying, 'Don't answer now, darling,' before the line went dead. The scene was painfully clear. How revolting, I thought loftily, behaving like that. Anyway, if Catherine had got some new man, as it seemed she had, I doubted very much that she would be interested in tracking down missing chums. Did no-one have a sense of responsibility except me?

The kittens, who had been chasing each other round the sitting-room, came to a halt at my feet and then jumped up onto my knees. They really were terribly sweet. I began tickling them under their chins and had just got two steady purrs going when the bell went again. Sighing, I dumped them on the floor and went over to the intercom. 'It's me, Jack,' said my ex irritably.

'You'll get used to living in Piccadilly Circus,' I explained to the cats and buzzed him in. 'All right, Emily, what happened last night?' demanded Jack, barging in a minute later and pecking me on the cheek.

'How nice to see you, how's your mother?' I asked.

'Oh she's fine, in plaster but she should be out of hospital in a couple of days,' said Jack, stalking into the sitting-room. 'Since when have you had cats?'

'Since about half an hour ago,' I said, sitting down exhausted. One of the cats was progressing up Jack's leg and the other had perched on his foot. Jack melted. 'How sweet,' he crooned, picking both up and perching one on each shoulder. 'Aren't you going to offer me a coffee, Emily?'

I stomped into the kitchen, poured him a cup and stomped back. Jack had established himself on the sofa and was making gootchy-goo noises at the kittens. 'Chh chh chh,' he said. 'Who's a sweet little kitten then? Shmuh shmuh shmuh. Man's talk,' he said briefly as I sat down. 'Now, what happened last night?'

'Oh, you know, the usual,' I said reluctantly. 'We went out to dinner and then, you know, I went back for a drink at his place.'

'And at what time exactly did you get home?'

'Uh, well, I think it was about an hour and a half ago.'

'Oh Emily!' cried Jack angrily. 'When are you going to learn to control yourself? You are going to get yourself into real trouble one day if you go on behaving like this! And I hope you realize Alexander's a friend of Gary's.'

'Yes, well, as a matter of fact, I have worked that one out,' I snapped. I was in no mood to be lectured at by exes. 'And thanks very much for telling me about Gary in advance. You seem to be making quite a habit of warning me about people the morning after the night before. I still haven't forgiven you about Buzz. Which reminds me.' I told him about the events of this morning.

'Well, it sounds as if they deserve one another,' said Jack when I had finished. He did not look even remotely mollified and in the mood for a gossip and indeed he was not. 'And another thing, Emily, if you have to keep going off with people, the least you could do is make it with people I don't know. How do you think I'm supposed to feel?'

'Well, how do you think I felt about the other night with that Australian bimbo?' I demanded.

'She's from New Zealand actually, and she's not a friend of yours. And anyway, I told you nothing happened.'

I sat back and took a slurp of coffee. This was quite unlike Jack. 'Do you know, I do believe you're jealous,' I said eventually.

'Of course I'm not jealous!' snapped Jack. There was a brief pause. Jack broke it by gently putting the kittens on the sofa and moodily prowling round the room. 'And whose is that cup,' he snarled, noticing Nigel's mug on the table beside Natasha's.

'Oh, just Nigel's, he was waiting for me when I got in,' I said lying back and shutting my eyes. 'He wants to help me sort out what's in my head right now.'

'And he's another one! Look what happened when you went off with him. Emily, will you not shut your eyes when I'm talking to you!' thundered Jack. I opened them to find him kneeling on the floor in front of me. I reached out and stroked his floppy blond hair back. Jack looked up and grinned at me. 'Well, maybe I am a bit jealous, actually,' he said. 'So you're going out with Gary tonight?'

'Yes.' Suddenly I was not absolutely sure I wanted to.

'And do you like him?'

'I guess so, I hardly know him. What are you doing?'

'Going to a party, it's at someone from work's. Shame you're going out with Gary, I could have taken you.'

'Well you should have asked before,' I said irritably. I would have quite liked to go.

Jack, obviously feeling he had been quite jealous enough for one afternoon, scrambled to his feet. 'I better go. But what are you going to do about these kittens?'

'Keep them, I guess. I can hardly turn them out onto the street.'

'Yes, but they can't get outside from your flat.'

'I know, but what else can I do?'

'Well, I was just thinking that I have a roof terrace,' said Jack. 'If you found them too much they could always come and live with me. In fact, you all could.'

166

'What, you mean *us* living together?' I said staring blankly at Jack. There had once been a question of us living together years ago but seconds after we had decided to, Jack had announced that he was not ready to make a commitment. 'You're asking me to live with you again? You know, after what happened last time, I think that's a bloody nerve.'

'Calm down, calm down, it's just a suggestion, that's all,' said Jack, hastily picking up his jacket which he had chucked onto the floor. 'Bye, Em, I've got to go and visit my mother. I'll call you tomorrow.' And with that, he was off.

13

I peered intensely into the little mirror in my bathroom and began feverishly to rub foundation into my face. I didn't usually wear foundation, but with the advent of my date, my skin seemed to be overreacting and I was developing a very large spot beside my nose. I had just stepped out of a heavily bubbled bath (the second of the day but I felt like pampering myself) and was still dressed only in a towel. The kittens, exhausted by the afternoon's events and their trip across London, were fast asleep on the sofa.

It was about 6.30 and completely dark outside as I wandered back into the sitting-room to pour myself a gin and tonic. I knew that it was the mark of moral decline to drink alone, but I felt I deserved a treat. The room was dusky as I had just put on two lamps, which glinted in two corners of the room. The street lamps were twinkling outside. The kittens twitched an ear each as the ice clinked in the glass and I splashed the necessaries in afterwards. Faintly in the background, I could hear Dire Straights' music coming from Nigel's flat. I listened in irritation for a moment and then marched over and put some Abba on the stereo. That would annoy him.

As the strains of 'Gimmee, gimmee, gimmee a man after midnight,' filtered into the air, I relaxed, drifted back into the bathroom and vigorously began to apply face powder. 'Dum dee dum dee dum dee dee,' I sang as I dabbed on blusher. 'Tiddly tiddly tiddly, tiddlyompom,' I went on gathering volume as I put on eyeshadow. I stopped singing as I concentrated on the eyeliner and mascara bit and then stood back and began vigorously brushing my hair. It was well over my shoulders, I must remember to have it cut soon. After all, I could afford it now.

I gathered my gin, lit a cigarette and began to ponder on recent events as I stood surveying my wardrobe. Item one: I had lost my job and must find another. Item two: Henry was still missing and no-one really knew why. Item three: Natasha had had a fling with a suspicious character and had landed me with some cats. Item four: I had just had a fling with Alexander, was about to go out with Gary and had been invited to move in with Jack. That was definitely one to think about later. Item five: Camilla was having an affair with Buzz. Item six: Nigel wanted to help me sort out what was in my head right now. Well, if he can work this lot out, he's a better man than I, I thought, pulling on my underwear. Even though I had no intention of spending another night with Gary until I knew him better, I still put on my best black lacy underwear.

I selected a short clingy black dress from the wardrobe, put it on and stood admiring myself for a minute until I decided it was too obvious and switched it for black miniskirt and loose red silk blouse. I put on my shiniest tights and went back into the sitting-room and sat down with the kittens, whom I had named Kir and Royale. 'Now Kir, behave yourself,' I crooned, tickling the black one under the chin. 'And you too, Royale, oh Royale, stop it!' In a display of affection, Royale had dug her claws into my leg and laddered the tights.

Muttering to myself, I decided that the miniskirt was too obvious as well and changed it for a pair of black jeans. Then I went into the kitchen and began fiddling with cat food. Although she had brought the feeding bowls (all part of the present from Edward), Natasha, needless to say, had forgotten the kittens would actually need feeding and I had spent the afternoon stocking up on kitten provisions and phoning Jamie to ask how to take care of them. He was with his girlfriend, Charlotte, in the middle of the Lake District, but luckily he had his mobile phone on him. I must remember to buy one, I thought, after all, I could afford it now. Apparently the poor little things were going to need a lot of inoculations and the operations I had planned for them (I was not risking two lovelorn cats hanging around my flat) were going to be very expensive.

The kittens fell ravenously on the food I had set out for them. They may have been tiny, but the amount of noise they were making would have done an air defence platoon proud. I briefly considered topping up my gin and tonic, but decided to be strong-minded. It was nearly time to be going, anyway.

About ten minutes later I was heading towards Kensington High Street. Although it was as cold as ever, it was a very clear night. Leaves were strewn all over the pavement. I made out a star or two and then hurled myself in front of an oncoming taxi, gave it instructions and set off.

About twenty minutes later, the cab drew up outside The Woodman. I paid the driver and made my way inside. The bar in The Woodman stretched down the middle of the room, with some pool tables in the back. As usual, the place was packed. It was full of people in Barbour jackets pretending that they usually got away for the weekend but the bloody Volvo's broken down so what could they do? I sourly pushed my way through until, in response to a 'yoo-hoo', I saw Gary sitting in the back.

At first, it all went well. 'Hello Emily, you look lovely,' he said with a faint trace of surprise in his voice, standing up to peck me. 'I've been really looking forward to seeing you. Now what can I get you?'

'Gin and tonic, please,' I said, plonking myself down. Gary was looking nice too. Although he wasn't quite as tall as Jack, he had quite broad shoulders and rather attractive brown curly hair. I felt myself warming to him. As he fought his way over to the bar, I pulled my jacket off and looked around. 'Well, it was really amazing,' said a stout person with very red cheeks sitting near me and slurping a pint of Guinness with a group of his chums. Like almost everyone else in the place – although not, mercifully, Gary, who was clad in chinos and a dark blue shirt – he was wearing green cords and a pink-striped shirt that totally failed to distract attention from a very receding hairline. 'Arabella said to me there's this fabulous girl you must meet who's heard all about how eligible you are – phnaw haw haw – but when I met her she turned out to be a real dog. Woof woof! Wouldn't even let me buy her a drink! Woman's obviously a lesbian. Anyway I said to Bella . . .'

Bored, I turned around and froze. The door had just opened and making their way in were Alexander and, please God no, Camilla. Was I fated to bump into the woman wherever I went? I may have finally sussed her out, but this was not the time to do anything about it. I attempted to scramble under the table, realized there was no room, bumped my head and came up again. 'Mr Guinness' shot me a look of astonishment, and then leant forward and muttered to his friends. I caught a sound of, 'Extraordinary. And she hasn't even had a drink.'

I leapt up and then sat down again, grabbed a paper that someone had left on the seat next to mine and peered out from behind it. I just had time to wonder what on earth Camilla was doing here – I thought that every Saturday night without exception was spent at a ball, place in the country or very chi–chi dinner party – when to my relief I saw her hail a group of people on the other side of the pub and go over and start talking to them.

Not so Alexander, however. To my appalled horror, Gary had also seen them come in and had bellowed across to Alexander. Alexander looked a bit uncertain, and then made his way over to Gary. There was some vigorous hand shaking and then Gary motioned in my direction.

I smiled across at the two of them extremely weakly from behind my paper and sank back against my chair. I trusted Alexander to be discreet, but I wasn't sure whether the story was that we had met briefly the night before or not at all. Must make sure to sort these things out in advance in the future, I thought, but how the hell was I supposed to know that ex-flings were going to start crawling out of the woodwork everywhere I turned? And what about Camilla? She was about as discreet as a *News of the World* reporter confronted with the evidence that a senior politician was having a serious relationship with a sheep – and a damn sight more effective at disseminating the information at that. I was just going to have to play it by ear.

'Emily! What a coincidence!' said Alexander, sensing my discomfort and seizing the initiative as he drew up a chair. 'I was just telling Gary we met last night! Small world!'

'Yes, very,' I said, seizing my drink and gulping. 'And how are you?'

'Oh fine, fine,' said Alexander.

Gary was looking at us curiously. 'So how exactly did you meet?' he asked.

'Through Jack,' I said hastily, 'you know, the same person who introduced us.'

'You seem to see quite a bit of him,' said Gary, slurping his pint and eyeing me suspiciously.

'Yes, well, we're very old friends,' I said. 'Anyway, I was celebrating. Oh, of course, I haven't told you, I lost my job yesterday.'

'Oh, well done, I remember you said you hated it,' said Gary. 'And how did you get involved in the celebrations?'

This was addressed to Alexander. Gary was beginning to seem distinctly unimpressed by the fact that I had made a new friend.

'I know Jack as our two banks have done a few deals together; we were having a drink and Jack invited Emily along,' said Alexander uncomfortably. There was a short silence. It was broken by all three of us beginning to talk at once. 'No, no, you go first,' said

Gary and Alexander simultaneously, and then lapsed into silence again. I was about to break it by pointing out that my glass was nearly empty (what with all the emotional drama I was drinking quite quickly, although the other two seemed hardly to have touched their pints) when Gary roused himself and tried again.

'You know, here's something funny,' he said. 'Alexander's flatmate – you know, Camilla? – works in the same place you do, or did, rather. I've been meaning to mention to you that we had someone else in common.'

'Yes, I know,' I said uneasily. 'We worked that one out last night.'

At this moment, needless to say, Camilla herself decided to stage an appearance. I had not noticed that there was an extra drink on the table – it looked horribly like orange juice, typical of the sanctimonious little cow – which Alexander had obviously been instructed to get. She loomed up behind the chaps just as I finished speaking. 'Emily, what a lovely surprise,' she said, happily taking the situation in at a glance. 'I hardly recognized you with your clothes on. Hi, Gerry, how are you?' She kissed him on both cheeks and sat down.

Gary looked rather startled. 'With her clothes on?' he said. 'But I thought you two used to work together. It must have been quite an office.'

'Oh, no, no, I was talking about something quite different,' said Camilla vaguely and then gazed intently at me. 'So Emily, how are you coping with life on the dole?' she purred.

'Oh, very well, thank you. Actually, I've had a few offers already,' I said loftily. This was completely untrue and I felt like punching the old cow, but I thought it might look a bit bad in front of Gary.

'Really? What?' asked Camilla.

'Oh, this and that,' I said. 'Anyway, what are you doing here? I thought you'd be at a party or something or spending a romantic evening somewhere. I can't remember if you told me if you have a boyfriend. Do you?'

Camilla shot me a filthy look and sipped her orange juice. 'Actually I am going to a party but since Alexander was at a bit of a loose end, I said I'd have a drink with him on my way there. But you're right, I don't go to pubs as much as you do, Emily.' She unbuttoned a very smart black coat with a fake fur trim at the edges to show off a discreet little black number underneath. As usual, she looked immaculate: smooth auburn hair, pearl earrings and carefully manicured nails. I looked down at mine and noticed they needed cleaning.

Gary, unfortunately, had stopped being suspicious and now seemed to be in the mood to play the Good Samaritan. 'You're at a loose end, Alexander?' he asked. 'We're off to a dinner party just round the corner. Why don't I give them a call and ask if I can bring you along?'

'Oh, no no, I couldn't possibly,' said Alexander quickly.

'Of course you can, they're very hospitable and they told me it was going to be a big bash, very informal, so I'm sure there'd be no problem in fitting you in. Emily, Alexander must come along, mustn't he?'

'Oh, uh, yes,' I said.

'I'll call them right away,' said Gary. He got up and started pushing his way through the crowds before anyone could say another word.

Oh no, I thought, what now? 'Well, Emily, how lovely for you to be able to spend an evening with two of your admirers,' commented Camilla, taking a sip of her orange juice.

'Don't be such a bitch, Camilla,' said Alexander shortly.

'Only pointing out the obvious,' responded Camilla, stroking back her smooth auburn hair and gazing intensely at me.

'Oh, do give it a rest, Camilla,' I said, draining my glass.

There was, however, no stopping Camilla once she was on the warpath. 'I'm just trying to help you, Emily,' she purred, leaning forward. 'Your behaviour can give rise to all sorts of misunderstandings, you know. After all, look what happened when you ended up with that ghastly man in the office the other day. I'm surprised he hasn't turned up as well.'

'What man at the office?' asked Alexander suspiciously.

'Oh, it would be better if Emily told you about that herself,' purred Camilla. She was about to say something more, but stopped as Gary loomed up behind us. 'It's all settled, they'd love you to come along,' he said to Alexander.

'Well, this will be an interesting evening,' said Camilla standing up and slipping on her coat. 'Have fun all of you. Try not to wake me up in the morning, you two! Bye.'

'Eh?' said Gary, looking after her. The remark had quite pointedly not been addressed to him. 'What's the woman talking about?'

'She's got a very original sense of humour,' replied Alexander in a slightly strained voice. I wondered if he was thinking about what Gary had got up to in the locker room. Maybe it had involved violence. 'I'll just go and get another round,' he added hastily, leaping up and pushing his way towards the bar.

Gary looked at me. 'You know, I get the feeling that there's something going on and I can't quite work out what it is. How well do you know Alex?'

'Oh, hardly at all,' I said uncomfortably. 'We just met last night.'

'And what's the situation with Jack?' persisted Gary.

'Oh, we're just friends,' I said irritably. Gary was showing a far greater insight into my life than I wanted, just for the moment. 'Why? Do you mind me having male friends?'

'Oh, no, not at all,' said Gary seriously. 'Actually, Emily, there's something I wanted to talk to you about. It's a bit of a shame that Alexander's here – though I don't think it would be a big surprise to him – but I'll try and say it quickly. Yesterday I made a big decision. I—'

'Here we are then,' said Alexander, dumping the drinks onto the table. 'Gin and tonic, pint of bitter and that's mine.' He pushed the relevant drinks around and then looked at us intensely to gauge the atmosphere.

'Thanks, mate,' said Gary, slurping. I waited for him to go on with his sentence, but he was obviously not going to do so in front of Alexander. 'So, it's packed in here,' he went on brightly.

'Yes, it's full of ghastly old Sloanes,' I said and then changed tack when I realized they were both looking at me disapprovingly. I had forgotten they shared an old school tie. 'I got two cats today,' I continued lamely.

'I didn't get the impression your lifestyle would accommodate pets,' said Alexander.

'No, nor I,' said Gary.

'Oh yes, I've decided to settle down and be responsible,' I said. 'Anyway, Jack said they could live with him if they were too much for me.'

'Just what is this with you and Jack?' asked Gary. 'I don't think you're telling us the full story, you know. And why get cats if you're not sure you want to keep them?'

'Well, I didn't exactly, I was more landed with them,' I said. Throwing caution to the winds, I told Gary the story of Natasha and Cosmo, Henry and Edward. After all, Alexander knew already and Gary was not a friend of Cosmo's – at least, I thought he was not. I had no idea so many of my old and new acquaintances were acquainted.

'No!' exclaimed Gary when I'd finished. 'And this was the woman I met the other night? Well, I can see why she's got so many admirers, I thought she was very attractive, but to go off and leave him like that? And you say he still hasn't turned up?'

'I think this Edward has something to do with it,' said Alexander seriously, harping back to last night's little idea. 'I think someone should check out his story.'

'How though?' I asked. 'He's spent the last year in Brazil, we can't exactly nip over and follow his tracks.' I had to admit, though, it was beginning to seem increasingly likely that Edward was involved.

'I say we should all go and confront him,' Alexander said excitedly.

'Oh, but we can't without Jack!' I cried. It would have been unforgivable if he had missed out on the fun.

'It would be a little unfair, since he's played such a pivotal role,' said Gary. 'Anyway, I hate to mention this, but we are all invited to a dinner party tonight and I think we'd better drink up. My friends will be wondering where we've all got to.'

14

'Come in, come in,' said Gary's friend, opening the door and ushering us into a little hall. The house was just round the corner from The Woodman and was typically Battersea. On the left there was a door into a double sitting/dining-room, through which I could see a crowd of people mingling amongst a lot of chintz. I was pleased to see that there were a lot more men than women present. Straight ahead, at the end of the hallway was a kitchen. I could make out a large Aga and a friendly looking figure, whom I supposed to be the lady of the house, stirring something. Casually dressed, in jeans and a stripy shirt, and with a long dark ponytail, she was obviously in the middle of an intricate manoeuvre and did not turn around, but stuck an arm out behind her back and waved at us.

Gary's friend, who turned out to be called Michael, led us through. 'Actually, it was supposed to be a sit-down dinner but we ended up inviting so many people we decided to make it a buffet,' he explained, picking up glasses from the sideboard and sploshing wine into them. 'So we were delighted you were able to come along as well,' he added hospitably to Alexander and looking at me slightly curiously. 'So you're the new woman Gary's been telling us about. He said he was sure you'd understand.'

'Uh, yes,' I said, wondering what on earth he was talking about. Alexander, as so often happened in Battersea circles, had seen someone he knew and had gone off to talk to them. 'Lovely house,' I added, hoping to change the subject. I had been glancing round the room as he spoke, and was gazing at a photograph in a silver frame on a shelf over one of the radiators: at first I thought it was an extremely beautiful woman, but when I looked more closely, I saw it was actually a man with very delicate feminine features. I supposed it was Michael's brother.

'Oh thanks,' said Michael, smiling as he followed my eye. 'We're just in the middle of doing it up. My partner works in Sotheby's, so we're developing quite an eye for some quite decent stuff but as I work in publishing, for us it's Sotheby's taste and Habitat money, unfortunately. Still, it's amazing what you can pick up if you go out to antique fairs at the weekend.'

'The room's looking good,' said Gary, looking around. 'Weren't those pictures hanging in the hall last time I was here?'

'Yes, we're going to put up some new stuff in the hall – photographs,' said Michael. 'There's a bloke I know who's just been travelling in Brazil who's got some amazing scenes. He's here tonight, actually.'

'Travelling in Brazil?' I asked.

'Yes, that's how I know him,' Michael replied. 'He's a professional photographer, done some really good work in the past, and my firm publishes his books. Would you like to meet him?'

'Would he by any chance be called Edward Dickinson?' I asked.

Michael gaped at me in astonishment. 'Good heavens, how extraordinary! He only got back to the country a few days ago. Edward, there's someone here who knows you!'

We had been standing in a huddle at the sideboard, on the right side of the door, which is why I hadn't seen Edward before. He was sitting near the window, with a chap sporting a very large moustache, and had his back to us. When Michael shouted out, he stood up and turned around. 'Emily, what a lovely surprise,' he said, walking towards us and kissing me on both cheeks. 'I seem to have bumped into you every night this week. And Alexander too!' he continued, as Alexander, noticing the fuss, disengaged himself from the people he was talking to and rejoined us. 'Are you here together?'

'Uh, not exactly,' I said uncomfortably. Edward seemed to have an extremely good memory for names. 'Actually, I'm here with Gary.' I made the necessary introductions, in doing so interrupting Alexander, who seemed to want to say something to me.

Gary, however, did not seem to be at all concerned with the niceties of the situation. 'Why on earth should you be here with Alex!' he said.

'I'm so sorry, I didn't mean to put my foot in it, I just assumed that after last night you were here together,' said Edward.

This did nothing to calm Gary down. 'Will someone please tell me what's going on!' he yelled.

The room fell silent, people looked round and then began to whisper. 'Well, we bumped into Edward last

182

night when we were all having a drink, you know, I told you,' I said.

'Yes, but I'd forgotten! Just how many people did you bump into last night?' shouted Gary.

The other guests, sensing fun, had gathered around us in a circle. 'You're not the woman Camilla told us about, are you?' said a complete stranger who I could only identify as the person Alexander had been speaking to a minute ago.

'Camilla?' I said, with dread in my voice.

'Yah, Camilla, Alexander's flatmate. She said he brought home a new woman last night.'

There was silence for a second and then everyone started shouting. 'How could you!' yelled Gary. 'When you were seeing me tonight!'

Alexander was shouting, 'Oh thanks a lot, Paul!' to the stranger, who was looking slightly pleased with himself.

Edward was shouting, 'Will you all please calm down!'

Michael was shouting, 'Would anyone like another drink!' I was pleased to see that in the middle of all this, he had not forgotten his duties as a host.

Gary was gaining in volume, though. 'I can't believe it!' he yelled. 'We seemed to be getting on so well together! And there was I, thinking you might be involved with Jack! Ha!'

He fell silent, and all the heads in the room turned to me, rather in the manner of a tennis match. It was my volley. 'Well, I'm sorry!' I shouted and then lowered my voice as I realized everyone else was still quiet. 'But it's not as if we were going out or anything. It was just one of those things. I didn't mean to upset you!' I looked around. Everyone was holding their breath to wait for Gary's response. 'Look,' I said hastily, 'can't we talk about this somewhere privately?' The room took this badly and started muttering.

Gary, however, saw the point, took me by the elbow and guided me into the hall. 'I'm not upset!' he hissed. 'I just think you've behaved very badly! No wonder Jack warned me off you!'

Jack had done what? I drew breath and opened my mouth to respond when I saw him turning in a third direction. It was clearly someone else's turn. 'Stop being so ridiculous, Gary!' shouted Michael, who had finished topping up people's glasses and had followed us into the hall. 'You obviously haven't told her!'

'Told me what!' I yelled. The way things were going, it would not have surprised me in the slightest if Gary was about to announce his engagement to Camilla. As it turned out, I was wrong.

'I'm gay!' shouted Gary.

'Whaaa?' I said. The door in the sitting-room swung slightly open. Behind it I could see the crowd holding their breath and getting as close as possible to hear what was going on. I suddenly realized that almost everyone there was a man. I could see only two other women present, who I assumed were friends of Michael's partner. She still had not made an appearance. 'But what about the other night?' I said. There was a shocked gasp from the crowd. I marched over and pulled the door to again, and looked pointedly at Michael who was still standing beside Gary.

'Oh, let him stay,' said Gary, looking fondly at Michael, 'he's been helping me to come to terms with it. I've known for a long time, well all my life really, but I've never been able to admit it openly before. It was meeting you, Emily, that made me decide to come out. You see, I thought you were a really lovely girl and very attractive but I just couldn't fancy you. You must have realized that the other night, when I couldn't, well, you know. And I thought, here's someone I really liked, and I could just see us settling down and getting married and having children and then me leaving you for a younger man. And it made me decide I couldn't go on living a lie any longer. I didn't want to ruin your life, Emily. I really hope we can still be friends.'

'What?' I said gaping at him. 'Ruin my life? But we'd only met twice. Maybe I wouldn't have wanted to marry you. Maybe I'd have been the one to leave with a younger man. And you couldn't, you know? Why didn't you tell me before? I've been trying to remember exactly what happened all week! And what do you mean, Jack warned you off me? Anyway, how could you have lived a lie all this time! What if you'd gone on doing so! What effect would it have had on our children! And if you're gay, why on earth were you so angry just now?'

'Yes, well sorry about that.' Gary had completely calmed down. 'It was just a bit of a shock, that's all. You see, I've been pretending to be heterosexual for so long, I guess I just had a heterosexual reaction without thinking about it. Actually, I'm very pleased about you and Alexander since it obviously can't work between Us.'

Oh, puleeze, I thought. First I find that I, Emily Whitelake, have been responsible for bringing a man out of the closet, then I am publicly informed that nothing had happened between us and then I find I am supposed to be upset about our non-existent relationship. Michael, though, seemed to be taking a different attitude. 'What Gary actually means,' he said sploshing some more wine into my glass, 'is that he was all set to make this big revelation and he finds he's been upstaged by events overtaking him. I trust you're not too heartbroken, Emily.'

'You poor darling,' said a voice from behind me. I turned around and gasped. Michael's partner had finally appeared, and looked even more beautiful than in the picture in the sitting-room. 'I'm Steven,' he said softly. 'Honestly, darling, men can be so awful. Imagine Gary letting you think he was straight. Bitch!' he snarled at Gary, who was looking hurt but understanding. 'Come into the sitting-room and have another drink, darling.'

'But—' I said, as he led me through the door back in to the main room. The assembled crowd leapt back as the door swung open and pretended to be chatting to one another. 'But I thought, I mean, I thought . . .'

'What did you think darling?' said Steven, pouring me a drink from a bottle on the table and putting his hand on my knee as we sat down together on the sofa. 'Did you think you'd met the man of your dreams and then he just turns out to be a bastard? Tell me, darling. I've been there too, you know.'

'No,' I said weakly, 'I mean you. I mean I thought about you. I mean, well, I thought you were, um, a, a . . .'

'A woman?' said Steven, stroking his hair coyly. 'Yes darling, a lot of people have thought that when they see me from behind. But tell me, darling, are you very very very upset? About Gary, I mean?'

'Not even remotely,' I said, shooting a venomous glance at Gary, who had reappeared and was deep in conversation with Alexander. 'No, it's just, now listen, how do you keep your hair looking like that?'

'Just lucky, I guess, darling,' said Steven. 'I just pile on tons of conditioner, you should try it.' He flicked my hair consideringly. 'Now I want you two to kiss and make up. Gary!' Gary broke off his conversation, came over and sat down. 'Be nice to one another, darlings,' said Steven and moved off.

'Honestly,' I said, 'you could have warned me. No-one likes to be informed in front of zillions of people that they're responsible for turning someone gay.'

'Oh, you didn't turn me, I told you, I've always known,' said Gary. 'You just made me decide to come out. I've never had a gay relationship, actually, just one experience years and years ago. It was at school, in the locker room.'

'So that was it!' I cried.

'What, you mean you knew about it?' asked Gary uncomprehendingly.

'I knew something had happened in the locker room, Camilla's been spreading the word all about town. Anyway, I hope you'll be very happy.' Gary grinned at me. 'But look,' I continued, 'what did you mean about Jack? How did he warn you off me?'

'It was yesterday, at work,' said Gary, drawing on a cigarette. 'I was in the computer room at the bank, when Jack wandered in, which was unusual in itself. He said, "So I hear you're seeing Emily tomorrow", and I said, "Yes". Then he told me that you led a very complicated life and that I'd find that out if I had a relationship with you.'

'What a bloody nerve!' I could hardly believe that my old friend Jack would do such a thing.

'Yes, but Emily, I don't think you should take it like

187

that,' said Gary earnestly. 'He wasn't being unkind about you at all, he sounded really fond of you. I think he was just concerned about you.'

'As well he may be,' I said, sitting back exhausted. My attention was then distracted by one of the two other women present, who plopped herself down on the sofa on my other side. 'Men,' she hissed at me in an American accent. 'You poor thing, being publicly dumped like that. I'm surprised you still have the nerve to speak to her!' she cried at Gary, who took the hint and moved off. 'But I wasn't dumped,' I began resentfully, before she cut me off – obviously a woman with a story to tell.

'Take me,' she said gulping a swig of wine. 'I've been duped – duped! But I still love the guy. I'm Laura, by the way.'

'I'm Emily. Go on, tell me about it.' I resignedly sat back and lit a cigarette. There was clearly going to be no chance of escape so I thought I might as well get it over with.

'Well, it's a sorry tale,' said Laura. 'I've been involved with someone for three years now. I even moved across from the States to be near him. All this time he's been promising he'll leave his wife. And has he? Has he hell!'

'Well, why don't you stop seeing him then?' I asked unsympathetically.

'I can't. I love him. Also, he earns a hell of a lot of dough and I don't want to give up on that kind of investment. And we work together at a bank and I'm worried he could make trouble for me.'

Although I was obviously talking to an American version of Natasha (albeit one who had not planned her financial strategy quite as carefully), my ears pricked up. Surely it wasn't possible, but – 'Oh really? Where do you work?'

'You wouldn't know it. It's an American place called Interbank.'

'What's the chap's name?' I asked, trying to sound nonchalant.

'Buzz. Bastard!' said Laura, bursting into tears. 'And he's got all that money!'

I briefly debated telling her what a bastard he really was, but decided against it. Instead I shoved a hanky at her, got her another drink and calmed her down, which she did right away. In fact, so much did she calm down, that practically as soon as I finished saying, 'There, there,' she spotted someone she knew across the room and pranced off, leaving me sitting alone on the sofa.

I looked around. I hated being left alone at parties, it made you look such a failure, even if it did seem that quite a few people present were not likely to be interested in me. Mercifully Edward, who I had almost forgotten amidst all the drama, seemed to have been lurking nearby, waiting for the chance to have a chat: he zoomed up and plonked himself down beside me. 'Well, what an evening. Actually, I'm glad we bumped into one another. I'd like to have a little word.'

'What, about Henry?' I asked, helping myself and him from a bottle on the coffee table.

'Oh, Henry, no I still haven't heard from him,' said Edward sipping gravely. 'No, I'd like to talk to you about your beautiful friend.'

'What, Natasha?' I asked irritably. The last thing I felt like doing was discussing Natasha all night.

'Yes,' said Edward seriously, offering me a cigarette

and then lighting one himself. 'I wouldn't normally be so indiscreet but she told me you're her closest friend and obviously you did see us together last night.'

'Closest mug, more like,' I said crossly. I wanted to talk about myself. 'What do you want to know?'

'I hope I'm not asking you to break any confidences, but I wondered what the situation is between her and this man she was living with. Last night I got the distinct impression they had split up for good, but this morning – I'm not being indiscreet, but she told me she tells you everything – after I had made her an impetuous little present, she screamed and said, "Oh my God, what's Cosmo going to say?" Are the two of them still together?'

I was not absolutely sure what to say. Edward seemed a very nice chap, and I didn't want to hurt his feelings, but for years now I had seen Natasha giving people the wrong impression – a bit like me, according to Camilla. Also, he did know about the Henry incident, after all. 'Well, the thing is,' I said hesitantly, 'Natasha and Cosmo have been together for a long time. But they do have a lot of rows, and, um, you know about Henry and everything . . .' I trailed off.

'So they are still together,' said Edward. A black look crossed his face.

'Uh, yes,' I said.

Edward was silent for a minute. 'Oh,' he said eventually, 'I hadn't quite realized that. What a shame. Do you think this relationship is going to last?'

'As long as Cosmo's trust fund continues to deliver the goods,' I said and could instantly have bitten my tongue. My lack of tact was making itself felt yet again.

Edward looked at me soberly and bit his lip. 'What about you?' he asked, making an obvious effort to pull himself together. 'You seem to have had an interesting evening tonight.'

'Yes, well it's all a bit embarrassing, actually,' I said. 'A friend of mine, oh of course, you've met him, you know, Jack, he said I was going to get myself into trouble if I carried on like this.'

'Well, you weren't to know that Gary was going to choose this evening to make such a significant announcement,' said Edward, chuckling. 'You poor girl. You're not upset, are you?'

'No, I'm bloody not,' I said irritably. If there was one thing worse than turning someone gay, it was having everyone think I'd be upset about it. 'No, I don't think that's quite what Jack meant, anyway. But he's behaving in a very strange way. I've just found out that he's warned Gary off me, and he was furious when he found out about Alexander and he mentioned something ridiculous about living together. He obviously didn't mean it, though.' I was on the verge of telling Edward that I thought Jack might have been overcome by the sight of the kittens, and stopped myself just in time.

'Well, you know, it sounds as if he's a good friend,' said Edward. 'Anyway, it looks as if food is served.'

He was right: various steaming casseroles had appeared on the dining-room table. Gary materialized at my side and the three of us went across. I was seriously impressed – there were various huge pots of *boeuf bourguignon*, several more casseroles of mashed potato and red cabbage, salad and two kinds of bread. It all looked so delicious I even managed to control my fury when I heard that Steven had baked the bread himself. The only thing was, I had already had so much to drink that I did not feel that hungry.

We all heaped our plates and trooped back into the sitting-room. I rather anxiously noticed that Alexander, Gary and Edward were all grouped together and starting to hiss at one another. Michael took my elbow and steered me to the sofa. 'So, quite a night,' he said.

'Yes, I'm really sorry about that little scene earlier, I do hope we didn't embarrass you too much,' I said, beginning to nibble on a bit of red cabbage.

'Not at all, I haven't enjoyed myself so much in years. In fact, I'm extremely relieved it all turned out the way it did, when Gary told me he'd met a nice girl, invited her out on a date and then decided to come out, I was concerned you might be a little upset. Tell me, if you don't mind my asking, exactly who are you involved with?'

'Well, I'm not absolutely sure myself. Obviously not Gary, and I'm not sure what's happening about Alexander. How is it that you managed to meet Steven and settle down and be normal?'

'Lack of imagination on my part,' said Michael. 'Actually, that's extremely unfair: I just got sick of waking up in strange beds on Sunday morning and luckily I met Steven. Sometimes I miss the single life, though.'

'It's not all it's cracked up to be,' I said, thinking of Nigel.

At this point, voices began to be raised on the other side of the room. 'That is a very offensive suggestion,' said Edward angrily. I swallowed the mouthful of mashed potato I had just forked into my mouth and Michael and I both leapt over to the trio standing by the door.

'What's going on?' asked Michael.

Edward breathed heavily and turned to us. 'Emily,' he said, struggling to contain himself, 'your friend Alexander has just accused me of being somehow involved in Henry's disappearance.'

'Oh, for heaven's sake!' I cried.

Alexander was looking irritable but unrepentant. 'I did not. I just said it was funny that he vanished at the time that Edward turned up.'

'Alexander, give it a rest,' I said. I did not think that this was either the time or the place to start on that one. Alexander and Edward both opened their mouths to retort something at each other when there were further raised voices from the other side of the room.

'I don't believe it!' shouted the American woman I had been chatting to earlier. 'He loves me!'

'I tell you,' said the stranger called Paul who had broken the news about my location this morning to the room earlier, 'he's having an affair with Camilla. Isn't that right, Alexander?' he called across the room. 'You told me the other day, Camilla's seeing some American guy called Buzz? It's obviously the same man.'

'For God's sake Paul, can't you keep your mouth shut about anything?' demanded Alexander furiously as he bounded across the room. 'Yes, though, I'm afraid it's true,' he added to Laura.

'I won't have anyone else getting their hands on that money!' shouted Laura. 'I've worked for a long time on that investment!'

Michael and Gary scampered off to join in the fun. There was absolute uproar now, everyone seemed to be getting involved. Edward and I stood watching, I felt very tired and I did not want to join in. 'I'm sorry about what Alexander said,' I said to Edward. 'He didn't really mean it, it's just high spirits and he's getting carried away by a jolly good mystery.'

'It was both of them, actually, Gary seems to think I know something about Henry as well.' There was a crashing sound from across the room as Paul, who did not seem to think he was getting enough attention, threw a glass into the fireplace to attract everyone's notice. 'You know, though, I don't know anything about it,' continued Edward, thoughtfully mopping up a few drips of wine – the glass had been full when it was hurled – from his jacket. There was another crash as Laura tried to punch Paul and was forcibly pulled back. 'It's just as big a mystery to me as to everyone else. Oh, no more, thank you.' This was to Steven, who, seemingly completely unperturbed by the fact that Paul had now mounted a chair and was roaring at the assembled multitude, was offering round more wine. I looked at my glass: surprisingly it was still full.

In the background, I could hear Gary counselling the woman. 'Confront your feelings about him,' he was urging. 'Confront Camilla. Take heart from me: if I can publicly come out of the closet then you can be strong enough to break it off.'

'Oh, ignore me then,' shouted Paul, jumping off his chair and landing on Alexander. They both fell over.

'Temper, temper,' chastised Michael helping them both up. 'More drinks, anyone?'

'About time too,' roared Paul, refilling his glass and hurling it into the fireplace. 'Will no-one pay any attention to me?'

'Do you know how much this dress cost!' shouted Laura, who had got drenched as the glass flew through the air. 'You're paying for the dry cleaning!'

Edward mopped some more drips from his jacket.

'You know, it's getting a bit noisy in here,' he said, stepping aside as Paul raced past, pursued by Laura. 'I feel like a quiet chat and I know a little place in Chelsea which stays open to all hours. Do you fancy a quick drink there?'

I glanced at my watch. It was getting late. I couldn't remember who I was supposed to be at the party with. I looked toward Gary and Alexander, who were huddled together whispering to each other, oblivious of anyone around them. Thousands of people seemed to be milling about. The whole thing was becoming a bit of a blur. 'Yes, I do,' I said.

'Come on then.' We made for the door.

15

Someone was snoring. At first I thought it was me, but then I realized that my mouth was shut and that I was awake. Keeping my eyes tightly screwed up, I cautiously stretched out a hand and felt the bed beside me. To my astonishment, it felt like my own bed, and there did not seem to be anyone else there. But where was that snoring coming from, then? I stretched out my hand a little further under the covers, moved it around the bed, withdrew it slightly and then something pounced on it.

I squeaked, sat bolt upright and opened my eyes. Two tiny sets of eyes peered back at me. The kittens were perched on the bed looking at me expectantly: the sound I had heard was not snoring but purring. I moved a foot under the covers. Both kittens chased it and leapt on it. I lay back against the pillow and entertained all three of us for a few minutes by moving my legs backwards and forwards, with the kittens frantically chasing them. Royale, the piebald, got so excited that when whirling after my leg, she caught sight of her tail and vigorously pursued that as well, turning herself into a little twirling ball of orange and black. Then we all got bored and calmed down: I rolled over onto my side and the kittens snuggled up against my leg, curled up and started purring again.

It felt funny to wake up in my own bed. What is wrong with me, I fretted. I must be losing my touch. I go to a party on Saturday night, and I wake up all by myself, although admittedly the crowd I was with last night was not exactly teeming with prospective partners. A second later I jumped out of my skin as there was a gentle tap on my bedroom door. Oh no, I thought, it's Nigel or even worse . . . 'Emily?' said a voice. 'Are you awake?'

'Uh, yes,' I said, sitting up and hurriedly adjusting my nightdress. The door opened and Edward appeared, fully dressed and bearing two steaming cups of coffee. 'I hope you don't mind, I raided your kitchen,' he said, coming in and handing me a cup.

'No, that was very sweet of you, do sit down,' I said, motioning to the opposite side of the bed. Then I squeaked again in dismay as I caught sight of the kittens: I had forgotten where they had come from.

'Don't worry, Emily, we discussed that last night,' said Edward, putting his mug down on the floor, sitting on the bed and stroking them. 'Don't you remember?'

'Oh yes, of course,' I said putting my hand to my head, which was throbbing slightly. I took a sip of coffee: it relieved a slightly aching throat. 'Did you sleep well?' I asked. It was beginning to come back to me that I had put Edward up on the sofa bed in the sitting-room.

'Very well, thank you, although I have a bit of a headache,' said Edward. 'I'm glad we had that little talk.'

'Oh, so am I,' I said. I could not remember a word

but I was sure that it would come to me eventually. We both lapsed into silence and slurped our coffees thoughtfully.

'I'm glad the kittens have got a good home,' said Edward after a while. 'I suppose it was jumping the gun a bit to give Natasha a present like that. I didn't know she was allergic to cats.'

'I am sorry about that.' I was beginning to remember that after a drink at a louche spot deep in the heart of Chelsea, I had brightly invited Edward back for a drink at my place, forgetting about the presence of the kittens. I only remembered when I opened the door and they flew out at us, occasioning a long and embarrassing explanation, some of which – Natasha's allergy, for example – was total invention on my part.

We both fell silent again. Then Edward looked at his watch and said, 'Well, I suppose I should be making a move. Thank you for putting me up. I've put the sofa bed away and left the sheets and blankets in the bathroom. Now, don't forget about my party next weekend, and I'll give you a call if I hear anything about Henry.'

I opened my mouth to start making goodbyes when we were both riveted by the sound of a key in the lock. 'Who on earth?' I said, and then froze.

'Don't worry, Emily, it's only me,' called out a horrible Birmingham twang. My bedroom door was right next to the front door in the tiny hall, so the second Nigel came into the flat he was in full view of us. And vice versa.

'I don't believe it!' he cried, standing at the door and surveying the scene. He looked even worse than usual. Nigel's weekend dirty protest always lasted the whole weekend, which meant that there was now two day's growth on his spotty chin. Unfortunately, his beard did not grow consistently, which meant there were large blotches of red skin on display. And to set it off, he was sporting a bright yellow T-shirt, with black shiny trousers. Nigel's appearance apart, however, I had to admit that to someone who had just walked in it looked a bit compromising: me in bed in my nightie and Edward sitting beside me.

This thought was overtaken by a flash of absolute fury. 'What the hell are you doing, barging in like this!' I shouted.

Nigel ignored the question. 'I can't believe it!' he cried again. 'After what happened between us the other night and all the problems that you've had since then and I tried to get you to confront your manizing yesterday and you've gone and done it again. I have to verbalize my anger, Emily.'

'Look, I told you I had a date last night,' I spat out furiously.

'Oh so this is him, is it?'

'No actually, it's someone else.' Then realizing that this was not quite the way to explain the situation, I added, 'Anyway, he's just a friend. Not that it's any of your business. Just what do you mean by barging in like this?'

'I was going to cook you a surprise breakfast,' said Nigel coldly. 'But now I think I won't.'

'You bet you bloody won't!' I shouted. 'I don't eat breakfast! And I want my keys back now!'

'No!' He shoved them in his pocket and jumped as the cats leapt off the bed and strolled over to say hello. 'Those are cats!' he shouted.

'Yes I know they are,' I snarled. 'Give me my bloody keys.'

The kittens, having sniffed Nigel, very sensibly decided that *odeur de Brummie* was not for them and leapt back onto the bed. Nigel fixed them with a gimlet eye. 'You know pets are not allowed under the terms of the lease.'

'What the hell has it got to do with you?' I demanded.

'Well, I don't want to live in a house with cats in it,' said Nigel. 'They could bring in rats and disease. In a very real way, pet-ownership is a form of abusing your neighbour.'

'I thought you were a vegetarian.'

'I care deeply about animal rights but, like, that's not the same as having to live with them,' said Nigel gravely. 'What is this, Emily? You care more about two smelly bits of fluff than you do about me? I'm going to have to ask you to get rid of them or I will have to complain to the managing agent.'

'You wouldn't.'

Nigel, realizing that he had got one-up on me, gave me a lofty look and turned to go, but he had reckoned without Edward. Edward had been sitting entirely quietly while this exchange went on, but at this he leapt up, grabbed Nigel by the scruff of his very scrawny neck and spun him round. 'I think I heard Emily say she wanted her keys,' he said quietly.

Nigel opened his mouth and then shut it again. 'This is between me and Emily,' he finally responded sullenly.

'Well, I am also a friend of Emily's and I notice that she does not like strange men barging in on her at all times of the day and night,' said Edward heavily, tightening his grip. 'And in your case, I can certainly see why. Now hand over those keys immediately.'

Nigel tried and failed to shake his hand off. Edward was obviously a jolly strong chap. It must have been all that lugging photographic equipment around the Amazon basin, I thought. Needless to say, Nigel was neither a match for him physically nor personality-wise. Eventually, and very slowly, he put his hand into the pocket of his tracksuit trousers and produced the keys. Edward grabbed them and handed them to me. 'Yours, I believe.'

'Thank you,' I said, looking at him in awe. Nigel stood for a moment rubbing his shoulder, which had been released. Then he straightened his puny frame and glared at me. 'I meant what I said about those cats, you know,' he said, and stalked off, slamming the flat door behind him.

'What an objectionable little creep,' said Edward. 'He's not one of your exes, I hope.'

'Good Lord no,' I exclaimed, scrambling out of bed. 'He just lives next door. Anyway, that was so nice of you. I've been worrying that he'll come in here at the dead of night, or alternatively when I'm out that he'll start going through all my possessions. Now look—' I was cut off mid-sentence by the doorbell. I went out into the hall and pushed the intercom button.

'It's me, Jack.'

Oh hell, I thought, and pushed the button. There was no back way for me to push Edward out, no wardrobe big enough to hide him in and I rather suspected Jack would recognize him if Edward bounded past on the stairs. Edward, probably think-ing the same, chuckled and walked into the sitting-room. A moment later Jack appeared. 'Wotcha,' he said, pecking me and striding past me into the sitting-room. 'Now look Emily, I've been thinking and – what the hell are you doing here?'

'Hello Jack, how are you?' said Edward standing up and stretching out his hand. 'Beautiful morning.'

'Not from where I'm standing,' said Jack, ignoring the hand. 'Emily, what is going on?'

'Edward just rescued me from that repulsive jerk who lives next door,' I said brightly.

'And what was he doing here in the first place?' demanded Jack.

'Look,' said Edward, picking up his coat from a nearby chair and sliding into it, 'I think I better leave you two to sort this out. But Jack, I assure you, this is completely innocent. I slept on the sofa bed. Good-bye, Emily, thanks again for putting me up. I hope to see you both again.' With that, he disappeared.

'Well?' said Jack.

'He told you. He slept on the sofa bed.'

'Well, it doesn't look slept-in to me.'

'He folded it up and put the sheets and blankets in the bathroom.'

Jack looked at me, went through the hall into the bathroom and returned a minute later. 'Oh,' he said.

'How's your mother?'

'Fine, I popped in to see her on the way here and she's coming out of hospital today. My father's collecting her later. But don't try to change the subject, I haven't finished talking about you.'

'Look, Jack, what is all this?' The kittens, who had been eating in the kitchen – Edward had obviously made them breakfast – came back into the room and leapt up beside me.

'How was your date?' asked Jack, ignoring the question.

'Well actually, Gary is gay,' I said.

'He's what?'

'Gay. He outed himself last night, in front of a roomful of people. It was quite an event, actually.' I told Jack the full story of what had happened, including bumping into Alexander, Camilla, another girlfriend of Buzz's and going for a drink with Edward as well as Edward's treatment of Nigel. Jack, to my relief, returned entirely to his usual self and burst out laughing. His very blue eyes, which had been almost black with fury, were their usual sparkling form. 'What an interesting evening, I wish I could have seen it. My party was extremely dull in comparison.'

'Yes, well— but look, Jack, what was this Gary told me about you warning him off me?'

'Sneaky little sod, he wasn't supposed to say anything about that. Well, I didn't exactly warn him off you. I just said that you lead a complicated life and he might find you a bit hot to handle.'

'Thanks a lot. But why did you say that?'

'If you really must know, I suppose I was jealous,' said Jack. 'I didn't want you to go out with him.'

'Why not?' I asked slightly shakily.

Jack ran his hand through his floppy blond hair and started striding around the room. The kittens and I watched from the sofa. 'Well, I suppose I don't want you to go out with anyone else,' he said eventually. 'You know, when we were going out together, I was a lot younger—'

'Oh no you weren't, it was only two years ago,' I cut in.

'Yes but there's a big difference between thirty-two and thirty-four,' said Jack illogically. 'Especially when

203

you're a man. You've got a lot of wild oats to sow, you know.'

'Women have oats too,' I said defensively.

'Yes, and you've sown quite enough of them over the last week,' snapped Jack. 'That's what made me start thinking. I was really pissed off about you and Gary and then when you started adding God knows who else to the list, it was really beginning to upset me. Be quiet, darling, this is important.' I had tried to butt in at this point to make it clear that nothing had happened between me and Gary. 'I made a mistake, Emily. I didn't want to settle down then, so I mucked things up between us and I really regret it. I know we've been just friends for ages, but I don't want us to be just friends anymore. I want us to get back together. In fact, there's nothing I'd like more than for you to move in with me. It's not as if we don't know one another well enough to have to wait ages to decide, I am already fully aware of your irritating habit of never cleaning the bath.'

'Yes, well you never replace the milk.'

'I promise to have a word with my local milkman, if he exists, first thing tomorrow. Now, what do you think?'

I looked at him. Jack was looking achingly hand-some but the emotion welling up in me at the sight of him was not at all what I expected. I was absolutely furious. 'How dare you?' I cried. 'After everything that happened between us before! Honestly Jack, the last time I agreed to live with you, you celebrated by taking a three-week holiday in Australia and telling me it was all over the second your plane touched down! I may be stupid, but I'm not that stupid! I have absolutely no intention of agreeing to live with you ever again!'

'I've already told you a thousand times, it wasn't a holiday, it was work!' said Jack heatedly. 'I just got that tan because I did a bit of water-skiing at the weekends. You can't hold it against me for ever.'

'God may forgive you, but I never will,' I said firmly. 'No, Jack. You can't just come up with this out of the blue and expect me to move in just like that. I quite like being single. Actually, I've had a most entertaining week.'

Jack sighed and wandered over to the window. 'Well, I suppose I can't really blame you for thinking like that,' he said eventually, looking outside. 'Your windows need cleaning. Anyway, I wish you'd give it some thought.'

'I have and the answer's no,' I said haughtily. 'Kindly do not comment on my domestic prowess.' We glared at each other, and then both jumped when the phone rang. We ignored it for a minute, but I had turned my answering machine off and it was difficult to continue in a more in anger than in sorrow stance with a shrill bell going off in your ear. I picked up the receiver.

'Emily, thank God you're there!' shrieked Natasha. 'Don't go anywhere! I'm coming right over!'

'Natasha, hang on, it's not convenient,' I said – too late, as she'd already hung up.

'Oh, for heaven's sake,' said Jack when I put the phone down. Natasha's voice had been easily audible to anyone in a five-mile radius. 'What on earth does the woman want now? Anyway, you'd better get dressed, my darling. We wouldn't want Nat to think there was anything going on between us.'

I looked at him: he was grinning at me. 'Please to remember there isn't,' I said loftily. 'You may make me some coffee while I'm in the bath.' I stalked out of the room to begin my ablutions.

16

'It was just, well, frightening,' breathed Natasha huskily, leaning forward and looking at us intently. 'I've never seen him behave like that.'

The three of us were in my sitting-room, drinking black coffee, which, along with wine, seemed to be forming the staple part of my diet. It was quite like the old days, when Natasha and I had been at university together, except I had not known Jack then. He was sitting on the sofa, listening patiently as Natasha told us the story of the night before. I, now dressed in usual weekend attire of black miniskirt, thick black tights and large red sweater, was sitting beside him with the kittens on my knees.

Natasha, in cream jodhpurs, cream sweater and brown boots, was sitting opposite us. The usual red slash of lipstick had been toned down into something that made her mouth look tawny and voluptuous. She was quivering with emotion – well, Natasha's version of emotion, anyway, which meant she feared a future in which Cosmo's trust fund played no part – and was looking pleadingly at Jack. I felt a stab of jealousy, which disappeared as Jack reached out and started stroking the back of my neck.

'And then he said, "You're going to make me do something stupid one of these days," and just marched out. It wasn't as if he was upset in a normal way, he wasn't shouting or anything. He was just completely cold and he ignored me when I said neither of them were serious. He was quite icy, and usually he shouts when I've really upset him. He was shouting earlier.'

'Well, what on earth made you tell him in the first place?' I asked. Natasha had been round for about half an hour. She was telling us about the quiet and romantic supper she had had with Cosmo the previous night, which had all gone horribly wrong when Natasha decided to make a clean breast of her recent misdemeanours.

'I was just angry,' said Natasha, drawing deeply on a cigarette. 'It was that trust fund business. I mean, why doesn't he want us to have a joint account? If he really loved me, he would. That's what I told him, and when he told me that he really did love me but he wasn't ready for bankruptcy proceedings, which would be sure to follow if I got my hands on his inheritance, I just snapped. I told him that I had plenty of other opportunities, and if he didn't pull his act together, I would have to reconsider my position.'

'Well, you didn't need to make it sound as if you were resigning from your job,' I said.

'Sometimes I think it's a full-time job keeping Cosmo happy,' said Natasha seriously, ignoring Jack, who had been unable to suppress a snort in the background. 'Anyway, he asked "What other opportunities", and I was so angry by this time I told him everything, including that Edward is easily as rich as he is – I found that out the other night, Emily. Did you know that Edward's father is in shipping? Anyway, that made him even madder and he shouted that he was glad Henry had disappeared, that he hoped he was at the bottom of the Thames and that he wished he'd had a hand in it himself. Suspicious or what?

'So of course, I accused him of actually being involved in Henry's disappearance, which is when he started being really cold. First he wouldn't speak to me and then when I said at least it was all out in the open, he just laughed bitterly, got up and walked out of the restaurant. And you know what he'd done? He'd left me with the bill. I mean, can you believe that? He actually left me with the bill. I had to pay for dinner myself!'

'To be absolutely honest,' Jack burst out, obviously able to stand it no more, 'I think you're bloody lucky he didn't punch you in the nose. And I am not advocating violence towards women,' he snapped as I opened my mouth. 'I just can't understand why you treat him like that, Natasha. Cosmo loves you. He wants to marry you. Why are you so surprised that he's upset when you cheat on him?'

'Well, if he wants to marry me so much, why won't he open a joint account?' persisted Natasha. 'Anyway, you're one to talk. Look at the way you treated poor Emily.'

'Oh, don't you start too,' said Jack wearily. 'Believe me, I have already been made more than aware of my failings in that department. Anyway, I was never unfaithful to her.'

'Yes, Natasha, don't bring that into it,' I said irritably. I was getting fed up with people talking about me as if I weren't there, and after the little scene I had just had with Jack, I did not feel it was an appropriate time to mull over our past relationship.

Natasha looked at us suspiciously. She realized something was afoot, but as ever, her own problems rose to the fore. 'Anyway,' she continued, 'not only did he leave me with the bill, but now he's disappeared too. I went home, and I thought he'd probably follow to make sure that I was all right, but he didn't. He didn't come back and he didn't ring or anything. So this morning, I rang Joe – you know that friend of his? – because I thought he might have gone round there. But Joe didn't know anything about it. So then I rang everyone I could think of, including you, Jack, there's a message on your machine when you get home, but no-one knew anything. I tried his parents, but his mother just said he's bound to turn up. The old cow didn't sound remotely sympathetic. She's never liked me, you know. So then I panicked and I came round here.'

'Yes, well, the door's always open to you,' I said wearily. 'Maybe he bumped into Henry and they've decided to go off and do some bonding since they've obviously got so much in common.'

'Don't be irritating, Emily.'

'Well, look,' I said, 'if you're really worried you should call the police.'

'I don't want to do that, it might look funny,' said Natasha. 'How am I expected to explain that I'm responsible for the disappearance of two people in one week?'

'Henry was not necessarily your fault, although of course the police might think otherwise,' said Jack, standing up and stretching. 'I'm starving. Have you got any food, Emily?'

'How can you think of food at a time like this?' protested Natasha. 'Anyway, he said something most peculiar as he walked out: he said, "You're not the only one considering your position. I have lots of other opportunities too." What do you think he meant by that?'

Jack and I exchanged a glance, but he clearly felt it was better to be diplomatic. 'I should think it was an off-the-cuff comment designed to annoy you, which it obviously did and I'm thinking of food because I was going to suggest eating something, and then the three of us can go and scout round your area. I haven't had breakfast and it's well after lunchtime,' he said, walking into the kitchen and opening my fridge. 'Ugh, what is this, Emily?' He was looking at something dark green and squooshy, which seemed to be breathing gently in the middle of the top shelf.

'I think it used to be a lettuce,' I said. Jack picked it up gingerly and dropped it into the rubbish.

'There's hardly anything here,' he said. 'And Edward's used up all the milk. I'm going to the shops to get something and we'll go out afterwards to look for him, OK?' He picked up his jacket and vanished.

I stopped stroking the kittens for a minute so that I could light a cigarette, then lay back against the sofa and realized that Natasha had fixed me with a gimlet eye. 'Edward used up all the milk?' she repeated.

I sat bolt upright. Since her arrival, we had solely been discussing Natasha's troubles and I had not had a chance to tell her about the night before. 'Is that Edward, who used up all the milk?' she asked again.

'Yes, I was going to tell you. He stayed here last night, but it was completely above board. He slept on the sofa bed, he was talking about you all evening and absolutely nothing happened.' I knew from experience that Natasha was extremely possessive about

211

men who simply admired her, let alone those she had actually had flings with.

'And just how did he happen to be here in the first place?' said Natasha, raising her eyebrows. 'I was under the impression you had a date with that chap Gary, who if you ask me is gay. He showed no interest in me at all.'

'Well, you're right there, actually,' I said. I told her about the events of the previous night.

Natasha was obviously totally fascinated, especially when I told her the bit about the public outing, but was unwilling to give up the moral high ground so quickly. '*Et tu*, Emily?' she inquired loftily when I had finished. 'Is there no-one I can trust anymore?'

'Natasha, please,' I said unhappily. She was a pain in the arse sometimes, but still my closest friend. 'I told you, absolutely nothing happened. He just stayed here because it was so late. Honestly, it's you he's interested in, he went on about you all night. It was quite boring, actually. And I'm not remotely interested in him.'

'Oh really? And just who are you interested in now that your new boyfriend has outed himself?'

'He wasn't my boyfriend,' I snapped. 'And if you really want to know, I'm not interested in anyone.'

'Oh yes you are,' said Natasha in an extremely superior tone, lighting another cigarette. 'You're interested in Jack.'

'No I'm not,' I said firmly.

'Yes you are.'

'No I'm not.'

'Yes you are.'

'Nat, do you absolutely have to make this sound like a pantomime?' I complained. 'Anyway, I'm not.

If I was, I would have said yes when Jack asked me to live with him just now.'

'He did what!' demanded Natasha. She was interrupted as the door burst open and Jack appeared, laden with groceries. 'I thought I'd make piperade,' he said. He slung his jacket off, went into the kitchen and started fiddling with eggs, tomatoes, green peppers and onions. One of Jack's many good qualities was that he was an excellent cook. A couple of moments later a very satisfactory smell of olive oil heating up in a frying pan wafted in.

Natasha, who seemed to have got over her attack of bad temper, came over to me and started whispering, 'Just what's going on between you two?'

'I told you, he asked me to live with him,' I hissed back.

'Why aren't you going to?'

'Because I'm not going through all that again. You know how pissed off I was the last time around.'

'Well, you should think about it, you're not getting any younger,' said Natasha in a normal tone of voice. 'Anyway, it's as plain as day that you've never even remotely got over him. And he's not at all bad-looking, you know.'

'Yes, and I might even be prepared to open a joint bank account,' shouted Jack, who had obviously heard every word from the kitchen. 'Will someone lay the table, please?'

About an hour later we finished eating. Jack had also bought bread, which we heated up in the oven, cheese and salad, and we opened a bottle of Meursault, which had been the only other occupant of the fridge along with the lettuce and a couple of tins of cat food. 'Just think, Emily, if you came to live with me, you could feast like this every day,' said Jack, lighting a post-prandial cigarette.

'I thought you had a job, which means you couldn't cook every day,' I said. 'I hope you're not thinking of giving it up, I would have even less intention of living with a pauper.'

'No, absolutely, you mustn't do that,' said Natasha, also lighting a cigarette.

'OK, OK, I promise to stay in work,' said Jack, 'although I've always fancied being a kept man, you know. Couldn't you get a well-paid job, Emily, if I'm prepared to be a house-husband?'

We both burst out laughing at the look on Natasha's face. 'I think he's joking,' I said. 'Anyway, Natasha, wouldn't you keep Cosmo if he lost his job?'

'I'd like to see him try,' said Natasha darkly. 'He was threatened with redundo about a year ago and he didn't dare come home for three days. I told you about that, didn't I, Emily? Anyway, the BBC's a lousy payer, I don't know what we'd do without that trust fund.' She stretched back in her chair and shut her eyes.

I shifted impatiently and kicked the table leg. 'Shall we go now?' I asked.

I looked at the two of them. No-one moved. 'I mean, we are all worried about Cosmo.'

'Yes,' said Natasha reluctantly, 'but it's getting dark outside.'

I got up and started carrying plates into the kitchen. 'And Henry?' I continued, 'I mean, we are still worried about him?'

'But I'm a bit sleepy,' said Natasha. 'I think I'll go and have a quick nap.'

'But Natasha . . .' I began. Natasha ignored me, stubbed out her cigarette, got up and walked into the bedroom. The door closed behind her. Jack and I looked at one another in despair and then we both went and curled up on the sofa. I was feeling a bit sleepy too. The kittens leapt up beside us and arranged themselves on our legs, which had got rather entangled. 'Just forty winks then,' said Jack, curling around me. I vaguely thought about pushing him away, but for some reason I didn't really want to. We both dozed off.

Some considerable time later – I had no idea how long – a siren went off in my ear. 'Aargh,' I said, reaching out for the phone. Jack, who had also been fast asleep, jerked upright and began rubbing his eyes. 'What is it?' I said sleepily, picking up the receiver.

'Well that's a nice way to talk to your brother,' said Jamie. 'Were you asleep? It's a bit early for you to be going to bed, isn't it?'

'What time is it?' I demanded.

'Just after seven. What was that?' Jack had muttered something in the background and headed off into the bathroom.

'Just Jack,' I said.

'Oh right,' said Jamie, sounding curious. 'I haven't interrupted anything, have I?'

'Of course you haven't,' I said crossly, 'although I quite want to talk to you about it. Anyway, I thought you were in the Lake District. What's up?'

'I was, we just got back an hour ago,' said Jamie. 'I'm calling because I'm coming up to London tomorrow. David was supposed to be speaking at a conference but he's just rung to say he's ill and can't make it and can I go instead.' David was Jamie's partner at the surgery. 'I thought that now that you're no longer in gainful employment you might be free for lunch.'

215

'Yes, well I probably would have been able to make it anyway. That's the whole point about PR: it's a job where you are supposed to interpose your liver between the client and the whole of Fleet Street. I could just have said you were someone very important.'

'In Bristol, I am,' said Jamie haughtily. 'Old ladies with sick poodles hang on to my every word. Where shall we meet then?'

'What about Alison Small, it's ages since you've taken me anywhere expensive.'

'Glad to understand your criteria in choosing a restaurant, you sound just like that very attractive friend of yours. No chance of her coming along too, I suppose?'

'No, there bloody isn't,' I said crossly. It was a bit much when even my own brother started lusting after Natasha. 'Listen, I'll call them tomorrow to make sure they've got a table. What time can you make it?'

'Say 1.30 to be on the safe side. If they're full, you choose somewhere else. You can get me on my mobile.'

'Fab, see you tomorrow,' I said and put the phone down. Thank heavens Jamie was coming to town: I thought it was about time I had a sensible chat with someone, not least about what to do about Jack.

The man himself reappeared at this point, followed by Natasha, who had also been woken by the phone. Although we must all have been asleep for several hours, she looked fresh as a daisy. 'Well, I'm glad Jamie thinks I'm very attractive, and actually I am free for lunch tomorrow,' she said, smirking at me.

'You were listening on the extension!' I burst out.

'I thought it might have been Cosmo, trying to

track me down,' said Natasha. 'Speaking of which, I do think we should go and try to find him now, I'm worried about him walking around in the dark by himself. I'm still worried he's going to end up in the arms of some low-class tart.'

'Well that would make a change,' I said nastily. 'Joke, joke,' I added hastily. 'Don't be so sensitive.'

'You're one to talk,' said Natasha, lighting a cigarette. 'Anyway, I don't want anyone else getting their hands on that trust fund. Come on, let's go.'

'Isn't it getting a bit late?' said Jack, returning from the kitchen where he had been making yet more coffee. 'I was going to suggest that Emily came back to my place for dinner. I seem to remember that she promised to cook for me a few days ago.'

'You wouldn't leave me alone?' said Natasha, her eyes filling with tears. 'With Cosmo gone, me all alone in that great big house?'

Jack looked pained, but he was a very kind chap. 'Oh all right then, but we're not going to stay out for very long and we'll only go on the condition that we can talk about me for a change,' he said. 'Emily, does that suit you?'

'What about the cats?' I asked.

'I'm sure they can look after one another,' said Jack.

I hesitated and then went and set out bowls of food and water, ignored the huge pile of washing-up from lunch, and joined the others in the sitting-room. They had already put on their coats. Jack held out mine. 'Come on then,' he said. We all made for the door.

Our first port of call was Cosmo and Natasha's house. Whenever I went round, I could always see why she was so keen to hang onto him. It was not really my style – the furniture and paintings were extremely modern and I did not like steel kitchens – but the effect was incredibly impressive. The front of the house was normal Pimlico-style dowdy, but inside it had been gutted. You stepped into a huge entrance hall that rose two storeys with enormous paintings hung around the walls. Beyond was a large corridor with stairs taking you up to the other floors on one side and a sitting-room on the other. Large futuristic pieces of furniture were dotted around.

We walked into the sitting-room, which had rush matting on the floor, and some huge white sofas with cast iron arms and legs. I plonked myself down in one while Jack went to sit in a large chair that looked like a tomato. 'Help yourself to drinks, I'm just going to listen to the answering machine,' said Natasha, flitting off into the kitchen.

The drinks cabinet was a large mirrored affair with a tiny freezer for making ice. I knew it well. Luckily Jack had left his car at home, and we had taken a taxi on the way over, so he didn't need to worry about driving. I went over and started making gin and tonics while we eavesdropped on the answering machine, quite clearly audible from the kitchen next door.

'Hi Natasha, it's Chris,' came a voice. 'Just checking you're all right. Is it true you've split up with Cosmo? Give me a call.' The tone beeped. Jack raised his eyes to the ceiling and grinned at me. His smile vanished when the next call began. 'Hi Natasha, it's Catherine,' said my friend. 'Have you heard about Emily? Apparently her new boyfriend outed himself at a party last night but someone told me Jack wants them to get back together. What's going on? Anyway, I've got some mega news for you too. Call me.' The tone beeped again.

'Bloody gossips,' said Jack, stalking over to the fireplace, which was in the middle of a large funnel-shaped structure in the centre of the room. There were a couple more messages from her mother and assorted admirers, but no word from Cosmo.

'I won't be a minute,' shouted Natasha. We could hear her leaving a message on Chris's answering machine ('I don't know what the situation with Cosmo is. I'm very upset and confused') and calling a few of Cosmo's favourite haunts to find out if he was there. I strolled over to stand by Jack before beginning to snoop around the room. 'Jack, look,' I said, struck by something on a side table. We peered at a little card. It had Edward's name, address and telephone number on it. Jack held it out to Natasha as she came back into the room. 'Wasn't it a bit unwise leaving that lying around?' he asked.

'Oh, Cosmo's used to me leaving bits of paper out,' said Natasha vaguely, pocketing it. She gestured around the room. 'You know that's an early Hockney over there,' she said. 'And that's a Schnabel. I am not giving up this place without a fight. Come on, you two, time to search in earnest.'

'Aren't you going to call Catherine?' I asked.

'Can't be bothered. I do not wish to spend the entire evening indulging in vulgar gossip,' said Natasha loftily. There had always been a bit of rivalry between her and Catherine. 'Are you two coming?'

I downed my gin and tonic. 'Let the hunt begin,' I said.

17

I spread out in bed. Where's Jack, I thought, blearily. Oh, there he is. I rolled over and put my arms round the figure slumbering beside me. Funny, it did not feel like Jack at all. In fact, it did not even feel like a man — 'Emily, what the hell are you doing?' asked a voice.

I sat bolt upright in bed. I could not work out where I was and for a second I did not recognize the figure sitting up beside me. Then I did. 'Nyahah!' I shouted, leaping out of my side of the bed. 'Nyahah!' shouted Natasha leaping out of her side. Then we both collapsed on the bed in a fit of giggles. 'Look, what on earth are you doing here?' I asked. 'I know times are tough but I'm not that desperate. And where are we, anyway?'

'We're in Jack's spare room,' said Natasha, 'you should recognize it. And I'll have you know a great many people would pay good money to be where you are now.'

'Yes, and you'd probably take it too,' I said. 'Oh yes, so we are.' I was beginning to recognize the shapes in the darkness and stretched out a hand to turn on the bedside light. There was only a bit of grey coming from behind the curtains, it was still very early. At that moment there was a knock on the door. Jack himself appeared, bearing a tray with a *cafetière*, mugs and a jug of milk. He put it on the bed and sat down beside me. 'Not intruding, am I?' he asked.

'Not at all,' said Natasha, eyeing him up. Jack was wearing only a pair of brightly striped boxer shorts, which showed off his tan. Although he was in his mid-thirties he still had an almost flat stomach and very slim legs. His blond hair flopped forward into one eye as he began to pour out the coffee. I shot Natasha rather a nasty look, but Jack, as ever, was impervious to her charms. 'What are you going to do about Cosmo?' he asked bluntly, handing her a steaming mug.

'I don't know,' Natasha replied fretfully, lying back against the pillows.

I blinked and rubbed my eyes. 'Don't you think you should try to find him?' I asked.

'What?' said Natasha, gaping at me. 'But we did find him, last night, don't you remember? Really, Emily, you are impossible.'

Jack laughed and moved over to put his arm round me. 'Now you mustn't criticize poor Emily, it's been a tough week and it's no wonder the poor thing's having a problem remembering things. You remind her, Natasha. Anyway, it's nearly seven and I must start getting dressed. At least one of us has a job to go to. I shall hog the bathroom briefly, but there will be plenty of hot water for both of you when I've finished. There's plenty of coffee in the kitchen.' He squeezed me and padded off towards the bathroom.

'Natasha, what happened?' I asked.

'Do you really not remember? You don't remember that floozie?'

'Oh yes!' I cried. It was all coming back to me now.

We had done a tour around some of Natasha's and Cosmo's favourite haunts in Pimlico and Chelsea, with complete lack of success. Then just as we had decided to call it a night, a nearby pub door opened and Cosmo lurched into view, very much the worse for wear and wrapped round the antipodean bimbo who had been chatting Jack up a couple of nights before. It emerged, appropriately enough, that they had met in a pub called 'The Australian' earlier in the evening. 'Ha!' he had cried on spotting Natasha, 'you're not the only one with opportunities! I've got someone else to share my trust fund now! I might even think of opening a joint account! Ha!'

Natasha's cool and calculated reaction had been to punch him on the nose, which had not succeeded in calming things down. The bimbo had counselled Natasha to allow Cosmo his own space, which would have resulted in a further punch had Jack not restrained her. I, meanwhile, extremely irritated by the bimbo's appearance on the scene, had found myself compelled to be extremely proprietorial towards Jack, as well as making lofty remarks about people who really understood poetry, which had resulted in harsh words from the bimbo and an exasperated look from Jack.

Cosmo then announced that he and the bimbo, who, it emerged, was called Elayne – 'with a "y"' emphasized Elayne – were going off to see someone who Natasha knew very well indeed. And no, he wouldn't tell us who it was and frankly he wished that Natasha would engage in carnal relations and then expire on the spot, except he did not put it quite as politely as that. And then he and Elayne had leapt – or rather staggered, in Cosmo's case – into a nearby taxi and disappeared. Natasha, who did not just get mad in these situations, but also even, was on the verge of rushing straight into the arms of Edward, but was persuaded not to do so by Jack and me. Jack then took charge and shepherded us both into a taxi and we ended up back at his place, where it was deemed improper that he and I should share a bed with someone else *in situ*.

I groaned and lay back. 'Well, it's all very well for you to groan, but what about me?' demanded Natasha. 'I'm the one that insufferable cow was gloating over.'

'I wouldn't worry, Cosmo didn't look capable of misbehaving and from what Jack's told me, won't have wanted to,' I said wearily. 'Anyway, what are you going to do?'

'Go home and change the locks,' snapped Natasha.

'You can't,' I protested, 'it's Cosmo's house.'

'Well, he should have thought of that before,' snarled Natasha. 'I can't possibly go to work today, I'm going to have to call in sick.'

'Why do they let you get away with it!' I burst out. 'You spent most of last week off sick as well. You can only have been in the office about three days this year so far.'

'In a design consultancy they understand if you're a sensitive person, not that you'd know anything about sensitivity, Emily. I can't believe that you have memory failure every time something terrible happens to me.'

'Well, you shouldn't have insisted on having a drink in every bar we stopped at on the way,' I snapped. 'And what's this about design consultancy? I thought you just helped people choose their curtains.'

'There's a lot more to it than that, you have to understand about primary colours,' said Natasha loftily. 'Anyway, are you free for lunch?'

'No, you know I'm meeting Jamie,' I said and then regretted it. Natasha's eyes lit up. 'I could come too,' she said.

'Natasha, look, I really want to see him by myself. I want to talk to him about Jack.'

'Why, what's there to talk about?' asked Jack. I had not noticed that he had reappeared in the doorway, now dressed in yellow striped shirt, dark blue and yellow tie and very dark blue trousers. He was holding some gold cufflinks that I had given him years ago and had not seen him wearing recently. 'Can you help me with these?' he asked me, handing over the cufflinks and extending an arm. 'So you want to discuss me with your estimable brother? I thought you had already made your feelings clear.'

'Will everyone insist on eavesdropping on my private conversations?' I burst out. With very bad grace I began to shove the cufflinks into the allotted slots. Natasha drifted off towards the bathroom.

Jack seized the opportunity and slid his free arm round me. 'What is it you want to discuss?' he said drawing me very tight and beginning to nibble gently on my ear.

I giggled and attempted to break free but Jack was stronger than me. Anyway, I did not particularly want to escape. 'I can't kiss you, I haven't brushed my teeth yet,' I complained.

'Greater love hath no man,' said Jack and began kissing anyway. We were interrupted by Natasha reappearing.

'Oh don't mind me,' she said as we jumped apart,

'my life is in crisis but you two young things just enjoy yourselves.'

Jack laughed and held out his other arm so I could do the other cufflink. I was feeling extremely taken aback. 'Why don't you call him,' he said soothingly. 'You know perfectly well you just need to crook your little finger and he'll come running.'

'Yes, but then I'd think he was weak,' said Natasha, petulantly sitting down on the bed.

'Well, at least we'd know he's all right,' said Jack, peering in the mirror and straightening his tie. He pushed his hair back out of his eyes. 'Now look, I'm really sorry, but I'm going to have to go. Emily, you know I think you should stay here but if you want to go back to your own flat, there's a spare set of keys for you to lock up with on the kitchen table.'

'Oh my God, I'm going to have to go!' I said, struck by a sudden thought. 'The kittens!'

'Plenty of room for you all. Bye, my darling, I'll call you later.' He kissed me goodbye, pecked Natasha and disappeared.

Natasha looked grudgingly impressed. 'Well he's certainly keen,' she said, looking after him. 'What on earth's holding you back, Emily?'

'I told you, I'm not going through all that again,' I said, making off to brush my teeth. Suddenly I was not totally certain that I had done the right thing, but I pushed the thought to the back of my mind. 'Fancy another quick coffee before we go?'

A couple of hours later I pushed open the door to my flat and was instantly hit by two enraged balls of fluff. Kir shot straight up my leg, came to rest on my shoulder and started mewing very loudly in my ear. Royale, who was a more adventurous type altogether, shot straight past me and down the stairs. I grabbed my keys and Kir and raced after her. Luckily I had shut the front door of the house. 'Royale, come back!' I shouted. 'Come and have breakfast!' Royale came to a demure halt beside the door, waited till I had nearly reached her, dodged my grasp and set off back up the stairs again. I skidded to a stop, cursed and began chasing her back up. My flat was on the first floor and there were another three in the building: I could see that I was going to get very fit if I remained a cat owner.

I paused beside my flat to deposit Kir inside and then set off up another two flights of stairs. Royale was waiting for me at the top. As I reached out for her, she dodged my grasp and began racing downstairs again. I followed. As we reached my landing, my next door neighbour's flat door opened. Nigel appeared. 'Can you keep the noise down, I'm reading a seminal work on the inter-reactional social strata of the urban development complexes in Newcastle,' he began self-importantly. 'Emily, what was that?' Royale had streaked between his legs into his flat.

'My cat,' I panted, pushing past him. To my horror I saw that Royale had leapt onto his sofa and was using a little paperback called *Council Estates in the North East* as a lavatory. She stopped as soon as she saw me, leapt off the sofa, came and butted her head against my legs and started purring.

I had every sympathy with her critique of the book, but Nigel thought otherwise. I saw him aiming a trainer. Just in time I bent down and scooped her up. 'Don't you dare kick her,' I hissed.

'That stupid animal, peeing on my book!' shouted Nigel.

'How much was it?' I demanded.

'What?'

'How much did the bloody book cost?' I repeated.

'Eight ninety nine,' said Nigel.

My handbag was still on my shoulder. I transferred Royale on to my other shoulder, rummaged for a tenner and thrust it at him. Nigel snatched it and glared at me. 'Who's going to clear up the mess?' he demanded. I marched over, gingerly picked up the book, and holding it well in front of me, made my way out.

Back in my own flat, I disposed of the book in the rubbish bin, put food out for the cats and then went to run a bath. In the background I could hear loud sounds of kittens eating. My flat felt awfully small after Jack's. Wandering between the bedroom and the bathroom, I pulled off my clothes, pulled my hair into a small knot and sank into the bubbly water and shut my eyes. What am I going to do? I wondered. I could not work out what I felt about Jack at all.

I was roused from my reverie by a small scratchy sound as the kittens raced into the bathroom, leapt up onto the loo seat, which was right beside the bath and peered curiously at me. 'It's called cellulite,' I informed them. 'You'll get it when you're older – oh no, I don't suppose you will, will you?' I sank back against the bath again. I'm going mad, I thought, telling cats to worry about cellulite. The kittens, unaware of my worries and joining in the general bath time atmosphere, began washing themselves.

We all continued our ablutions for a few minutes when I heard the phone ring. I had heard someone say somewhere that you had to be a real optimist to get out of the bath to answer the phone, but there you had it. I was. I leapt out of the tub, grabbed a towel and raced to the phone in the sitting-room, ignoring the kittens, who were mewing loudly as I had showered them with water. 'Hello,' I panted, picking up the receiver.

'May I speak to Miss Whitelake, please?' said a strange voice.

'This is she,' I said cautiously.

'Miss Whitelake, this is Grenstone Holdings,' said the voice. 'We have been informed that you have two animals residing in your flat. Is this correct?'

'Um, ah,' I hedged wildly. 'Sort of.' Grenstone Holdings were the managing agents.

'Miss Whitelake, are you aware that under the terms of your lease you are not allowed to have pets?'

'Um, sort of. Well they're not really pets. I mean they're not here for long. I'm just looking after them for a friend.'

'Miss Whitelake, are you aware that if you contravene the terms of the lease, you could be deprived of the leasehold of the property?'

'*What?*' I said. The flat belonged to my parents, and it did not even bear thinking about what they would do if it was taken away from them because of me. It would be even worse than that time Natasha crashed the brand new car they had given me for my birthday.

'Miss Whitelake,' continued the voice, obviously not to be messed around with, 'you have twenty-four hours to get the animals out of the flat. If we discover they are still in residence at the end of that period, we will have to review the tenancy.'

The line went dead. Oh no, I thought, what am I going to do? The kittens were going to have to move in with Jack, even if I did not. Luckily, he was a cat lover – 'So independent,' he had said to me once, 'you just feed them, go out for the night and when you come back the next morning they're really pleased to see you' – a comment which, coming as it did three months after we had split up, I did not appreciate at the time. I was beginning to see his point, though.

Not that it was the morning any longer. Glancing at the clock on my video, I squeaked in horror as I realized it was quarter to one, and rushed into my bedroom to get dressed.

Three-quarters of an hour later, exactly on time, the taxi drew up in front of Alison Small. Luckily I had remembered to call them and make a reservation. I pushed open the door, and raced up the long wooden floor to the back, where I had seen my brother, sipping a large gin and tonic. He stood up and threw his arms around me. 'You're looking well, Emily,' he said in a surprised voice as I collapsed onto my steel and leather chair. 'How does it feel to be free from corporate communications at last?'

'Wonderful,' I said, ordering a gin and tonic myself and relishing the envious looks from a couple of women at the next table, who obviously had not quite worked out our relationship. Jamie was a nice-looking chap: he was tall and broad and although his hair was the same mousy brown mine would have been if I had left it alone, it was made up for by an extremely pleasant-looking face. Jamie was the only person I knew who always seemed to be smiling, even when he was angry – which was quite frequently, actually, we had the same short temper. He was wearing a tweedy jacket, brown and blue tie and brown corduroy trousers. 'I thought you were supposed to be delivering a lecture,' I said critically.

'Oh, they expect vets to dress like this, it makes

them feel as if you've rushed straight from the surgery,' said Jamie. 'So what's going on?'

'I've got all sorts of other problems I want to talk to you about,' I went on. 'But anyway, how are you?'

'Oh, very well,' said Jamie pinching one of my cigarettes. 'I see you haven't given up yet, you old reprobate. I nearly have, I just smoke other people's now. Now, you must tell me everything, but shall we order first?'

We both started studying the menu – very modern European. I always enjoyed going out with Jamie. We were so close that it was equally easy to squabble, gossip and sit in companionable silence, as we were doing now. Jamie was a couple of years older than me, Jack's age, and had always protected me from wrathful parents, school bullies and anyone else he felt was treating his little sister harshly. He had once even rung Jack up and shouted at him when we split up a few years ago. They had long ago made up, at my instigation, but I appreciated the thought.

We both ordered, Jamie chose a bottle of wine and then we sat back. 'Now come on, Em, what's going on? Out with it.'

'Well . . .' I began.

We were interrupted at this point by one of the waiters. 'Emily?' he said peering at me. 'Remember me? Marco from Saturday night?' He looked approvingly at Jamie and winked. 'Glad to see you've got over Gary. Not bad.' He nudged me and disappeared.

'What on earth?' said Jamie, looking after him.

'Oh, he was just at a party I went to on Saturday night,' I said irritably. I vaguely recognized him as the moustachioed chap Edward had been talking to, but we had not actually spoken ourselves. 'The person who took me, Gary, used the occasion to out himself.'

I was on the verge of explaining more, when Marco reappeared, followed by a whole bevy of waiters bearing plates and wine. They had all obviously been apprised of the situation. 'Mmm, nice,' said one, setting down the soup. 'Fast work,' said another, proffering bread and pepper. 'You know, I'm not really a waiter,' said Marco, making eyes at Jamie, 'I'm really an actor. Shall I join you for a drink after lunch and you can tell me all about how the two of you met?'

'We met,' I said irritably, 'because we both happen to have been born to the same parents.'

'No!' said Marco excitedly. 'So this is a forbidden love thing?'

'It certainly bloody isn't,' said Jamie heatedly. 'I am up in London for the day and I am taking my little sister out to lunch.'

'Oh,' said Marco, deeply disappointed. 'Well if you want anything, call me.' He vanished.

'Honestly, Emily,' said Jamie wearily, beginning to slurp his soup. 'Glad to see your life is as calm as ever.' We both jumped at the sound of crashing noises. 'What on earth was that?'

Down at the other end of the restaurant, at a table by the window, there was the sound of a woman shouting, followed by the sound of a second glass breaking. The voice was horribly familiar. My ears pricked up. 'How dare you, you senile old man!' yelled Camilla.

Silence fell with a thud. All the other diners craned their heads to watch. 'But Camilla, be reasonable,' I could hear Richard saying. 'We can't have another scene like that, we'd end up as a laughing stock.'

'We're not going to have another scene! That woman will never come near the office again!' shouted Camilla.

Whatever was happening, this was too good to miss. 'That's Camilla and Richard, you know, my old boss,' I babbled to Jamie. 'I must find out what's going on.' The other diners had piped up again, drowning out the row. I leapt up and skidded down the room to my erstwhile colleagues. 'Richard, Camilla, what a lovely surprise,' I panted.

Both jumped when they saw me. Camilla was not behaving at all like her usual calm self: not only was her hair ruffled – the first time I had seen it so in our entire acquaintance – but she thrust an arm in my direction and cried, 'It's her! It's all Emily's fault! She was there on Saturday night, too, she probably put her up to it!'

Although neither had invited me to join them, I pulled up a chair and sat down. 'What on earth's going on?' I said. 'What's my fault?'

Richard sighed and dragged his hand through his hair. 'Emily, how lovely to bump into you,' he said wearily. 'Nothing's your fault. We're just having a quiet chat about work.'

'So I can see,' I said.

Camilla was breathing heavily. 'Richard,' she began.

'Don't you mean Gramps?' cut in Richard mildly. I held my breath and waited.

'That was just a joke,' said Camilla angrily. 'And I don't know how she found out about that. It was a minor pleasantry. Look, Richard, can you tell Emily to go away?'

'Emily, my dear, I'm sorry about Camilla's

rudeness, but it might be better if you did,' said Richard kindly. 'Give me a call this afternoon and we'll arrange lunch. I wanted to talk to you anyway as we seem to have lost details of your time sheets and we need to work out how much to bill Interbank. Camilla was supposed to have back-up copies of everything but they seem to have disappeared. Do you know, I'm beginning to think I might have acted a little hastily last week.'

I grinned at them, stood up and made my way back to Jamie. I was not going back to my old job for love nor money, and I had no intention of helping them with their billing arrangements, but it was nice to see that I was being appreciated retrospectively. By the time I got back to the table, the waiters had cleared away the first course and brought on the second. Jamie was looking hungry, but he had politely waited for my return before digging in, which he did the second I sat down. 'What on earth's going on?' he asked through a mouthful of fish.

'Not sure, but it doesn't look good for Camilla,' I said gleefully. 'Look, Jamie, do you have your mobile on you?'

Jamie nodded, rifled through his briefcase which was on the floor at his feet and produced it. I took it, dialled Klinker Dorfmann's number and a moment later was answered by the receptionist. 'May I speak to Ian Goldsmith?' I asked. Ian was usually lunching with clients or down in the pub with George at this time of day, but just for once, miraculously, he was at his desk.

'Emily! I was going to call you. We've had quite a row here this morning, and I thought you should be the first to know before someone accidentally leaks it to *The Times* Diary. That reminds me, I must get their number.'

'Well, funnily enough I'd rather guessed that,' I said. 'It's the most amazing coincidence, but I'm with my brother in Alison Small and you'll never guess who's having a row and a half in the very same place. Richard and Camilla!'

'Oh so that's where they've gone,' said Ian, chuckling. 'Really, Emily, you should have been there.'

'Go on, tell me, what on earth's happened?' I demanded joyously, mouthing apologies at Jamie, who grinned and consumed another mouthful.

'Well, we had our usual Monday get-together this morning,' began Ian. The Monday get-together was a nightmarish weekly event where all the consultants sat around and boasted about how much money they were making for the firm under the pretence of keeping their colleagues informed about new business. My own contribution to these sessions had always been minimal. 'Well, Camilla was there for the first time,' Ian went on.

'She had just started explaining some idiotic idea about how we should target first-time buyers of English merchant banks because there seem to be so many around at the moment, when the door burst open and this psychotic American woman burst in. She shouted, "Where is that home wrecker?" saw Camilla and lunged at her. George and I stepped in to stop her – sorry, Em, I know you'd probably rather we had left them to it – and she started screaming and shouting about Buzz Copenhager. You'll never believe it, but it turns out that Buzz and Camilla have been having an affair. You wouldn't have thought she'd go for a chap with a name like that, would you? Well, anyway, at first we assumed that this was Buzz's wife, but then it turns out that she's another Interbank employee who's also been having an affair with Buzz! Somehow she found out about Camilla and turned up to make her feelings felt.'

'No!' I said. 'Actually, I have a feeling that I might know who she is. Is she called Laura, by any chance? But go on, what happened next?'

'Yes she is,' said Ian gleefully. 'Well, then a real slanging match started. I didn't know Camilla had the vocabulary to express herself in quite the way she did: I can't tell you her exact words because you're much too young to know what they mean but the general gist of the conversation was that this American woman had been born out of wedlock, had sadly not completed her educational studies and had obviously been spreading her favours a little too liberally to warrant respect. Oh, and Camilla added that it was entirely possible that those favours were exchanged in return for hard cash, that this woman had mannish qualities and her present shape was only due to a sex-change operation and that she was sleazy, slimy, lousy, stinky and any number of further adjectives that momentarily escape me.'

'Oh, how fantastic,' I said. 'What did Laura say?'

'Well, she didn't seem to be taking any of this too well, after calling Camilla a low-down little tart and pond life, she hurled a pot of coffee at her. Went all over Camilla's jacket.'

'It wasn't the yellow one, was it?'

'Yes, it was actually. I suspect that it's going to be rather difficult to clean. I believe she went home to change it. Anyway, that was a little while later. I still haven't got to the best bit. Well, you can imagine how the others were taking this. Richard actually began to shout, "What the hell's going on?" I've never heard

235

Richard shout before, it was quite frightening. Donald was even angrier, though. Some of the coffee had got on his tie, and you know what a vain bastard he is. He began yelling, "What has happened to this firm? We are going to become a laughing stock," and then he told Richard that he had always warned him that this kind of thing would happen if you promote women.'

'Well, that sounds about par for the course,' I said. 'And then?'

'Well, first Richard tried to control this American, at which point she started shouting that Camilla despised everyone she works with and called Richard Gramps behind his back – I never knew that, did you Emily? – and so on, which shut Richard up for a minute. Wonder how she knew that?'

'Probably heard it on Saturday night,' I said. 'She was at a party I was at and some jerk told her about Buzz and Camilla. I saw the havoc she managed to create then.'

'Yes, well, she certainly made her feelings felt at our place. Anyway, to top it all, Buzz himself turned up at this point. We found out later that she left a note for him saying she was going to Klinker Dorfmann to confront his bit on the side. Both Camilla and this woman started shouting at him, Richard was saying that he did not want to work with adulterers and then, really Emily, you will never believe this, Buzz's wife turned up.'

'I wouldn't have thought the boardroom would have been big enough to hold all Buzz's women friends. But why did the wife turn up? And how did she know where he was?'

'Because Laura, who seems to have planned all this down to the ground, rang the wife at home and told her everything, including that she was going to Klinker Dorfmann and that she fully expected to see Buzz there too.'

'Blimey,' I said in awe. 'Puts my little scene last week into the shade.'

'You're telling me it does. Anyway, the end result of all this is that Camilla is to be demoted if she's lucky, that Richard will not work with Interbank unless he deals with someone other than Buzz, that Buzz's job, you will be pleased to hear, is also at risk because someone, I can't imagine who, got on the phone to Buzz's boss at Interbank and relayed the whole sorry tale (I think you owe me a drink there, Emily) and that Buzz is now formally separated, the locks have been changed on the South Ken des res and that the wife has informed him she will take him for everything he's got. She must have moved bloody fast this morning. A most satisfactory outcome all round, I think you'll agree.'

'It certainly is,' I said. '*Après moi, le déluge.* Anyway—' I caught Jamie's eye, he was beginning to look impatient. 'Look, we must meet up and talk about it more, but I better go, my brother is still here.'

'Yes, I've got a few phone calls to make myself,' said Ian thoughtfully. 'Normally, of course, I would be very concerned about a story like this damaging the reputation of the firm, but I don't think I mentioned that I resigned this morning? Going to work for Green Knight for megabucks. I have a funny feeling George might be going there as well. I'll talk to you soon.'

'OK, 'bye,' I said, clicking off the phone. I hastily started digging into my lamb, noticing guiltily that Jamie had completely finished already.

'I assume you won't mind if I nick another of your cigarettes,' he said.

'No, not at all, if you don't mind me eating while you're smoking.'

'Feel free,' said Jamie. 'What on earth was all that about?'

'Divine retribution. Terrible chaos at my beloved ex-employers, involving that woman over there you see walking out.'

Jamie followed my gaze. Camilla, who had been yelling again, turned at the door for one last blast. 'You can stuff your bloody job!' she shouted. 'I will not work as a receptionist, I'm a consultant!' With that she stepped outside and slammed the door.

'Dearie me,' I said, scooping up another forkful of potato and was promptly riveted by the sight of who was coming in the door. 'What the hell are you doing here?' I demanded of Natasha as she appeared at our table.

'Oh, I just wanted to talk,' said Natasha meekly. 'I knew you wouldn't mind if I popped in for a chat. Hi, Jamie, how are you?'

'He's very happily involved with his girlfriend and has been for years,' I butted in irritably. Jamie was looking at Natasha with the kind of glazed expression so familiar to those of us who had charted her progress over the last decade. I noticed crossly that yet again she was wearing something I had not seen before – the woman seemed to have as big a wardrobe as Camilla – this time a fitted black bouclé suit. The jacket was buttoned up to the neck, with a round curvy collar, on which there was an enormous silver brooch, and the skirt was even shorter than mine.

She ran her hand through her short black hair and pouted at Jamie. 'You're so lucky,' she breathed. 'I wish we all had such good news in our lives.'

Jamie sighed slightly. 'That's very sweet of you to say so,' he said, looking at her wistfully. 'I do hope you'll come to the wedding if we ever get round to it.'

'Of course,' said Natasha, lowering her voice so that it became slightly husky, 'but I should warn you that I always cry at weddings.'

'Oh, for God's sake,' I said pushing my now empty plate aside and lighting a cigarette. 'The only time I've ever seen you cry at a wedding was when Catherine turned up wearing the same thing as you.'

'Well, she did it deliberately, the little cow,' said Natasha, returning to normal. 'That's the last time I ever tell anyone where I shop. Anyway, I really do want to talk to you.'

'Can I listen in too?' asked Jamie hopefully.

'I think you're supposed to, she always performs better to a wider audience,' I said spitefully. 'No thank you, I'll just have coffee.'

Marco had been hovering. He had produced a third glass for Natasha, splashed the remains of the wine into it (I was a bit irritated, it was a delicious New World Chardonnay and I was rather hoping for another drop myself), took orders for coffee from all of us, made eyes at Jamie again, and disappeared. 'Well, I don't know if Emily's told you, but I've been having a few problems recently with Cosmo, my boyfriend,' she began.

'No, actually, I didn't tell Jamie, we had far more interesting things to talk about,' I butted in.

Natasha shot me a nasty glance and went on. 'Anyway, last night we had a terrible scene, and he went off with another woman,' she breathed.

'Only because he found out you'd been going off

239

with practically every man over the age of sixteen in Greater London.'

'Don't be so horrible, Emily,' said Jamie. 'You poor thing, how awful for you. He must be crazy.'

Natasha shot him a faltering smile. 'Oh thank you. Anyway, he's gone missing again, he's not come back to our house, he's not in work and I just don't know what to do. And then, something else awful happened.'

'What is it?' asked Jamie, looking deeply into her eyes. I could see why he was so popular with the blue-rinsed brigade in Bristol, if his bedside manner with poodles was anything compared to this.

'Well, it's rather a long story, but a friend of Emily's and mine went missing last week, we've been trying to find out where he was and this morning his mother rang me. She said they hadn't heard from him for days, and did anyone know where he was.'

'Well, shouldn't someone call the police?' asked Jamie.

'No, we can't,' said Natasha firmly, 'but it's too complicated to tell you why.'

'Well, surely there's no harm now that Cosmo knows all about him,' I said.

'Must you bring that up?' asked Natasha irritably. Jamie, guessing the history of this, looked slightly crestfallen but went on being caring. 'Look,' he said, 'why don't we all go back to Emily's flat and decide on a plan of action.'

'What?' I said indignantly. I had been planning on doing a bit of pleasant shopping in the afternoon.

'Well, we can't stay here and I've decided I don't need to go back to Bristol till tomorrow, I was hoping you could put me up,' said Jamie. I looked around. He was right, we could not stay there. It was after three o'clock, and we were the last people in the restaurant. Richard had stalked off a couple of minutes after Camilla.

'Oh, all right,' I said with very bad grace. I wanted to get back and ring Jack to explain the kitten situation anyway, although I had been hoping for a little peace and quiet, which was the last thing I could expect with those two around.

'Good girl,' said Jamie, 'for that I'll buy you lunch.'

18

The phone began ringing just as I inserted my key in the lock. I pushed the door open and raced into the sitting-room, leaving the other two to chase the kittens, both of whom had made a dash for freedom. 'Emily Whitelake,' I said automatically.

'Hullo Emily, it's Alexander. How are you?'

'Oh, very well, thanks. Did you stay late on Saturday?' I asked.

'Yes, a whole group of us did. I noticed you'd disappeared. They've got a couple of spare rooms, so Gary and I both spent the night there. We had to share a bed actually, although of course nothing happened, and we thought we should help clear up the mess in the morning.'

'Was there much to do?' I asked.

'Surprisingly little, just a bit of smashed glass. Michael said the evenings usually get much more chaotic than that. He's a nice chap, Gary seems to have some very nice friends.'

'Yesss,' I said cautiously.

'Anyway, it's because of Gary really that I'm ringing,' said Alexander. 'He rang this morning to suggest we had a drink tonight, and I thought you might like to come along too.'

'Wouldn't I be a bit *de trop*?'

'Don't be silly, Emily, we're just good friends,' said Alexander with a self-conscious laugh. 'Well sort of, anyway. No, the reason I thought you might like to come along was that we've decided to check out this Edward character once and for all. If your friend still hasn't turned up, there's something funny going on and we think he's in on it.'

'What do you mean, check him out? He didn't seem too pleased when you asked him about it on Saturday night.'

'Exactly! It made it seem all the more suspicious. But we weren't planning on confronting him, we just want to go down to the area, ask if anyone knows anything about it, that sort of thing. The only trouble is that we don't know where he lives, so we were hoping you'd come too.'

'What, you mean you're going as a sort of lynch mob?' I demanded.

'Don't be silly, Emily, nothing like that, we just want to nose around the local cellars and make sure there are no dead bodies, that sort of thing. Come on, it'll be fun.' I hesitated. I was quite curious to see what was going on myself, and I did not see any real harm in going along. 'Well, on condition that Jack comes too,' I said.

'Excellent,' said Alexander. 'Now, where shall we meet?'

'There's a little wine bar behind Holborn tube station,' I said. 'That's very close by.'

'Yes I know it, see you there at 7.30,' said Alexander and hung up.

I put the phone down. Jamie and Natasha, having

rescued the kittens, were standing looking at me curiously. I bent down and scooped up Kir, who was nosing round my ankles. 'Well?' they said in unison.

'That was Alexander, he and Gary are going to check out Edward's story tonight to make sure he's got nothing to do with Henry's disappearance.'

'And you're going too?' asked Natasha.

'Yes, thought I might.'

'Then I'm coming along as well,' said Natasha firmly, plonking herself down on the sofa and lighting a cigarette.

'Mightn't it be a little awkward, given your relationship with Edward?' I asked.

'Relationship with Edward?' repeated Jamie. He was looking increasingly disillusioned.

'Yes, I think Natasha forgot to mention that that was one of the factors that led to her little disagreement with Cosmo.'

Natasha's black eyes flashed in my direction. 'Well, that's why I think I should come too,' she said. 'If there's anything to get out of it my womanly wiles should help.'

Jamie was rallying bravely. 'If you two are going, I'm coming along too.'

'Look, how many of us are going down there?' I asked.

'Safety in numbers, you never know. Edward might be dangerous,' said Jamie.

I snorted. 'He seems an extremely charming and amiable chap to me who has had the great misfortune to get caught up with a group of lunatics.' I slumped wearily into a chair and glanced at the phone. It rang instantly. 'Emily Whitelake,' I said automatically.

'Hello, darling, it's me,' said my mother. 'Now,

first things first. How did your date go on Saturday night? Any wedding bells on the horizon?'

'Mummy, for heaven's sake,' I burst out. 'It was only a first date and anyway, to tell you the truth, I don't think we've got a great deal in common.' I was buggered if I was telling my mother Gary chose the occasion to out himself. 'I think we're just going to be good friends.'

'Hm,' said my mother consideringly. 'Well, I suppose that's just as well, darling, after all he is a computer programmer. Now look, darling, I was just ringing about the New Year. Now you know there was some question of you staying up here for a week.'

'Don't tell me,' I said, 'the Hendersons have asked you to celebrate New Year in their little beach house in Barbados.'

My mother gasped with astonishment. 'Good Lord, darling, how did you know that? Well never mind, you're quite right, they did. Now look, darling, I know you and Jamie want to make plans and so I just thought I'd mention it to you. Now, if you really want us to say no . . .' She paused.

'No, no, Mummy, you go,' I said resentfully. My little guess was supposed to have been sarcasm, not getting it right first time. 'Actually, Jamie's come up for the day, he's here if you want to talk to him.'

'Oh darling, how lovely, it's so nice when families are together. I really don't have time for a chat, but give him my love and say I'll ring him in a day or two. Now not to worry about the date, darling, I'm sure the right man will come along.'

She hung up before I could say another word. I turned to Jamie with a black look. He grinned at me. 'Now, Em, which would you prefer, lording it over the neighbours with a tan in January or spending a night with us?' he asked. 'Anyway, we can go down to Bristol and celebrate there.'

'Well, I know which I would choose,' said Natasha thoughtfully. 'I wonder if Chris would be free over the New Year if Cosmo doesn't turn up?'

'Sometimes, even now, you have the capacity to surprise me, Nat,' I said. Jamie was looking disillusioned again. 'Anyway, I'm ringing Jack, I want him to come along too and I've got to sort out this kitten business. Do feel free to make yourselves at home. I'm calling him from the bedroom.' I stalked out of the room.

Jack was, as ever, in a meeting when I called but apparently he had especially instructed that I should be put through. I felt rather flattered. 'Hullo darling, how's it going?' he asked.

'Oh, everything's in a state of chaos.' I told him about Nigel sneaking about the kittens and the little search party this evening.

'How ridiculous, but I suppose we'd better go along,' said Jack when I'd finished. 'Anyway, I can't stay on the phone, but Emily, you're going to have to do something about the kittens. I really think you should take them to my place. If you don't want them to stay there permanently, you can decide what to do about them later.'

I could not think of what else to do. 'All right,' I said, 'shall I see you at the wine bar?'

'Absolutely, and I want to have a little talk to you after that. See you later, darling, 'bye.'

'Bye.' I put the phone down and jumped as I noticed that Jamie and Natasha were both quite shamelessly earwigging at the door.

'You know, I'm beginning to think he really is quite keen,' said Natasha, 'and he's got a very nice flat.'

'You know, there is more to life than just material possessions,' I responded irritably.

'So I'm told, but you've got to think about the future,' said Natasha grandly, drifting back into the sitting-room. I followed them in and began to pack up the kittens' belongings. It took some doing, trying to catch them both and get them into their carrying cage, but luckily Jamie's veterinary expertise came to the fore: slightly to my horror, he grabbed them both by the scruff of the neck and dropped them in. Shortly before he had done so, Royale managed to ladder Natasha's tights, so I had to produce another pair for her to stem the flow of abuse. The litter tray, feeding bowls and assorted tins of cat food went into a box that I had been keeping in case of emergency. I rang for a taxi, pulled on my coat and glanced at my watch. 'Good Lord,' I said, 'it's after five o'clock. I think the best thing is if we all meet up there.'

'I'll be delighted to look after Natasha,' said Jamie gallantly.

'Yes, well just remember you're living with some-one,' I said. The doorbell rang. I picked up the intercom; 'Taxi for Miss Whitelake,' said a voice.

'Be right down,' I said. Jamie helped me carry the cage, from which the kittens were issuing some very pitiful mewling, to the car, I gave him instructions about where we were all going to meet, and we drove off.

About ten minutes later, most of which were punc-tuated by the driver informing me that he did not like carrying animals in his vehicle, we drew up in front of Jack's flat. I paid the driver, automatically asked for another receipt, and carried everything up to the flat, which was on the first floor. Jack lived in a much smarter house than I did: there was a wide staircase in the middle of the hall, which led to a landing with doors on both sides. The kittens managed to kick a bit of litter out of their basket and onto the chic cream carpet in the hall, but otherwise we got into the flat without mishap.

I put the litter tray in the bathroom, poured litter into it, and thinking of Natasha's instructions, hauled the carrying cage in after me and released the kittens into their new home. Although they could not get out to the street from the flat, Jack's large kitchen, which was opposite the bathroom, opened on to a roof terrace where they could play once they had got used to the place.

I mooched around for a moment and then peered into the bedroom. A couple of large chests of drawers were dotted about, with clothes spilling out of them. I went to sit on the large, neatly made-up bed, and then noticed with a jolt that a picture had appeared on the bedside table. It was the same picture of Jack and me at a wedding that I had on my desk at home. I had forgotten that Jack had a copy. I picked it up, stroked the bit with Jack in it and then put it down and smoothed down the bed.

Then I padded up the hall into the large, airy sitting-room. There was a grand marble fireplace in one wall, with painted white wooden cupboards on either side filled with books – mostly unread. Several comfortable sofas dotted the wooden floor and there were watercolours around the walls. Rugs and plants were in abundance. 'Maybe Natasha has a point after all,' I said to the kittens who, having investigated the rest of the flat, had followed me in. 'What do you think?' Both arched their backs and started purring. I knelt down and tickled them for a bit, and then remembered that I was supposed to be joining a search party. My inclination to leave the flat was minimal, but heaven knows what Gary and Alexander were up to and I also didn't want to miss out on the fun. 'I've got to go, you two,' I said, straightening up. The kittens accompanied me out to the hall and, slightly to my surprise, did not try to escape: they sat down and continued purring as I put on my coat, picked up my bag and opened the door. At this they both stood up, chirruped at me and padded back into the sitting-room. I switched off the hall light, pulled the door to behind me and left.

19

Settling the kittens in had taken longer than I thought. I glanced at my watch, realized I was going to be late, ran up to Holland Park Road and flagged down a taxi. 'Holborn tube, please,' I said to the cab driver and scrambled in.

'Wot you in such a hurry for then?' demanded the cab driver, stepping on to the accelerator. 'Got a date?'

'Not exactly,' I said, settling back. 'I'm not exactly seeing anyone at the moment.'

'Wot, a young girl like you?' asked the cabby, peering at me in the mirror. 'Nah, you're too young to settle down. Play the field, that's what I say. Plenty of time before you should fink of settlin' down. My missus was just like you when we was courtin', but that was a long time ago. I turned to her the other day, and said, look gel, why don't you try to make somefink of yourself? You was never like this when you was a young lady. And you know what she said to me? She said, if you was 'alf the man you used to be, 'Arry, then I wouldn't have let meself get to the way I am. See, what I fink. . . .'

I lit a cigarette and listened as the cab driver gave me a brief lecture on his life and times, his disappointment at the reality of conjugal bliss and his hopes and fears for his son, who was also about to get married. Eventually he pulled up outside Holborn tube and I alighted. 'Anyway,' said the cabby, softening considerably as I gave him a large tip, 'I'm sure you will be very happy. Good on yer!'

With that he drove off. I am not going to be like that, I thought firmly, as I began to make my way up the little alleyway beside Holborn tube, and I am not having Jack turn into half the man he used to be – not that that was remotely relevant. I had decided not to live with him anyway. At that point I nearly jumped out of my skin as there was a bellow behind me. 'Emily!' shouted a voice. 'Wait up!'

I turned around, and there was Jack himself, bounding up behind me. Before I had time to even think about it, he had grabbed me, whirled me around and began to kiss me. I kissed back for a minute, and then broke away. We looked at each other slightly shakily. 'Come on,' said Jack, after clearing his throat a couple of times. 'We better not keep the others waiting.'

We pushed open the door of the wine bar. It looked packed. I made my way in, with Jack behind me, and stopped, shocked. 'Oh, good God what's happening?' I said. Just about everyone I knew seemed to be in there. There were Alexander and Gary, sharing a bottle of wine and laughing together at some joke. Natasha and Jamie were sitting opposite them, but who was that at the next table? Nigel! And Catherine was there, sitting beside him, chatting amicably to George and Ian, who were also on the same table. It felt as if it was about a year since I had seen Catherine, although it was less than a week since our little get-together at the

Bleeding Heart. 'What on earth?' I demanded striding over to the tables.

'Em!' shouted George, standing up and giving me a bear hug. 'What a huge coincidence! Ian and I decided to come here to conspire – I gather Ian told you all about our little drama at work today, and I do suggest you read tomorrow's *Times* Diary – as we thought it was far enough away from the office not to be seen, and we bump into Catherine and Natasha. And Jamie too! We haven't met up for years! What's the big occasion?'

'Uh nothing, we're just meeting up for a drink,' I said, disentangling myself from Ian, who was also giving me a bear hug. I thought it might look a bit silly if I told them what we were really there for. 'But I didn't know there were going to be so many of us.'

Jack was shaking hands with Jamie and exchanging greetings with the others. I waved across the table at Gary and Alexander, who were ordering more wine and glasses, and saw Natasha making agonized looks in Nigel's direction and mouthing 'sorry'. He had supplemented his usual tracksuit garb with an anorak that had seen better and cleaner days plus a pair of extremely dirty jeans and had seized the opportunity of a gap in the conversation to start boring Catherine rigid with one of his latest theories about the world. 'It's socio-political environmentalist situations that define people's aspirational self-data,' he droned. 'Take Me, for example, I had my choice of careers – I could have been a banker or an engineer or a politician or anything, but I thought that, like, my true vocation was guiding my fellow human beings on a voyage of self-discovery. Oh hello, Emily.'

'What are *you* doing here?' I demanded. Jack had

taken his coat off and wisely wedged himself in between Natasha and Jamie on the adjacent table.

Nigel looked at me with a hangdog expression. 'Well that's not a very nice greeting. I've just come along to be supportive.'

'Supportive of me?' I spat. 'Well that makes a nice change. Oh, by the way, you needn't worry about the cats anymore, because they've moved out. And what are *you* doing here?' I asked, staring at Catherine.

'Blimey, friendly or what?' said Catherine, draining her glass and refilling it. I saw that there were a number of empty bottles on the table. She dragged a chair from a third table to her other side, found a clean glass and poured some wine for me. 'Sit down,' she invited. 'Not that you deserve it after that greeting, but I had some information I thought might interest you. I called your flat, Natasha answered, and she said you were going to be here later and I was going to be in the area anyway. I don't think I'll tell you now.'

'Oh don't be such a pain,' I said.

'Honestly, Em, she told us and you'll want to hear!' boomed Ian. He and George were looking even cheerier than usual.

Catherine looked at me haughtily and then relented. 'Well, there are two things actually, but I'll save the second till another time, it's a bit public here,' she began. 'The first is about a job. You do want to rejoin the ranks of the gainfully employed, don't you, Emily? Or are you thinking of remaining a lady of leisure?'

'Go on,' I said, interested in spite of myself.

'Well you've always drivelled on about how you want to do something arty instead of working in that terrible profession – oh, sorry,' she said to George and Ian.

'Not at all, we think the same thing, we're just better at hiding it than Emily,' said George airily.

Ian beamed at her. 'And better paid,' he added.

'Well anyway,' said Catherine hastily, as I glared at the boys, 'a magazine that I used to work for is looking for someone to write for their arts pages. I heard about it this morning and said that I might know someone suitable because I've got this dreadful friend who's just been sacked because she was too incompetent at sucking up to people, and also she drinks far too much, and they said perfect! Send her along.'

'You didn't really say that, did you?' I said, gaping at Catherine.

'No, of course not,' said my friend, lighting a cigarette. 'I said you had a good degree in English, very interested in literature, that sort of thing, and that you were looking for a change in profession. When I told them what you used to do, they quite understood. Here's the name and number, they're expecting a call tomorrow. I've been meaning to ring and tell you, but I didn't have a chance until now.' She pushed a piece of paper across the table at me.

'Gosh,' I said, pocketing it, 'thanks.' Although I was rather enjoying the feeling of not having to go into an office, I thought I needed to start plotting a new career, to say nothing of taking responsibility for my Harvey Nichols charge card.

'And you know, if you want to talk it through with anyone, I'm there for you, Emily,' added Nigel. Below the edge of the table, I could see him beginning to run his nasty greasy little hand up Catherine's skirt. Catherine did not say anything, she just put her hand with the lit cigarette under the tablecloth. A second later there was a yowl of pain from Nigel, who hastily withdrew his hand.

'Anyway,' continued Catherine calmly, 'there's much more I want to talk about, but I've really got to go. I'll call you tomorrow, Emily.' She got up, put on her coat, waved to everyone and disappeared.

I glanced at Natasha. She was directing the full force of her very dark eyes at Jamie, and telling him what a caring personality he must have to be a vet. Jack was telling Gary and Alexander that he thought it most unlikely we would find anything, let alone a body.

'What exactly is going on?' asked George curiously, who had also overheard him.

'Yes, Emily, you're not all just meeting for a drink, are you?' chipped in Ian, looking at me suspiciously.

I hesitated, but the desire to gossip won the day. 'It's a very long story, but the upshot is that a friend of mine and Natasha's has gone missing and those two over there' – I pointed to Gary and Alexander, who were giggling at yet another private joke – 'think another friend of ours is involved. It's all totally ridiculous, but Jack and I thought we'd better humour them. We're going to mount a search party.'

'And you didn't tell us?' demanded George. 'Emily, you rotter. After everything we've done for you. We demand to be allowed to come along.'

'Absolutely,' boomed Ian. 'We've never been detectives before.'

At this point, a general movement began at the next table. 'Come along, it's time to go,' said Alexander excitedly. 'And we're all coming along? Excellent. Now, shall we split into groups, or all go together?'

'Don't you think you're taking this a wee bit too seriously?' asked Jack.

'No, no, he's quite right,' said Gary. 'Now, Alexander and I will head the groups. Natasha's given us the address, by the way,' he said to me. 'Emily, you come with me, and Natasha and Jamie and you.' He motioned at George. 'The rest of you go along with Alexander. I say we take the streets on the left of Boswell Street and you lot take the streets on the right and then we meet at Edward's flat in an hour.'

'I thought we weren't going to confront him!' I said. I was feeling a bit snappish, and I did not want to be separated from Jack.

Jack looked as if he felt pretty much the same. 'Yes, an hour is much too long and it's completely unfair to turn up like this on the poor bloke's doorstep,' he complained.

'All right,' Alexander relented, 'well, let's say half an hour and we'll meet at the bottom of Boswell Street. Let's synchronize watches, Gary!' They began feverishly comparing their wrist-wear. Oh, for heaven's sakes, I thought. This is getting more like *Boys' Own* by the minute.

Jack came over to me as everyone began struggling into their coats. 'It's just half an hour,' he whispered, 'and we'll go off for a drink on our own after that.' He kissed me and went off with the first group.

'Well,' said Natasha, looming up by my side, 'what's going on here? Are you moving in with him, Emily?'

'No I am not,' I said. 'And you two, what on earth is Nigel doing here?'

'Oh, I'm really sorry about that Emily,' said Natasha. 'He came out of his flat just as we were leaving and I stopped and said hello. Then he demanded to know what was going on and your brother told him we were going on a body hunt with you. He just insisted on coming along. We simply couldn't get rid of him.'

'All my fault,' said Jamie cheerily. 'Come on, we better get going, the others will have a head start.'

'I feel as if I'm taking part in a treasure hunt,' I complained as we left the wine bar. 'Shouldn't we have brought provisions in case we get lost?'

'Thought of that already!' said Gary, producing a hip flask. 'Whisky to guard against the cold. Shhhh, we're nearly there.'

We came to a halt at the bottom of Boswell Street. 'You know, I'm beginning to see why working in PR didn't suit you,' hissed George. 'All that sitting in an office when you could be out being a private eye.'

'Sorry about this,' I hissed back.

'Don't be ridiculous, I haven't enjoyed myself so much for years.' George accepted a proffered gulp from Gary's flask, then we all had one, just to get in the mood.

'Now,' hissed Gary, 'what we do is go up one street and down the next. We have to check all cellars and alleyways. Even if we don't find Henry's body, we have to be on the lookout for scraps of clothing or a blunt instrument. We stay together. This might be dangerous.'

This was greeted by a muffled snort from Jamie and a patient look from George, who was roughly the same dimensions as a small town-house in Kensington, and not a chap who looked as if he would be trifled with in the cold light of day let alone a dark alley, but Natasha seemed to take it on board. She squeaked nervously and took my arm. We turned our collars up – more as protection from the bitter cold than as a means of disguise. It had also begun to rain. 'Come on,' hissed Gary. We set off at prowling pace, still talking in whispers.

'Any further news of Cosmo?' I hissed at Natasha.

'No, but I forgot to tell you earlier that I changed all the locks this morning. That'll give him something to think about,' she hissed in return. 'Emily, this is getting scary. What are we going to do if we actually find something?'

'Don't know, but I'm sure our leaders have thought of a plan,' I hissed back. 'Come on, let's keep up with them, I don't want to be left alone round here.'

There were all sorts of dark little streets, running helter-skelter around the place. We turned into one. The boys started peering down flights of stairs leading to basement flats and into dark little corners. There seemed to be dark alleys all over the place: the boys went up each one, scouting carefully for anything that looked mysterious. Natasha and I followed nervously, peering over shoulders and prodding the odd bag of rubbish to show we were doing our bit. I fervently wished that Jack was there. 'Don't leave any stone unturned,' whispered Gary. 'We're sure to find something.'

'Look,' murmured Natasha, grabbing my arm. A bit further down the road was a row of garages, some with their doors open. Very much against my better judgement I left the boys, who were investigating a boarded-up building, and followed her. We snuck into the first one. It was empty except for a few battered old car parts and some soiled bits of cloth.

The second was not much better: it housed some empty crates and half a pane of glass. Both of us nearly jumped out of our skins when I banged into some dark object in the corner which groaned slightly and moved forward. It turned out to be an old-fashioned lawn mower, which was covered with rust. All the spikes were broken. Heaven knows what it was doing there, there could not have been a garden for miles around.

'Come on, there's one more,' whispered Natasha. She stole out of the dark dank building, and went into the next on the row, which seemed even blacker and colder than the last as we got inside. There was also rather an odd smell. We stopped just inside the entrance. We were both so nervous that our combined fear seemed to be taking on a presence of its own. Grasping each other's hands, we edged further and further into the garage, past more piles of boxes and crates.

In the gloom, we could see a dark shape on the floor towards the back. I glanced at Natasha: I could just make out a petrified expression on her face. We got to within a few feet of the object and then froze. It was quite clearly a body. The torso was twisted into some horrible position. The arms and legs were splayed out in a dreadful way, but we could not see the face, which was completely in darkness. Heaven knows what had been done to him.

By this time we were so scared we could hardly move. I opened my mouth to shout but no sound came out. Natasha was whimpering with terror. We were both shaking so badly it was a surprise we didn't fall over. We managed to back away until we finally got to the entrance of the garage. Then our strength returned and we both pounded up the road to the boys who were investigating an area under the raised ground floor of another boarded-up building. A man passing on the other side of the road turned around and stared after us as we raced along. I was in such a blind panic that I hardly noticed.

'What on earth?' said George as we collapsed breathlessly beside the group. 'Have you found anything?'

'Him!' gasped Natasha. She was too breathless to shout, which was just as well as there were still a few residents amongst the boarded-up buildings. 'We've found him! His body! In that garage over there!'

Everyone looked at each other and then the three boys started off at a run in the direction in which she was pointing. Natasha and I were obviously thinking the same thing: was it better to go back and confront those dreadful twisted limbs with three large grown men beside us or was it better to stand alone in a deserted building? It was not that difficult a choice. As one, we set off to follow them. The three had slowed down once they got to the garage and were peering in. 'It's in the back there,' I whispered.

Jamie straightened his shoulders. 'Come on, there are five of us. There's no reason to be scared.'

Even George was looking a little bit nervous, though. We prowled softly through the shadows till we got to the back of the garage. The body was still there. One arm looked as if it was nearly hanging off the body and a leg was twisted underneath the torso at a right angle. He must have been tortured horribly. Although I was absolutely petrified, I suddenly found myself thinking, but where is the blood? It must be too dark to see it. Natasha and I had stopped prowling and were clinging on to one another as the three men cautiously approached the corpse. Jamie stretched out a foot and prodded it. Quite suddenly, he burst out laughing. A second later the other two joined him. 'This isn't Henry!' he shouted.

To my absolute appalled horror, he aimed a powerful kick at the body. Horror turned to consternation as the body rose up into the air and plopped down on the ground a few feet away. A body that large could not have been that light and would not have made a plopping sound on the concrete. Tension released, the three men were shaking with laughter. Natasha released me and walked over to inspect it. After a moment she turned round. 'It's a guy,' she said matter of factly.

'What?' I asked.

'A guy,' said Natasha. 'You know, as in "Penny for the". It was Guy Fawkes night a couple of weeks ago, it must have been left here.'

'What?' I repeated. 'A guy? You mean we've been scared witless by a guy?'

'Honestly, you two,' said Jamie coming over and putting his arm around me. 'What a palaver. Henry's body, indeed. Come on, Em, you must admit, it's quite funny.'

I attempted to snicker and failed. Gary materialized beside me with the hip flask. 'Have a swig of that,' he said kindly, 'it must have been quite a shock. Come on, you too Natasha.' We did as we were told and began to cheer up a bit. 'Good old Em,' said George pounding me on the back, 'always one for a bit of melodrama.'

'Yes, well I was there too,' said Natasha, who had completely returned to her usual self. 'At least we found something, which is more than you lot did. Oh, yuk, I've got mud on my shoes.'

'Well you shouldn't be wearing designer wear on a night-time mission,' I said uncharitably. 'Bugger, so have I. Is the half-hour up yet?'

'More than,' said Gary checking his watch. Although there were more unexplored streets around us, the atmosphere of tension had dissolved completely. The discovery of the guy had brought us back to reality: it did not look as if we were going to find Henry around here.

'Come on, the others will be wondering where we've got to,' said Jamie. 'And I personally could do with getting inside somewhere and having a drink. It's bloody cold out here.'

There was a murmur of agreement and we all set off to the allotted meeting place. Jamie drew me behind the others and slid his hand through mine in my coat pocket as we walked up the road, a habit of his ever since we were children. 'Emily, what is going on between you and Jack?'

'Absolutely nothing,' I said crossly. Why did everyone in the world have to be so interested in us?

'What are you two whispering about?' demanded Natasha, holding back from the others to join us.

'I was just telling Jamie about your life, times and plentiful past relationships,' I said brightly. 'Ah, here we are.' We had turned a corner and found ourselves back at the bottom of Boswell Street where Gary and Alexander were conferring in whispers. George and Ian were discussing the packages they had managed to negotiate to join Green Knight. Nigel took the opportunity to engage Natasha in conversation. I could hear him asking her out on a protest march.

Jack was standing slightly apart from the rest. He came over to me. 'So I gather you made something of a momentous discovery.'

'Yes, well, anyone can make a mistake,' I said. 'It was very dark.' The three of us, Jack, Jamie and me, stood hunched in the wind as the ringleaders decided what to do. After a moment Gary turned around. 'We think,' he said solemnly, 'that while we're here we might as well go and look at the actual flat itself.'

Everyone hesitated. 'We won't actually go to the door,' added Alexander, 'but we might as well look at the cellar, if there is one. Come on, it will only take a minute.'

'This is ridiculous,' muttered Jack.

'Oh go on, it will only be for a minute,' said Ian.

'Yes, go on,' George urged.

'You know, maybe I could talk to him,' said Nigel, who had just been turned down by Natasha. 'After all, I'm a trained counsellor and I can get people to verbalize what can seem an insurmountable problem to them.'

Jack ignored him and looked at me. I looked at Natasha. We all shrugged. Gary and Alexander were obviously determined to go anyway. 'OK, but really only for a minute,' said Jack.

We spread out in a line and began to creep down the street. I could hear Alexander trying to convince Jack that a confrontation with Edward would bring everything out into the open while Jack quietly and firmly informed him that not only was there absolutely no proof that Edward had anything to do with Henry's disappearance, but that if you suddenly accuse a man of murder with absolutely no proof to back it up, it might constitute slander and thus be a very expensive accusation indeed. I was not too bothered either way as long as we were allowed to go off for a drink afterwards.

As we prowled further up the street, everyone poked their noses into any dark spaces around with complete lack of success. As we got closer to the building, we got quieter and more subdued. Our attempts at stealth were somewhat marred by the fact that I tripped over a dustbin, which clattered loudly as the lid fell off, but other than that we made it intact to the bottom of the stairs to the flat. A couple of old-age pensioners gave us a rather funny look as we stopped and started whispering, but I assumed they were used to eccentrics in that part of town.

'Now,' hissed Jack to Alexander, 'the flat's up there. We must be very quiet.'

Obviously enjoying the whole thing enormously, Alexander nodded and we rummaged around at the bottom of the stairs. I turned and to my horror, saw that Gary was beginning to creep up. I nudged Jack and pointed. 'Silly ass,' hissed Jack and began to follow. I crept after him and, glancing back, saw that everyone in our little group was queuing up to do the same. Jack kept trying to attract Gary's attention and draw us back, but without success. We got to Edward's floor and stole up outside the flat. The piece of graffiti had been painted over. The curtains were drawn and someone was speaking inside.

'It's all been so amazing,' the voice was saying. 'We actually met ages ago, but it wasn't till we both went to a supper party at Chris's on Thursday that it suddenly took off. We've hardly spent a moment apart since then. Luckily I'd taken the week off anyway. I was supposed to get my stuff from my parents, but I didn't even have time to ring them . . .'

'What!' I shouted standing up. 'I don't believe it. After all that worry . . .'

'Shh, shh,' said Jack but ruined the effect by bursting out laughing. 'Dead is he?' he demanded of the two of us between snorts. 'Doesn't sound very dead to me. Dead lucky by the sounds of it. And here are we, Hercule Poirot, Miss Marple and—' he paused, trying to think of a suitable name for Gary '—Inspector Clouseau, solving the mystery . . .'

It had gone very quiet inside. The voices had stopped talking and had obviously heard us. 'Jack?' said the one that had been boasting a moment ago, 'Jack is that you?'

The door burst open, and there was Henry, looking at us in total astonishment. 'What on earth are you doing skulking outside like this?' he demanded. 'You'll catch your death of cold. Oh, hello Emily. Were you thinking of coming to visit? You're lucky to catch me, I moved out last week.' He looked in astonishment at the crowd gathering behind us and caught sight of Natasha. 'Oh hello, Natasha,' he said coldly. 'Nice of you to look in. So it was you two just now. I thought I saw you pounding down the street a few minutes ago. What on earth is going on?'

At this point Edward loomed up in the doorway behind him. 'Oh, Henry's friends,' he said in amusement. 'Actually, Henry, they might have been coming to have a drink with me. We've met a few times recently, I haven't had a chance to tell you about it. And you've brought along quite a few more new friends, I see, and I'm so pleased to see you again, Natasha. I'm Edward,' he added, extending a hand to George, who was looking slightly dumbfounded. 'I'm delighted to meet you all. Do come in.'

20

We all trooped into the sitting-room. The scene of domestic bliss was absolutely delightful except for the fact that Cosmo was sitting in the background in a large armchair sipping a gin and tonic. He turned pale when he saw Natasha, got up and walked to the back of the room. A fire – one of those fake coal ones, but very effective – was roaring in the grate. There were two more gin and tonics on the table, in front of the two sofas where Edward and Henry had obviously been sitting, and a huge pile of photographs showing pictures of exotic climes. And who was that, skulking in the background, also slurping a gin and tonic? Catherine!

We all stood gaping with our mouths open. Happily, Edward had not forgotten his duties as a host. 'Drinks anyone?' he asked brightly. 'Luckily I'm well stocked up with gin although a few of you might have to use mugs rather than glasses. Then we can all sit down and have a little chat.'

'Yes please,' said Natasha and I simultaneously. Having greeted Edward with a wistful smile, she had transferred her attentions to Cosmo and was staring darkly in his direction. He was looking down at the floor. 'If that woman's here too I will not be answerable for my actions,' she hissed at me. There were further murmurs of assent as people started settling themselves in to chairs. Catherine, to my intense astonishment, went and perched on the back of Henry's chair and, rather possessively put her hand on his shoulder. Natasha shot her a nasty glance.

'You know, you can't have them all,' I hissed at her.

It was Jack, as ever, who did not co-operate. 'Look,' he said, as Edward started clinking ice into glasses, 'what the hell is going on?'

Yes,' chipped in Gary, who was looking absolutely crestfallen, 'why isn't Henry dead?'

'Yes,' George and Ian chimed, 'we were promised a body!'

'Yes,' added Natasha, 'where have you been? Why were you like that when I saw you on the floor? And what on earth are you doing with her?' This was all directed at Henry.

Uproar broke out. 'Natasha!' cried Cosmo. 'We must talk!'

'Dead?' cried Henry. 'Why on earth should I be dead!'

'You cow!' shouted Catherine. 'Why shouldn't we be together? We're in love!'

'There's no such thing as love, it's just a chemical inter-reaction between personalities,' yelled Nigel. 'But it's good you're all verbalizing your emotions.'

'Will you all calm down!' shouted Jack.

Edward, who had seemed to become accustomed to being blamed for other people's disappearances, could control himself no longer. He stood in the middle of the room, threw his head back, and began to roar with laughter. 'You've formed a posse,' he gasped eventually. 'What a delight! The last time this happened to me, I was taking pictures of industrial development in the Amazon basin and some of the local contractors cut up very rough. They were going to run me out of town, but that's a story for another time. Well, my friends, I am so sorry to disappoint you, but here you have living, breathing, flesh-and-blood proof of my innocence. My good friend Henry popped round this evening to sort out the little matter of unpaid bills and so on, and brought his charming new girlfriend to meet me. May I say how happy I am for them both. The two of them found Cosmo here, who has been staying with me, and we have all been getting on famously. It seems that we all have a great deal in common.'

'Actually, quite a few people here have a great deal in common,' I muttered. Luckily, no-one heard me.

Natasha, meanwhile, had been ominously silent. She could control herself no more. 'Why aren't you dead?' she demanded of Henry. 'What are you doing with Catherine, where have you been and why are you here?' This last was directed at Cosmo, who was quivering with emotion in the corner.

'I assume you're referring to my unfortunate disposition last weekend,' said Henry calmly, before Cosmo got a chance to speak. 'No,' he put a hand up as Natasha tried to interrupt, 'I gather just about everyone here knows about it, certainly our respective partners do, so we might as well discuss it publicly. I had a bit of a mishap on Sunday morning. For the first time in many years, I had an epileptic seizure. Yes,' he went on as we all gasped in shock, 'I have epilepsy. I hadn't mentioned it to any of you as it hasn't been a problem and I was hoping it would never happen again, but there you are.'

268

'But I thought you thrashed around and foamed at the mouth if you had an epileptic attack,' I said blankly.

'That's an old cliché,' said Henry. 'I don't wish to bore you with my medical history, but would you all like to know exactly what happened?'

'Yes!' shouted the room. Even Gary and Alexander fell silent as Henry began to explain.

'Well, I pieced it together myself afterwards,' he started. 'I was perfectly all right the first time Natasha left: in fact, I was woken by her slamming the door and then I went back to sleep again. The seizure must have started in my sleep, just before she came back the second time. My doctor says it must have been quite severe: I can't remember a thing about it, but I probably went rigid and then started to convulse. That sometimes happens, and I must have fallen out of bed while it was going on, which is how I assume this unfortunate misunderstanding occurred. When I came to, I found a bit of blood on my cheek. I had bitten the inside of my mouth.'

'So that's what it was,' said Natasha, gazing at him.

Henry gave her a black look and went on. 'Nat timed her second visit very well,' he said. 'The reason I wasn't moving is that one can fall asleep after a seizure, and in fact, coincidentally, as I briefly came to I heard the door slamming for the second time. You must have appeared just after the worst bit,' he informed her coldly. 'It took me a little while to realize what had happened, but as I said, I've known for ages that I have epilepsy: it's just that I haven't had a seizure in years and so I didn't really feel the need to warn anyone about it. I saw my doctor the next day, and he said it was probably brought on by the amount we had to drink.'

Natasha was looking so taken aback that she was incapable of speech. Jack stepped in again. 'But what happened then?' he asked. 'Where have you been all week? Are you all right now? We've been ringing everyone, even your parents.'

'I'm perfectly all right, I've just had to go back on to the medicine,' said Henry. 'And my doctors have told me not to drink so much. As far as everything else is concerned, my parents have been on holiday, they only got back last night. I rang them earlier this evening, it seems they were a bit concerned as well as I hadn't left a message, but I explained everything. I had dumped my furniture with them, stayed there for a couple of days, and then went to a supper party at Chris's on Thursday. Catherine was there too, and,' he simpered, 'the rest is history.'

Natasha took a different view. 'Oh no, it isn't,' she snarled. 'This is obviously a conspiracy. First I find that yet again Catherine is treading on my territory, secondly I find that Chris has had a supper party and hasn't invited me and now I find that I have had an affair with someone who has a medical condition and didn't tell me. Epilepsy! How dare you not tell me you have epilepsy when I've been worrying myself silly about where you are. And what if I had caught epilepsy too! And why have I kept seeing your ghost all week!'

Everyone started shouting again. 'I am not treading on your territory!' yelled Catherine.

'You can't catch epilepsy!' bellowed Henry. 'You can't have seen my ghost as I'm not dead – you must just have seen me around town. And if you were so bloody worried, why did you leave me in the first place!'

'It's so unfair, we thought you were dead!' shouted Alexander.

'This is a very interesting aggressional confrontational social inter-reaction,' commented Nigel.

'Don't be so mean to Natasha!' demanded Cosmo. Natasha had been looking pleadingly at him, he was obviously about to perform a climbdown yet again. 'It's all my fault,' he went on, striding into the middle of the room. 'I've been neglecting her, I should never have gone away last weekend. I'm sure she only left you because she was worried about me. She's always been like that, she's so selfless when it comes to other people's feelings. And I can understand that other people are attracted to her, she's so beautiful.' Natasha looked modest, and yet at the same time as if he were only mentioning an undeniable truth. Oh puleeze, I thought, but there was no stopping him. 'I have decided,' he continued solemnly, 'that I want to open a joint account!'

'Cosmo!' shrieked Natasha. She rushed across the room and threw her arms around him. 'Darling, I knew you'd come round! How could I ever have doubted you! Let's open it tomorrow!' The two embraced.

The announcement totally dispelled the atmosphere of tension. Everyone started talking quite naturally again. Edward was still pouring out drinks, he looked at me, grinned, shrugged and handed a mug of gin and tonic to Nigel, who sniffed it suspiciously and walked away. I went over to Catherine and Henry. 'Well you are a couple of dark horses. Why on earth didn't you tell me? And what's Cosmo doing here?'

'We haven't really had time,' said Catherine archly. 'I would have told you earlier but I didn't want to

271

make a public announcement and anyway I did try to get hold of Nat to tell her, I was worried she might take it like this.'

'Yes, well this has been very discreet,' I said.

'Much better that it all comes out in the open,' said Henry, happily. 'Anyway, I did try to ring you last week, but I was having problems with my phone.'

'Oh, well, that explains that,' I said. 'But listen, what about Cosmo?'

'Poor sap,' said Catherine sniffily.

'Yes, we all know that but why is he here?'

'He's been here since yesterday,' said Henry. 'When I got here I saw him – by the way, Emily, Natasha had told me they'd split up, that's why it happened, not that it matters now –' he added hastily, as Catherine glared at him, 'and I felt really uncomfortable, but Ed told me he'd also had something to do with her and Cosmo wanted to talk to both of us about it. Thinks it's all his fault because he hasn't made a proper commitment. Apparently he'd turned up absolutely plastered last night and Ed put him up for the night, which was going a bit beyond the call of duty, if you ask me.' Obviously the antipodean bimbo had been dropped en route, I thought. Thank heavens Jack and I managed to stop Natasha from racing into the arms of Edward. That would have messed up plans for the joint bank account.

'Anyway,' Henry went on, 'we all had a chat and, despite everything Ed and I could do to dissuade him, he'd decided he wanted to patch things up between them. He was all set to go and make amends when you all turned up here. I say, Em, you didn't really think Ed had pushed me under a bus or something, did you?'

'Good heavens no, that was just a joke,' I said. 'How's he taking all this Cosmo and Natasha stuff?'

'Thinks he's well out of it,' said Henry. 'Catherine's going to introduce him to her sister.' The two of them started simpering again.

The party was beginning to disperse. Gary and Alexander had loomed up beside us. 'I'm glad to have met you,' said Alexander, shaking Henry's hand, 'I didn't mean what I said. I'm very glad you're alive.'

'Yes,' said Gary pecking me, 'me too. Anyway, we're off to dinner, we have a lot to discuss.' They waved at us and disappeared.

Henry looked after them suspiciously. 'Is something going on there?'

'Almost certainly,' I said wearily, and was distracted by George and Ian.

'We're off too,' they boomed. 'Most enjoyable evening. Give you a call tomorrow, Em. Bye all.'

Natasha and Cosmo were the next to troop out. Nat was so pleased that she even managed to kiss Catherine goodbye ('She's always been jealous of me, you know,' she hissed darkly as she kissed me, 'but I'm prepared to overlook it this once,') before they disappeared. I looked round. Nigel was not stirring, he had made himself very comfortable in front of the fire with Edward, and was giving him a short lecture in the importance of semantics in sexual stereotyping. Jack and Jamie had been murmuring. 'Actually,' Jamie said to me, 'I've got some, er, friends I want to see so I'll be off. Don't worry if you're not back tonight, I've got my own keys to the flat.' He said goodbye to the happy couple and disappeared.

I fixed Jack with a gimlet eye. 'Just what did Jamie mean by that?' I inquired.

'Can't imagine,' said Jack, handing me the coat that I had earlier deposited in the corner. 'Come on, darling, I want to talk, and just for once, I really do not want to have anyone else around.'

I looked up at him. His dark blue eyes were glinting, and a bit of blond hair was flopping forward. I felt a sudden lurch. 'All right,' I said. We waved at Henry and Catherine, who had started cooing at each other again, and made for the door.

21

About half an hour later we arrived back at Jack's flat, having decided it was the only place where we could be relatively certain no-one would interrupt us. The first thing he did when we got inside was to switch the telephone off, then told me to go and wait for him in the sitting-room while he looked for something in the bedroom.

I wandered down the hall into the large dark room, slipped my shoes off, and plonked myself on the sofa without bothering to turn the lights on. It was totally dark outside, but the street lamps twinkled into the room and the light was on in the hall behind me. The kittens, having done a bit of exploring, followed me in and leapt up beside me. I gazed out of the windows, which were becoming slightly blurred by spots of rain. The wind was lashing the streets outside. I shivered, got up to light the fire (coal effect – very realistic) and returned to the sofa, where the kittens were now asleep. I began to doze myself and jumped as Jack bounded back into the room. I leapt up and we threw our arms around one another. The kittens opened an eye each and went back to sleep.

'You're sitting in the dark,' said Jack eventually,

disentangling himself. 'No, leave it,' as I went to switch on a light, 'it's nice. Go and sit over there.' He pointed to a large armchair in front of the fire. I padded over to it, and sat down, curling my feet underneath me. Jack plonked himself into the chair opposite me.

'Now listen,' he began. 'I've been thinking about this living together thing, and it's obvious you're not too keen and thinking about it neither am I.'

'I don't believe it!' I burst out. 'This is the second time you've changed your mind! You promised you weren't going to again!'

'Em, darling, will you shut up?' said Jack. He reached out and stroked my hand. 'I've never done this before, and I'd quite like to give it a clear run. What I mean is, I'm not keen about living together because I want it to be a permanent thing and I thought we might as well go the whole hog.'

'What do you mean?' I asked suspiciously.

'I'm going to do this properly,' said Jack. He got up, came and stood in front of me, and then dropped onto one knee and took my hand. He looked up at me, dark blue eyes flashing in the light of the fire. 'Will you marry me?' he asked.

'What?' I said.

'I thought I'd made myself clear, but I'll try again. Will you marry me?'

I knew that you were supposed to say, oh, I'll think about it and give you my answer in a week or so, but I didn't. 'Um, yes,' I said. Still holding my hand, Jack dug into his trouser pocket with his free paw and produced a small box, which he shoved at me. 'Open it,' he said.

I opened it. Inside was one of the most beautiful rings I had ever seen: two strands of seed pearls and rubies twined around each other to frame a large round diamond. The stones nestled in an intricate filigree gold setting. I stared at Jack. 'You really mean it,' I said.

'It was my grandmother's,' said Jack. 'My mother gave it to me last year in anticipation of just such an occasion. And you wear a lot of red, so I thought you should be the one to have it. My mother always said she hoped it would be you, by the way.'

'So you're proposing to me because the ring matches my wardrobe?' I said, looking coyly at Jack.

'Of course,' he said. 'And a few other considerations as well. Try it on, it can be altered if it doesn't quite fit.'

'You put it on for me,' I said, proffering the relevant hand.

Jack took my hand and slid the ring on. It fitted perfectly. 'There,' he said, looking at me, 'now we're formally engaged.'

I had never been a great one for masking emotion, and true to form, I burst into tears. Jack, who was looking quite emotional himself, slid into the chair beside me. 'You know, you're supposed to be happy,' he said, folding his arms around me.

'I am happy,' I sniffed, 'that's why I'm crying.' Jack kissed a few tears away, and then kissed me. 'But, Jack, why now?' I said eventually. 'I mean, what's made you decide you want us to get married?'

'Oh, lots of things,' said Jack. 'The first is that I love you, I always have, I always will and I was totally stupid before. But I guess things have changed recently for other reasons. First, I suddenly realized your behaviour over the past week was making me jealous as hell. Then I saw my parents in the hospital together. My mother was lying there in plaster, and my father was fussing around her, and I thought, "What if anything happened to either of us?" I couldn't bear not being there to look after you. And even though my mother was in a lot of pain, they seemed so happy together, even there, and I thought that's the way we should be. We should be married. I want us to be like them and stay together forever. I don't want us to be one of those ghastly couples whose only priority is to worry about the soft furnishings, we can still go out and have a lot of fun, but I want us to have fun together. I don't want to be without you anymore.'

'Gosh,' I said. We started kissing again. 'By the way,' said Jack eventually, 'I have a bottle of champagne in the fridge. I think this calls for a drop or two.'

He disentangled himself and went into the kitchen. I stood up and admired my ring in the light of the fire. The rubies glinted darkly and whichever way I turned it, the diamond filled the room with a rainbow of colours. A moment later Jack reappeared with a bottle and a couple of glasses. He eased the cork off, poured the liquid out and handed me a brimming glass. 'To the future Mrs Melbourne,' he said.

'And to the future Mr Whitelake,' I said, raising mine. Jack laughed, we clinked and sipped and then strolled over to the window. 'Actually, will you mind if I keep my name?' I asked.

'Not at all,' said Jack, 'as long as you don't mind me keeping mine. And will you mind living here, at least for now?'

'Not at all,' I said. 'When were you thinking of, um, you know?'

'What, you mean the actual ceremony?' asked Jack. 'A couple of years time? No, *joke*, Emily, I was thinking about the spring actually. What do you think?'

'Sounds brill,' I said. At this point we both got a little carried away, started giggling hysterically and did an impromptu waltz around the room together. Eventually we calmed down, linked arms and stood looking out into the night. 'Does this mean we have to start behaving responsibly?' I asked anxiously.

'I wouldn't have thought so,' said Jack, rubbing his cheek against my hair. 'I would have thought we have a few years of misbehaviour left yet. But any naughtiness will have to be with me.'

'What, you mean I have to give up other men?' I asked indignantly.

'You can't have the ring unless you do,' said Jack.

'Oh, OK then,' I said. We had another sip of champagne and began another clench. 'Well, kittens, you're going to have a father,' I informed Kir and Royale when Jack finally released me. They had taken absolutely no interest in the proceedings and were still asleep on the sofa. Both twitched an ear in acknowledgement.

Jack grinned. 'I think this calls for more than champagne,' he said, picking up the bottle and his glass. 'Come on, darling, pick up yours too. We can finish the bottle in the bedroom.' I giggled, grabbed my glass and we both raced up the hall.

Epilogue

The forest fire was catching up with me. I was racing, panting, sweating: anything to get away from the heat of the flames which were beginning to lick my back. I fell, crashed down on the boiling hot earth, struggled up and ran on. Everywhere I looked branches of trees, alight with a roaring fire, were crashing around me, the sounds of scorching crackled in my ears and nibbled my neck and – nibbled? Flames didn't nibble. Neither did they start murmuring. 'Emily darling,' they whispered. 'Emily darling, wake up.'

I opened my eyes. Jack was kissing me and stroking back my hair.

'Whaa?' I asked. 'Where am I?'

'Really, Emily, you are impossible,' said Jack, sitting up and looking at me in amusement. 'Now look, darling, if you're going to tell me you can't remember what happened last night I am going to take it very badly.'

I put my hand to my head and saw a glint of diamond. I could remember extremely well what happened last night. 'Did you really mean it?' I asked.

'I certainly jolly well did, and to prove it, after we've told our respective parents, I suggest we start thinking about announcements in papers,' said Jack firmly. He lay down again and we cuddled for a few minutes. 'Very unfortunately, though, I think I had better get up, if you want me to keep you in the style to which you intend to become accustomed,' he added, glancing at the clock on the bedside table.

'Excuse me,' I said haughtily, 'I do not intend to become a kept woman. Catherine has found a new job for me. You may bring me a cup of coffee.'

Jack laughed, kissed me again and went out into the kitchen. I lay back happily, and began to think about the day ahead.

A couple of hours later, having taken my time about getting up, I was sitting at Jack's kitchen table, surrounded by kittens, on the phone to the man himself. 'Go on, read it,' I said, gleefully crunching into a slice of toast. He had just got hold of a copy of the day's papers, and had found an absolutely fascinating article.

' "Strange goings-on at the normally staid US institution Interbank,"' read Jack. 'I suppose for staid they mean incredibly dull. Anyway, "Buzz Copenhager, who came over from the US to head up corporate communications just one month ago, resigned abruptly last night amid rumours of an internal power struggle. A spokesman from the bank refused to comment on the speculation last night, but said his position would be taken up by Laura Whittingale, who came over from the States at the same time." '

'Laura!' I said. 'That's the old bag who he was having an affair with. I bet Camilla's spitting with fury.'

'Yes, and there's more,' said Jack. ' "The bank has

also severed links with its longstanding public relations firm, Klinker Dorfmann Bergin Wallis, where coincidentally there has also been a spate of resignations. Ian Goldsmith and George Easterly are to join rival outfit Green Knight, while newly-promoted Camilla Dressingham-Whitstable has left to pursue other interests. Chief Executive Richard Dorfmann said, 'Of course we are sorry to see valued members of staff depart and we wish George and Ian every success in the future.' "'

'He didn't mention Camilla?' I asked.

'Nope,' said Jack.

'Blimey,' I said in awe. 'No wonder Ian and George are so good at their jobs. I've never been able to leak anything that successfully and that anonymously.'

'You're well out of it,' said Jack. I could hear him inhaling on a cigarette over the phone. 'Now look, darling, I'm taking you to dinner tonight alone. If any of our friends turn up, tell them to bugger off. I've booked a table for 8.30 at Le Caprice, I think it's about time we had a proper celebration on our own. Shall we meet for a drink at 7.30 in the American Bar?'

'Sounds fab,' I said.

'Right, see you later then,' said Jack. 'Don't forget to ring your parents, I'm about to call mine. Love you.'

'Love you,' I said shyly and put the phone down. I surveyed the kitchen. The kittens were asleep on the next chair, purring slightly. Outside it was a brilliantly sunny day, and beyond Jack's roof terrace, I could see a long wintry garden stretching out behind the neighbouring houses. The trees, almost bare of leaves, gave off a silvery glow where the frost had not quite melted. 'Isn't it a beautiful day?' I said to the kittens. 'A beautiful day to go shopping. I must get a new dress for tonight. Now where did I put my Harvey Nicks card? I wonder if they do wedding dresses there?'

But first things first. I dialled my parents' number. 'Helena Whitelake,' said my mother.

'Hullo, Mummy, it's me,' I said meekly.

'Darling!' said my mother. 'I was just thinking about you. Do you know, I heard last night that the elder Peterson's boy's marriage is in trouble. Perhaps you should come along on Boxing Day after all.'

'Actually, Mummy, that won't be necessary,' I said smugly. 'I have just become engaged.'

There was a short intake of breath over the phone followed by an explosion. 'No!' shouted my mother. 'I can't believe it! Darling, how wonderful! At last! Who is it, that computer programmer, Gerry or whatever his name is?'

'No it is not,' I said irritably. 'It's Jack.'

'Oh, darling,' said my mother softly. She sounded quite human just for a second. 'Oh darling, I really am pleased. I always thought you two should get back together, I was saying so to Jamie just the other day. When did you decide to get married?'

'Last night,' I said happily. 'And you should see the ring.'

'Now, we're going to have to have a big shopping trip,' said my mother firmly. 'You are not getting married in a miniskirt, Emily. When were you thinking about having the wedding?'

'This spring,' I said, and then stopped, struck by a terrible thought. 'That won't conflict with your skiing, will it, Mummy?'

'Do you know, I might even be prepared to do

without skiing – although only this once, of course,' added my mother hastily. 'No, I mean, of course we'll go skiing, but we'll just have to make sure the dates don't coincide. That really is wonderful news, darling. Now ring Daddy and tell him yourself, he'll be thrilled. I must dash, I want to ring the Hendersons and tell them the news right away.' She put the phone down.

I put down the receiver and looked at the phone. It rang instantly. I snatched it up. 'Hello,' I said.

'Emily, it's me!' shrieked Natasha. 'I've had a terrible row with Cosmo! He's prepared to open a joint account – but he won't have his trust fund paid into it! I've got to talk to you! I'm coming over right away! And listen! Don't tell anyone!' The phone went dead. I gazed at the receiver for a moment, and then, chuckling, went off to run a bath.

THE END

ADDICTED
by Jill Gascoine

'He stood, solitary, by the window, staring out at the well-groomed garden, feeling the luxury of the large, light, gentle house all round him. There was something about it, a forgotten experience of order from his childhood that he found dangerously seductive. It was a family home, basking in complacency . . . just asking for destruction'

It was the morning after Rosemary's fiftieth birthday party when she first met Ben Morrison. Rosemary was smart, successful, self-possessed and self-contained. She had her own TV show, a house she loved, and enough money to live as she wished. Men didn't really play a great part in her life-style.

Ben Morrison was thirty-three, an actor, a huge, dark bear of a man, half Spanish, half English. He was relaxed, attractive, casual and had once had a brief affair with Rosemary's daughter. On the face of it, he and Rosemary had absolutely nothing in common.

So when he erupted into Rosemary's life, smashing her tranquillity with an untamed, passionate greed, she was unprepared for her destruction. Gradually he eroded everything about her, personality, pride, sanity.

It took a full year for Rosemary to fight back, to be cured of Ben Morrison and his addictive, all-consuming sexual possession. It was a year she would never forget.

'Gascoine has written a page-turner which involves a glamorous heroine and lots of sex . . . without abandoning either sense or observation. The book has humour and a certain astuteness as well as narrative drive'
Sunday Times

'Sexy and poignant'
Today

0 552 14231 X

CATCH THE WIND
by Frances Donnelly

It was the wildest time, the wickedest time, the saddest time – it was the Sixties . . .

The three lost girls – reflecting the intertwined lives of their mothers before them – found themselves trapped in a zany lifestyle of rock bands, drugs, flower people, and – in Daisy's case – something more dangerous. Daisy was new into London, fresh from the hippy trail of California. Somehow she found herself labelled with the new woman of the Sixties' image – free-wheeling, aggressive, sexually uninhibited. It was an image that was hard to lose.

Annie had found her own niche in London as a dress designer – but somehow she just didn't fit into the vibrant mood of the Sixties. Shy, self-effacing, she was continually left behind when it came to men, and taken advantage of when it came to women.

But Alexia was the most bewildered of them all. With a neurotic mother who had dumped her at birth, with a sophisticated French background, and a suave, rich husband much older than herself, she was ripe for trouble. When rock star Kit Carson exploded into her life and she was thrown out by her husband, she could do nothing else but join the erotic, wild, sleazy lifestyle of a top rock band. For a while it was fun, then when she became pregnant she realised she had to take hold of her life if history was not to repeat itself.

The three girls, victims of the past, with old hang-ups, and old secrets still shadowing their lives, finally united into a friendship that was to hold fast and carry them into a happier time.

The compelling sequel to *Shake Down the Stars*.

0 552 13313 2

THE MAN WHO MADE HUSBANDS JEALOUS
by Jilly Cooper

Lysander Hawkley combined breathtaking good looks with the kindest of hearts. He couldn't pass a stray dog, an ill-treated horse, or a neglected wife without rushing to the rescue. And with neglected wives the rescue invariably led to ecstatic bonking, which didn't please their erring husbands one bit.

Lysander's mid-life crisis had begun at twenty-two. Reeling from the death of his beautiful mother, he was out of work, drinking too much, and desperately in debt. The solution came from Ferdie, his fat friend; if Lysander was so good at making husbands jealous, why shouldn't he get paid for it?

Let loose among the neglected wives of the ritzy county of Rutshire, Lysander causes absolute havoc. But it is only when he meets Rannaldini, Rutshire's King Rat and a temperamental, fiendishly promiscuous international conductor, that the trouble really starts. The only unglamorous woman around Rannaldini was Kitty, his plump young wife who ran his life like clockwork. Soon Lysander was convinced that Kitty must be rescued from Rannaldini at all costs, even if it means enlisting the help of the old blue-eyed havoc maker: Rupert Campbell-Black himself . . .

'Delicious . . . her bawdy humour shines through at all times . . . almost like an old-fashioned comedy of manners – with dollops of sex . . . settle down and have a rollicking good time. Satisfaction guaranteed!'
Jackie Collins

'Irresistible . . . I devoured it in a day . . . she's on cracking form . . . just read it and enjoy'
Susannah Herbert, *Sunday Telegraph*

'It is a happy, happy feckless romp . . . her fans, who are legion, will love it'
Maeve Binchy, *Mail on Sunday*

0 552 13895 9

A SELECTED LIST OF FINE NOVELS AVAILABLE FROM CORGI BOOKS

14309 X	THE KERRY DANCE	Louise Brindley	£5.99
12850 3	TOO MUCH TOO SOON	Jacqueline Briskin	£5.99
13397 3	THE CRIMSON PALACE	Jacqueline Briskin	£5.99
13558 5	AMBITION	Julie Burchill	£5.99
14103 8	RIDERS	Jilly Cooper	£6.99
13264 0	RIVALS	Jilly Cooper	£6.99
13552 6	POLO	Jilly Cooper	£6.99
13895 9	THE MAN WHO MADE HUSBANDS JEALOUS	Jilly Cooper	£6.99
13313 2	CATCH THE WIND	Frances Donnelly	£5.99
12887 2	SHAKE DOWN THE STARS	Frances Donnelly	£5.99
13266 7	A GLIMPSE OF STOCKING	Elizabeth Gage	£5.99
13644 1	PANDORA'S BOX	Elizabeth Gage	£5.99
13964 5	TABOO	Elizabeth Gage	£4.99
14261 1	INTIMATE	Elizabeth Gage	£5.99
14231 X	ADDICTED	Jill Gascoine	£4.99
14232 8	LILIAN	Jill Gascoine	£4.99
13872 X	LEGACY OF LOVE	Caroline Harvey	£4.99
99694 7	DROWNING IN HONEY	Kate Hatfield	£6.99
14285 9	ANGELS ALONE	Kate Hatfield	£5.99
14207 7	DADDY'S GIRL	Janet Inglis	£5.99
14208 5	FATHER OF LIES	Janet Inglis	£5.99
14331 6	THE SECRET YEARS	Judith Lennox	£4.99
13910 6	BLUEBIRDS	Margaret Mayhew	£5.99
13904 1	VOICES OF SUMMER	Diane Pearson	£4.99
10375 6	CSARDAS	Diane Pearson	£5.99
14123 2	THE LONDONERS	Margaret Pemberton	£4.99
14124 0	MAGNOLIA SQUARE	Margaret Pemberton	£4.99
14318 9	WATER UNDER THE BRIDGE	Susan Sallis	£4.99
13749 9	LIGHTNING	Danielle Steel	£5.99